DEDICATION

This book is dedicated to Evan.

For all the inspiration you give.
The motivation too—but most of all for love.
I can't wait to call you my husband.

LIAM

D J COOK

All rights reserved. No part of this book may be reproduced without written consent from the author, except that of small quotations used in reviews and promotions via blogs.

Liam is a work of fiction. Names, characters, businesses, events and incidents are either the products of the author's imagination or used in a fictitious manner. Any resemblance to actual persons, living or dead, or actual events is purely coincidental.

Cover design by Shower Of Schmidt's Designs
Editing by H.A. Robinson

Copyright © 2021 D J Cook
All rights reserved.
ISBN: 9798742187035

D J COOK ON SOCIAL MEDIA:

Instagram - @author_djcook
Facebook - @AuthorDJCook

ACKNOWLEDGMENTS

There are so many people who have contributed to releasing this book, both professionally and personally. I couldn't have done it without any of them! So here goes:

Heather. For being the most wonderful friend and editor anyone could ask for. You are a constant in my life and I don't ever want that to change. You will always be the reason I started writing, and I can't thank you enough for making me start that journey. I can't wait for more days out, dog walks, bad food eating and kick-up-the-ass writing days.

Eleanor. My crazy talented cover designer. Not only do you give me the book covers I've dreamed of—I've known you for just over a year now and you've become a great friend of mine. My world would be really different without you in it.

Ruth. My alpha reader and incredible friend. One of the only people that has eyes on my writing while I write. This book wouldn't be what it is today without your input, your gasps of shock, your encouragement and the occasional punch. Thank you for everything. I hope we continue writing together forever.

Thank you to my ARC readers: Blaire, Dayle, Riah, Nicola, Victoria, Sarah, Ruth, Jamie, Hannah, Sylwia & Abi. For taking the time to read this story, one I've battled to get out for the best part of a year. You guys are the reason I keep writing.

Thank you to my cheerleaders, my closest friends and family who ask how I'm getting on and encourage me to keep writing. Those who share my books on social media, leave reviews and tell your friends about me. There are just too many of you to name, but you know who you are and I do, too. I see every one of you and I love you all for it.

To my readers. Thank you for supporting this journey of mine and reading Liam. I hope you love his story as much as I do.

And, how could I forget about Evan? You have physically sat me down and forced me to write at times I just couldn't get the words out. You're my idea generator and the only other person who gets to read what I'm writing as I write—I couldn't be more grateful for all of your help and support. That's why this book is dedicated to you. I love you.

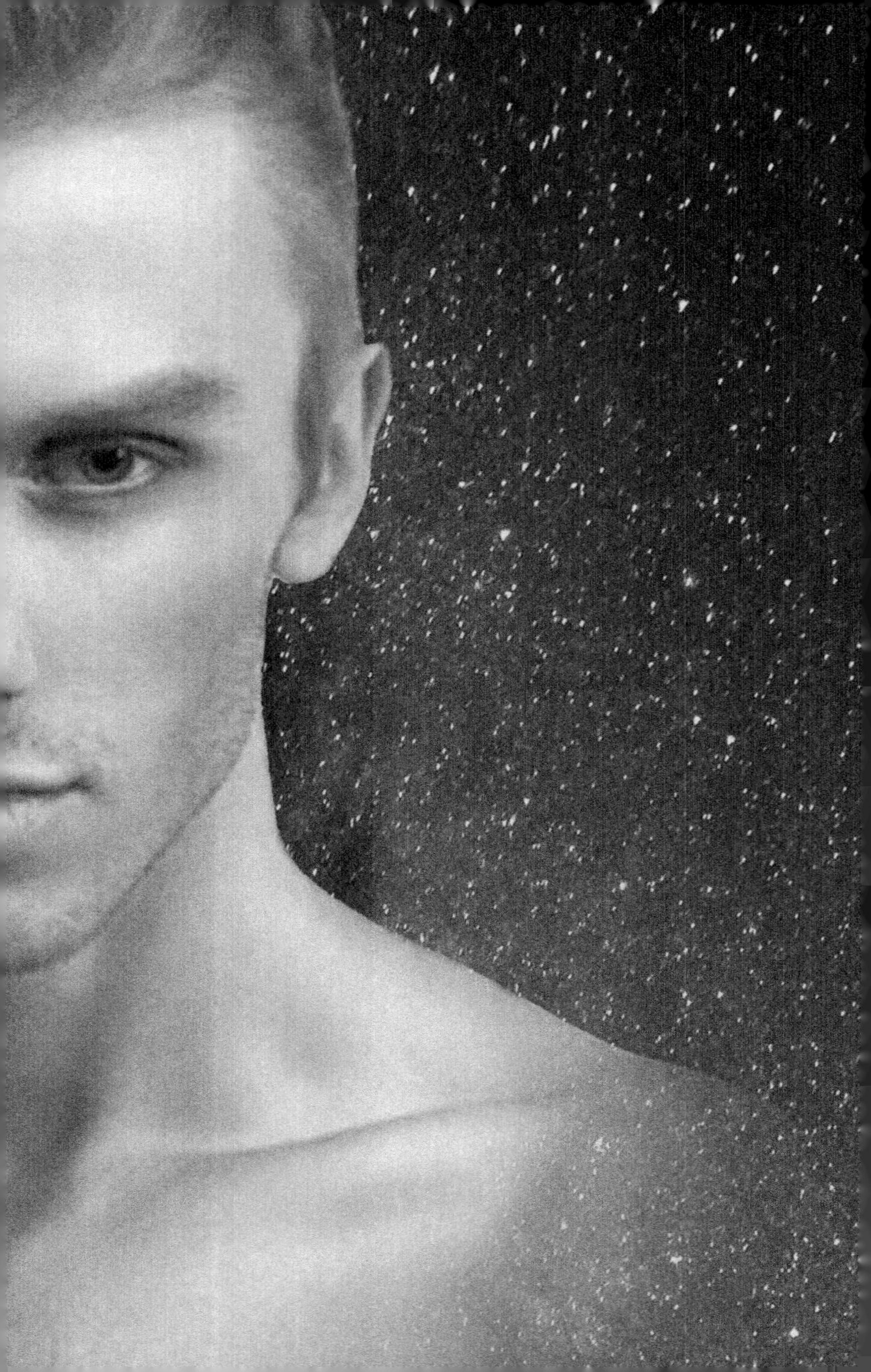

PROLOGUE

"Don't get up or you're dead."
Saliva shot from his mouth like a silver-laced bullet landing centimetres from my face, which was firmly pressed to the rough gravel. A crowd of school children surrounded us, but they didn't stop him. I didn't know much about him, just that he was in a few of my classes and made no effort to learn. I did know that for some reason, he didn't like me. I could tell by the repetitive beating my chest was taking from his foot, and this wasn't the first occurrence. Luckily, my face always escaped the punches from his worn knuckles, purely so the teachers wouldn't ask too many questions. Normally, I could turn anything into a joke, but not this. My body ached in agony with each drum to my chest, but I couldn't let my face show it. I wanted to cry, but that wouldn't have done me any favours. I knew if I

didn't react to his caveman idiocy, he would stop. Eventually.

So I lay there limply, watching his every movement and mentally bracing myself for each impact. Sweat dripped his pruned brow and all I could do was stare at him with his chiseled jaw forming a line directly to his pouting lips.

Maybe that's why he's beating me up?

Maybe I'd looked at him for just a second too long while we changed for P.E. Maybe his own insecurities were the reason he often used his brute strength against my flailing weakness. If my looks could have killed him, I'd have understood his reasons. I'd have placed myself on the ground for him for ease, yet instead, my looks were doing no damage to him and a whole lot to me.

I'd known I was different for a couple of years after trying to make friends with boys the same age as me. Not even sneaking money from our savings jar at home would have persuaded them to like me, something I'd learned the hard way. I'd spent years trying to convince them I was normal—that was until I realised that being normal was not to be sought after. It wasn't the repeated beatings that forced me to realise it—it was my best friend.

"What the hell are you playing at? Get off him, Dale." Tamsin ran towards us. In pain and full of shame, I tried not to cower on the floor beneath the bully.

"Back off, Tamsin. The queer deserves it."

Did I deserve it?

Queer. I'd heard that word enough times that the once scorching insult had become a slight burn—something I could brush off from someone who meant nothing to me. I could take his unimaginative attempt at name calling, but I couldn't take the punches. Yes, the pain was a factor I couldn't deny, but it was the aftermath I couldn't forget. Seeing the bruises consume my body at a rate quicker than I could accept them as part of me. The worry that came each morning and evening as I'd get changed in my bedroom, hoping that Mum would knock before she came in to see the purples and yellows of my skin.

"No, he doesn't!" I could feel her pushing and pulling at Dale above me, his hand still pressing my face to the ground with force. Tamsin had always been the pretty, quiet girl. Even through primary school she'd stood just inches away from the bullies insisting they stop. She had very few friends, and I'd once believed that it wasn't her choice. That was until she'd let me into her guarded life. She had her mum and that was all she needed, until she saved me.

"Get off him. Just because you've seen how small your dick is compared to his doesn't mean you have to take it out on him," Tamsin said as Dale's pressure softened, the spectators sucking in the air around them. Everyone underestimated the quiet girl, but not me. Tamsin only spoke when she had something to say, and she made sure she was heard.

A shallow sigh leapt from my mouth in relief, short-lived as Dale launched towards Tamsin. She squealed as his broad shoulders approached her. I tried desperately to fight the pain he'd inflicted to save her until I heard a familiar voice and my limp body fell flat to the ground.

"What's going on here?" Miss Chan yelled, making Dale jump and turn his attention away from Tamsin.

Miss Chan was my textiles teacher—my favourite teacher of all time. Textiles and art were the only lessons where I could truly express myself. Even when the curriculum dictated what I had to create, I still felt a sense of freedom I had in no other class. Dale looked at Miss Chan, almost apologetically, even though he had no such intentions. He fancied her; all the hormone ravaged teenagers in the school did, understandable even to someone not attracted to her. She was fresh faced, and always wore a low cut top, even in winter. Pencils would be dropped consistently, just so the lads could stare down her shirt at the breasts she did a poor job of concealing. If any other teacher had worn the same, it would have been inappropriate, but not for Miss Chan.

I admired her platform ankle boots that she'd paired with a vintage skirt as I caught my breath on the ground. The other boys were looking just a tad north of her skirt with their mouths agape. Crowds had been chanting and encouraging the imbecile. I didn't know if it was his parents or the popularity that had made him sour. It didn't matter I had just two people fighting my corner, because they always came to my rescue. She always found time for me, just like Tamsin.

"Miss Chan, Liam provoked me. He kept looking at me in that weird way. He clearly fancies me and it's gross." The other lads laughed as I pulled myself up from the floor and wiped off the bits of gravel that had stuck to my blazer.

"Really? So just a mere look warrants a fight now, does it?" she said in a stern manner, enough to dull the rumble of whispers surrounding us. "After school detention tonight, and no lunch breaks for the rest of the week. You'll be writing essays discussing why behaviour like this is unacceptable, no matter what provoked you."

"Okay, Miss." He looked pleased with himself. After all, he had just bagged himself a couple of extra hours with a hot teacher. As the crowd dispersed, Miss Chan pulled a pocket mirror from her Saffiano leather bag.

"Are you alright, Liam?" she asked, and held the mirror up so I could see my reflection. My once shiny hair had become dull, covered in dust, and not sat in its usual place. I wondered why I even bothered spending so much time making myself look presentable, as more often than not I was used as a punch bag.

"I'm fine, thank you. I didn't do anything. You know that, right?"

"Of course I do. Liam, bullies like him aren't going to make it very far in the real world. They are egotistical, have narrow minds and aren't going to like it when the people they used to bully excel quicker than them. The world has enough small-minded people like Dale, but I can promise you something: the world is changing, slower than we could hope for, but once you've grown up, the world will be ready for you. It will be ready for your expansive artistic mind and your clever unique personality. Be more like you, okay?" I nodded as the school bell rang. "Now, let's get you two to class." Tamsin and I followed sluggishly behind Miss Chan, who was racing ahead to get to her next lesson.

"She's right, you know? You are so naturally and wonderfully you. Don't not be yourself just because of a few idiot boys," Tamsin piped up. I used a stone as a football, kicking it along as I walked towards the school entrance.

"Is she right, though? You know I love her, but how is she so sure? What if I'm going to be used as a punch bag the rest of my life just because I like boys?"

"Maybe she isn't sure? Maybe she's just hopeful? I just know we need more people like her."

Hope.

Tamsin was right, and without thought, I held my head high, straightened the slouch in my back and stopped feeling sorry for myself. School kids were mean —some of them anyway—but I had my person, my best friend to see me through and help dust me off after all of the pain.

. . .

As the school bell rang for the final time that day, I grabbed my bag from under the wooden desk I'd etched my name into, and without hurry, placed my belongings within it. Everyone was eager to get home, but not me. Tamsin hung back as I waited for the school corridors to empty. I loved school, bullying aside. Although I had to hide myself a little at school, it was worse at home. I still hadn't told Mum or Dad about my sexuality. I could endure the punches at school, but I couldn't deal with their disappointment. Bile filled my stomach at each thought of ever telling them. Mum would never have a grandchild; Dad wouldn't be able to take me to the pub with *the lads* and talk about footie or the barmaid's boobs. These thoughts ate me up, so much so I couldn't face the reality of telling them. Not yet, anyway. Until then, Tamsin knew and she was all that mattered.

"Tamsin, sign up to drama club with me?" I asked as I stared helplessly at the glittered comedy and tragedy masks on the poster.

"No way. There's no chance you're getting me on a stage in front of people. I hate reading aloud in English, that's bad enough."

"Pleaseeeeeee. Pretty please with Zac Efron on top? I don't want to do it alone. It will be so fun. We can do all the group tasks together. You'll get to spend extra time with me..."

"Urgh. Fine. But I'm not happy about this, Wrighty." My nickname from an early age, for those who acknowledged I was there. My last name with a 'y' on the end, so not the most imaginative nickname you could have bestowed upon you.

I supposed it was better than being called Gayboy, the other nickname the bullies found too much joy in giving me.

"Yay!" With a quick scribble on the poster we were both signed up for drama club, practically handing the bullies another reason to beat me up.

"I'm going to the loo before the caretaker throws us out of school again. Wait for me near the car park? I won't be long."

I sat waiting on a cold concrete step that was already making my lower half go numb. Still, it was better than going home straight away. What felt like hours passed as I waited for her, looking up at the clouded sky above and across the car park. A car waited with the engine running not too far away from me. I saw Miss Chan walk over and step into the car effortlessly. I was about to wave to her as I usually would, when she leant in and kissed the female sat in the drivers' seat.

She's gay. Just like me.

Tamsin has been right.

Everything Miss Chan had said before was in hope. Hope for a changing world for me, for her and everyone else who had to confess, at some point in their life, to being homosexual like it was a crime. She was hiding from her true self, just like I was. She was living a lie that started and finished at the gates of the school. It was a convincing lie at that; I'd had no idea. Dale would be distraught. In fact, fifty percent of the school's population would have been if they'd found out. Her girlfriend was just as beautiful as Miss Chan—short blonde hair from what I could see, similar to mine. That was the happiest I'd ever seen her at school. Whether that was because she didn't have to deal with sexually charged teenagers or that she got to spend time with her partner and stop acting, I didn't know. I guessed it was a mix of both.

I ambled towards my house with Tamsin at my side, finding the smallest of distractions to keep us entertained on the monotonous route we walked to school. Houses lined the streets one by one, so kicking a plastic bottle across the road to each other couldn't have been more fun. Before taking to the final few streets to our homes, I ran towards the wooden park and launched myself onto a swing seat with force.

"Don't you just wish we could stay young forever and not have a care in the world like our parents have?" Tamsin said, also swinging as her brown hair made waves in the wind that trailed behind her.

"But I do worry, Tamsin. I worry about telling everyone that I'm gay. Why do I even have to tell people? Why don't you have to confess that you're straight?" I asked, angry at society.

"I don't know, but I think you should just get it over with. Your parents love you. It'll be fine! If not, just come and stay with me and my mum. She'll adopt you. She'd probably trade me in for you if she could." She laughed at herself. I did love her mum.

"Okay. I'll tell them tonight. Be on standby in case I need to escape. I'll buzz you on the walkie-talkie if it doesn't work out."

I pushed myself off the swing and marched myself home, waving back to Tamsin repetitively as she sat still swinging.

"Is that you, Liam? You're late. Tea will be on the table soon." Mum spent the majority of her time in the kitchen; even after cooking and cleaning she'd find a reason to be in there.

"Yeah, Mum, it's me. Is Dad home?" I asked nervously. I was in no fit shape to face the devastation my sexuality would cause our family, but I was also not ready to keep living a lie.

It was just three words.

I am gay.

"He's upstairs, sweetie. Why? You weren't told off by the caretaker again, were you? You got Tamsin into a lot of trouble last time," she asked, her voice coated with anger but her face sweeter than ever.

"Hey, lad, how was school?" My dad stomped down the stairs and wrapped one arm around Mum.

"I got beat up," I said simply.

"What? By who? Why?" Mum asked quickly, this time her face not looking as sweet.

"Did you stick up for yourself? Did you give him a good smack back?" Dad said, focused entirely on the wrong thing.

I'd never be the lad he wanted me to be. I had to tell him. Both of them. No more pretending.

"He beat me up because... I'm... I'm gay." Two words. Easier than three. I tried not to stutter. The words came out quicker than I'd imagined in my head, but even after I'd spoken them they lingered.

"You're gay?" Mum questioned, seeming like she didn't understand what I'd just said.

"Yeah. I'm gay. I've known for a while now, I just didn't know how to tell you both... I... didn't want to disappoint you," I said once the words wrapped around my tongue, welling up after bottling the emotions I'd hidden away for so long.

"Well, that's alright, isn't it? Are you happy?" Mum asked softly but my dad remained silent.

"I think so," I replied, trying to decide if I was happy about feeling this way about men. Yeah, it would've been nice to have a wife, a huge house surrounded by a picket fence, but none of that would have made me happy–– not like meeting the man of my dreams, anyway.

"Good. Look, go and run yourself a bath, put your music on full blast and relax. You don't need to worry anymore. I love you, okay?" Mum smiled as she looked into my eyes and then pulled me in towards her chest. She was filled with a warmth that pushed away the cold I'd felt for so long. I was already as tall as her, my chin resting on her shoulder.

"I love you, too, Mum," I said with a smile and took myself upstairs. The worst was over. I could relax. I jumped onto my bed and for a few moments I sat in silence before reaching out to Tamsin. A huge weight had lifted, and the worry about my peers finding out seemed to fade.

"Tamsin. Are you there?" I said between the crackling of the walkie-talkie.

"I'm here. How did it go? Do you need to come and stay with us?"

"No, it's fine. I've told them and I think it's all okay. I don't need to worry anymore."

"See, I told you it would all be fine. I'm so proud of you, Gayboy," she said lovingly.

If she can call me that then who cares who else will?

"You're always right. I hate that. See you tomorrow, Tams."

I sat in bed with the walkie-talkie in my hand, staring at my ceiling covered in glow-in-the-dark star stickers my dad had put up for me as a surprise one birthday. I loved the stars. They had been my happy place for as long as I could remember. I must have been daydreaming, brought back to the reality of my bedroom by a sudden crash of noise downstairs.

"It's okay, Jed. Calm down." I heard Mum shouting

and then the sound of breaking dishes filled my eardrums. I tried to cover my ears to make it all go away, but there was no escape.

"It's not fucking fine, Diane. That's not my son. He's been brainwashed. It's not normal."

That's not my son.

I couldn't help but sob. As my tears soaked the pillow below them, I prayed for the shouting to stop. I wished I could take back what I'd said, to be back in the closet. If I was wishing, I'd have been straight—anything to make my dad happy. I was right to have wished for a change, because I had no idea what the following morning would bring.

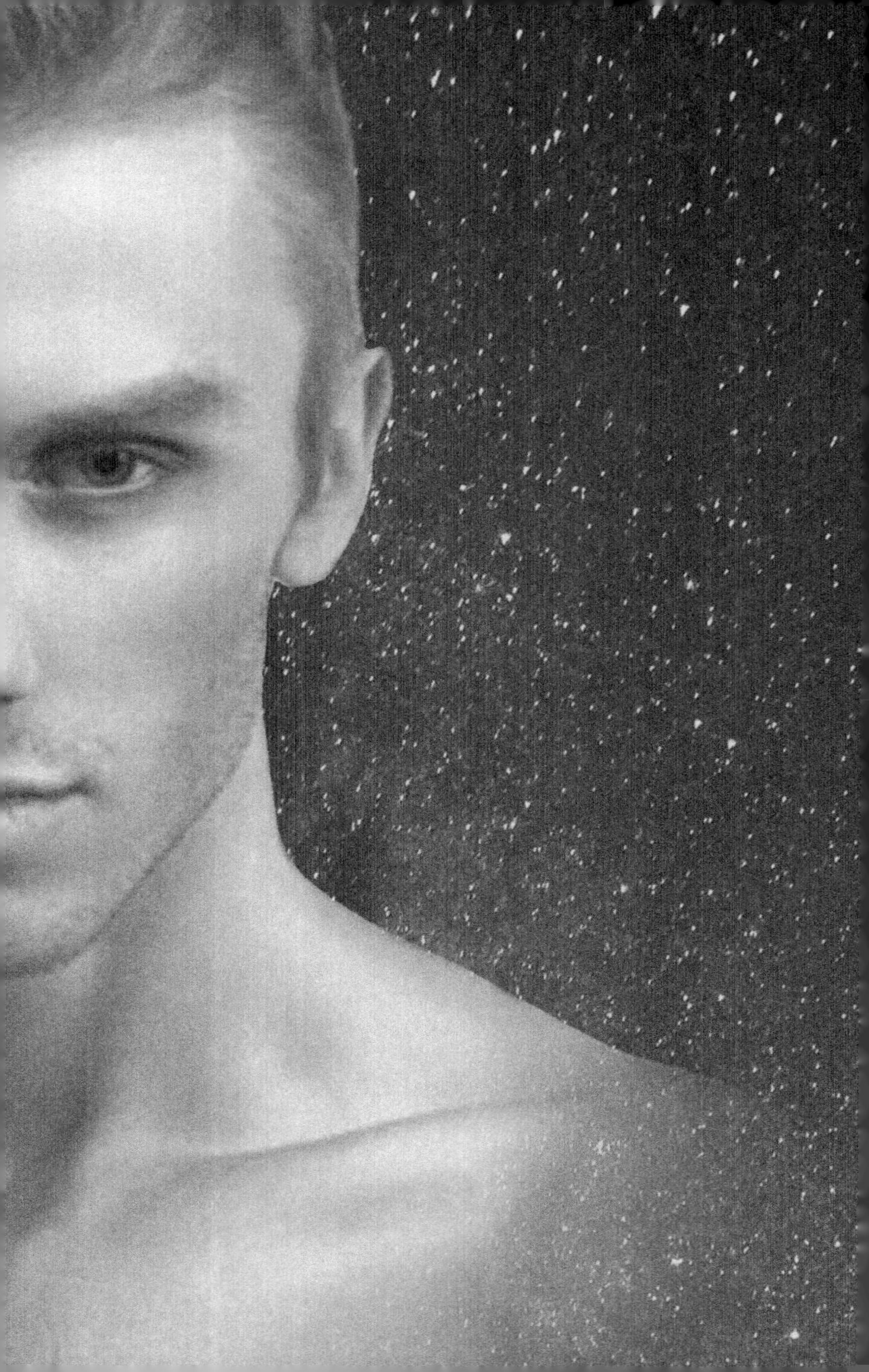

CHAPTER ONE

TEN YEARS LATER

Of late, I'd been too busy to find myself waking up in someone else's bed. It used to be a ritual—a tradition that every weekend, at least, I'd stumble out of bed the following morning in a stranger's room, half cut from the night before. My fashion business, Wrighteous, was booming like I'd never thought it would and because of that, things had changed. I was too busy to be drinking as often as I once had—too sensible to be jumping into a different guy's bed each week. That was unless the offer was just too good.

I lay next to Ab's, his light breath tickling the back of my neck. I didn't know his name. I'd learnt not to ask, especially using a so called dating app. Instead, I knew his user name, good enough for a one night stand. It's often said in the dating world that straight guys only want *one thing*. Gay guys were no different, the ones I seemed to attract, anyway. Tamsin and my previous accolades had told me I was attractive—fair hair, the bluest of eyes and a complexion that was sought after in the modelling world. For a while, I'd believed it. That was until my ex-boyfriend had come along in my first year of university and started dismantling my confidence like a finished jigsaw puzzle. Did I sleep with guys for validation? Absolutely, but I wanted more than sex. I used to be like all the other guys, but times were changing. I was getting older and everyone around me was settling down.

Ab365 was damn good in bed. It looked as though his abs had been manufactured to perfection and he had a face for television. Abs stirred a little and muttered, "Morning."

The cover grazed my bare skin as it moved in harmony with him. He groaned a little with each movement and then rested his hand on my waist. He seemed to want another helping, so I complied like any sex starved twenty-two year old would, and then hopped out of bed once we both groaned with pleasure.

"You can just say it, you know?" I blurted, as I straightened my blonde hair in the mirror above his bed. "You want me to leave, right?"

"No, it's not like that." His expression said different, and I'd seen it plastered on the faces of too many men to not understand what it meant.

"Please, your profile picture of that massive thing hanging between your legs tells me otherwise. I know I came here for one reason and it's fine. I had fun, but I'm not gonna hang around for that typically awkward conversation we'd be having in precisely ten minutes. So let's just cut to the chase, okay?" I couldn't stop myself. My defences were up and I was protecting myself.

"Whoa, I'm just not looking for anything serious at the moment." His eyebrows pointed, and he lifted his hands like he'd surrendered to me.

"Me either. Don't worry, it's fine," I lied as I gathered my clothes and continued to put them on with a stare from the guy who, just minutes earlier, had been breathing heavily on top of me.

Maybe I was wrong to have spoken to him with such confidence but for once, I wanted to leave a stranger's house with a shred of dignity intact, and not have the walk of shame filled with sadness. This guy wasn't to blame, though; it was all me. It was something internal that made me react the way I did, something wired deep into my brain and was too advanced for me to even try to change.

"Thanks for everything, Abs." My tongue turned my words sarcastic without intention and the door closed behind me. As I walked down the first few flights of steps, I remembered moaning about not being able to get the lift up to his flat. My stomach was at war with itself—the older I got, the worse those morning hangovers seemed. With my stomach raging and my legs sore from the stairs, my mind was fixated on leaving Abs behind. I didn't even feel better for my attempt at taking control of the situation.

Feeling sorry for myself and very late, I arrived at the unit I'd purchased a few months before, as my bespoke fashion business for drag queens outgrew my bedroom at Mum's.

"Hey, bestie," I croaked to Tamsin, already in the office drowning in paperwork on the desk she refused to tidy. She somehow managed to justify it, saying it seemed we were in demand to potential clients. Grade A logic.

"Hey, Gayboy. Oooh, someone is looking a little bit rough today. Do you need the hangover kit?" She held up a box personalised with a vinyl sticker that read *Liam's Hangover Kit*. She then pressed play on the sound system and by no coincidence at all, *Walk of Shame* by P!nk played. Tamsin laughed over the music filling Wrighteous HQ.

"Ha ha ha. You're so funny. You'd think after all these years of us being friends I would've expected a stunt like this." I began to lip sync to the music, and strut up and down the unit, the feel good music as infectious as Abs' kiss. A poisonous kiss.

"What can I say? Always full of surprises. So, go on, what was this guy's excuse? Was it him and not you? Already married? Moving abroad?"

She was my person. The only one I could rely on to be one-hundred percent real with me when it came to men. Entirely honest when I'd pour my heart out to her, having a sudden need for more with every man who took his top off in front of me.

"He just wasn't looking for anything serious. At least he was honest and didn't lie about moving abroad. Also, I've only slept with a married guy once, and I didn't know."

"Mmm Hmm. Home-wrecker," Tamsin hummed and coughed above her words, her head still glued to the paperwork in front of her instead of me. "Well, Gayboy, it will work out for the best. Hot guys often mean trouble. You'll find someone, I promise. Just stay off the bloody dating app, please? It does you no good." Truth. I couldn't deny it. I always ended up broken, the heart on my sleeve as worn as they came.

"You're right. We can't all have a hunk like Callum, can we?" I smiled at her, allowing a small sigh to escape me. I wasn't going to shrug off Tamsin's advice this time. I was going to listen to her. I'd focus on Wrighteous, putting my all into the business instead of wasting my time trying to find the man of my dreams and an occasional few minutes of pleasure. What I didn't know? The decision to listen to her was going to reshape my life entirely.

David Mirage
16th September 2019

[11:03]

Hiiii Liam. Fancy meeting up any time this week? It's been ages! We should catch up. You can show me all the outfits you're working on at the moment... x

I placed my phone swiftly back into my pocket after reading the message from Miss Mirage. She was an icon for Tamsin and me at University, and designing David's dress had been the start of my career. If it hadn't been for him, Wrighteous might not have existed at all. I had him to thank entirely and he knew it. Previously, I hadn't minded a quick fling with him—pleasure was pleasure—but I knew he wasn't the one for me. It was just sex, but even that had started to come off the list as one of my priorities. I had to stop giving myself away as freely as I had done in the past. I had to listen to Tamsin. I avoided messaging him back, and sat at the sewing machine to finish a garment for a well-known drag queen based in Scotland.

"We booked the DJ for the christening last night. You excited to get druuuunnk?" Tamsin yelled over the noise of the sewing machine that was weaving two pieces of material together to make one beautiful garment.

"If you'd have asked me any other day, I'd have said yes. But in the hungover state I'm in, absolutely not," I laughed, bearing a grin. I'd been so honoured when she'd asked me to be Godfather to Tess just after her birth. What didn't fill me with joy? The thought of being stuck in a freezing church for the best part of a day having religion shoved in my face. I'd had enough of that at my graduation ceremony held at Chester Cathedral. Those solid wooden benches did nothing for comfort. Maybe the whole point of them was they didn't want people to stay for long at all.

"Well… knowing you, you'll be having a drink tonight when you see the amount of orders we have. We've got a merchandise order from Ima Cuming, and it's a big one," Tamsin said, skipping over to me, waving the printed order.

"A big one, really?" I smouldered, insinuating a dirty pun to make Tamsin laugh. I then snapped out of it as my mind played the name over and over.

"I've heard of her! She's a big deal! Let's see." I snatched the order out of her hands, my eyes drawn to the figure at the bottom. "Oh my god. This order pays for all the bills and then some. I know we play to our strengths but I'm gonna need you to give me a hand with this."

The next morning, I found myself feeling brighter after not taking shot after shot of vodka and jumping into bed with another guy. I was brighter, until…

David Mirage
17th September 2019

[14:27]

Hey! Do you ever answer your phone? Don't make me come down there! x

I had every intention of replying... but I just didn't. I wasn't trying to be rude, nor did I want to alienate a popular local drag queen. My fingers were poised to tap a reply when the phone rang, and Tamsin was nowhere to be seen. I let her off as normally she'd never be caught slacking, so I answered the phone and cracked on with all I had to do until Tamsin arrived back at the unit and worked alongside me with Ima Cuming's order.

"Hiiiii, queens," David pronounced as he entered the work unit, his eyes immediately darting to Tamsin and me, piecing together fabric fans.

"Shit," I muttered under my breath, with Tamsin's mouth pointing slightly at the edges. "Miss Mirage, what brings you all the way over to the dark side?" I stood up and walked towards him with Tamsin waving behind, focused on attaching the fan design straight. If she didn't, there'd be Hell to pay.

"Well, I need a new dress, and I thought what better person than the king of drag fashion?" He lightly kissed each of my cheeks the way the French do in the movies, and made himself comfortable on a futon placed next to a coffee table.

"King of fashion? You're too kind. You didn't have to come all this way. We have your measurements. You could've just called," I said, trying not to seem rude while also casually insisting he didn't drop by without notice again.

"Don't be silly. I wanted to see you. Besides, you didn't reply to my texts. Is something wrong?" he said as

I placed myself next to him with his hand rested on my leg. This would have been the perfect opportunity to tell him I didn't want a relationship, nor was I going to jump into his bed at the drop of a message like I used to. I had responsibilities—I had my idea of a future and it didn't involve him, not the way he'd have liked it to.

"It's just been super busy here. I'm all good. So, this dress? Tell me more," I said, worming my way around being honest with him like a coward.

"I want a new outfit for my Christmas event. Up for the challenge?" His hand grazed from my knee up to my thigh in exactly the right way. A year ago, I would have pounced on him, but I had to change.

"Absolutely. I'm drowning in work but I'm sure I can fit in my favourite customer." I switched on my charm. The Liam Wright charm he'd fallen head over heels for when I was at university.

"Great. Looks like we're going to be spending a lot more time together over the next few weeks."

Yippee.

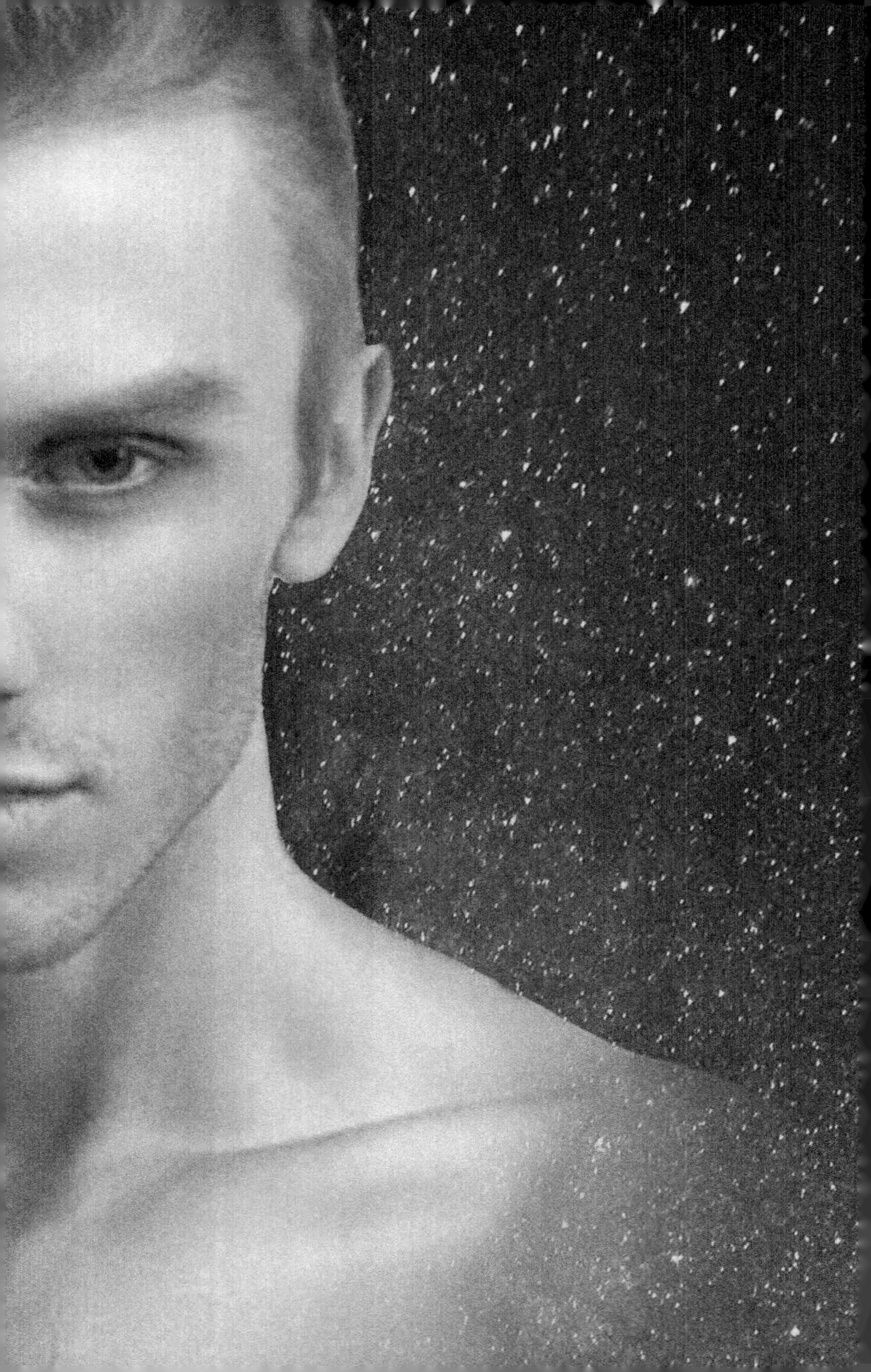

CHAPTER TWO

No matter how late I stumbled home from work, my routine stayed the same each time. I'd go to the fridge, re-heat a meal Mum had made if I hadn't been to the kebab shop down the road, and then I'd scroll on my phone with the sound of the TV filling the silent space of the living room. With the dating app deleted from my phone, I'd often find myself clicking on the app that had replaced it out of habit. I had been addicted.

Sleeping with men had become my thing, and I'd never truly wanted that. I wanted a prince to love me so much that he'd sweep me off my feet. I wanted a man who would treat me right and build me up instead of knocking me down. I knew I'd find it without the help of an app. I just had to wait.

"You're back late. How's the food?" Mum asked, popping the kettle on to make a pot of tea ready for her retreat to her bedroom. My nostrils flared at the smell of the home cooked food that sat in front of me, the whole house filled with a sense of comfort.

"It's incredible, thank you. You know you don't have to cook for me. I can just nip and get a kebab on the way home," I said, looking down at the nearly empty plate, trying to scrape as much gravy onto my fork as possible.

"Don't be silly. I won't have you going hungry, not in our house." Mum kissed my forehead and then carried her pot of tea upstairs, mouthing goodnight so she wouldn't wake up Jade. I knew I wouldn't be far behind her, so once I'd finished an episode of *Fashion Police*, I gathered my things and carried myself upstairs. I hovered outside Jade's bedroom as I listened to a light snore that seeped through the cracks of the door. I'd been so busy at work I hadn't even considered making time for her, so with hesitation I pulled down the handle, cringing at every squeak. I placed myself on the edge of her bed, her nightlight providing just enough of a glow so I could see her face.

"Goodnight, Jade," I whispered under my breath. "I hope you're dreaming about mountains of ice cream, unicorn rides and knights in shining armour. One day, I'll be there to make sure that knight never does anything to hurt you. I'll be like your fairy-tale bodyguard. Mostly fairy, but you'll realise that soon enough." I gave a silent laugh and Jade stirred a little as I stood up and placed my lips to her forehead, kissing softly, just as our mum did.

She was pretending to be asleep.

"Do you want to play lions?" She rolled over, throwing me a fake yawn. She was going to drama school. I knew it.

"You should be asleep."

"But I can't sleep and I want to play lions. Will you be my baby lion please?" she begged, her eyes looking tired as if she fought to stay awake.

"Not tonight, but I love you. Sweet dreams." I got up and walked towards the door as Jade mumbled that she loved me too, her words almost incomprehensible.

"I love you more, sweet dreams," I spoke as the door shut behind me. A single tear rolled down my cheek. I missed her more than anything, but I knew these long days at the office would pay off. A sacrifice I had to make. I didn't have time to play silly games with her.

She could play lions with her school friends.

I justified it as I walked into my room and fell straight to sleep, my dreams full of regret as wild lions attacked me in the dead of night. My conscience was attacking me.

―――――

Just a few weeks later and the orders were slowly completed, one by one, alongside all the merchandise for Ima Cuming's tour. The orders were pouring funds into Wrighteous and my savings quicker than ever. The downside——we were tired and ready to have some time off. Christmas was a couple of months away and I'd already planned to shut the unit down for two weeks to recover from our busiest period. We desperately needed to switch off from work, to spend time with our families without orders swirling around our heads.

"That's the last one done. Ima Cuming, you shall go to your tour," I chuckled as Tamsin packed the final fan away and swirled on her feet like Cinderella in celebration. "Look, I've just got to make some final adjustments to David's dress. Why don't you go home? I know you said you wanted to be here as a distraction, but just go and take some time off,"

"I know, but going home is the worst thing I could do. I'll get all depressed that I've had to spend a year without Mum. The unit's a mess and I can't leave it like this." She started picking up the cardboard and bubble wrap that sat as a protection for the concrete floor.

"Why? Your desk is always messy, so the floor being untidy for a while won't hurt."

"Ha! Besides, the amount of custom orders we have waiting is crazy. You need me here." She placed her hands under her chin and looked modest. I did need her, but I wasn't going to let her avoid grieving. A whole year had passed. The day meant something, and I knew she'd regret not making it all about her mum.

"I'm not taking no for an answer. The christening is this weekend, too. I bet you have loads to do? Just take the rest of the week off, that's an order."

"Not really, that's what Mother-In-Laws are for,"

she giggled, grabbing her bag and jacket, "but if you want me to leave, I shall leave as you wish." That time she spoke with grandeur, like someone out of a period drama.

"Good. Don't come back. See you at the Christening. Byeeeeeee."

David Mirage
7th October 2019

[12:17]

Hey, queen. Your dress has been finished ahead of schedule, and it's gorgeous. I can't wait to show you. When will you be free to nip here for a fitting? I'll get you booked in.

[12:20]
Hiiii. How does this afternoon work? I can head over in a few hours if you aren't too busy? X

I wasn't too busy. In fact, I'd put off starting any other orders because once I'd started them I'd want them finished. Instead, I'd been drawing designs in a huge leather bound book. Allowing my pencil to mark the page with different shapes, and then I transformed those shapes into something beautiful.

Nearly all of my outfits had a novelty aesthetic, a twist unique enough for any UK drag queen to fawn over. I should have been designing more drag fashion because that's what sold well, but instead, my hand had a brain of its own—sketching fashion only seen on catwalks and in the streets of the fashion capitals of the world. The pencil ran across the page as I envisioned a delicate embroidered lace that would run from shoulder to floor. Butterflies and flowers, created with cotton thread, would be embellished from the top down, leaving the detail to fade naturally. Before I knew it, the clock had taken three hours and I'd illustrated six other fashion designs, each with their own unique style and inspired by some of the most famous international fashion designers.

"Liam, my darling. So great to see you again." As David walked in, I placed the sketch book on the coffee table and stood up, ready to be greeted by kisses on my cheeks.

"Good to see you, too. Are you ready?" I asked as I made my way over to the mannequin. A rough cloth material sat over the outfit, ready for me to reveal it.

"Very. Unveil her, I can't wait any longer." He squeaked with excitement.

I swiftly pulled the material away. A silver sequin dress sat perfectly on the bodice of the mannequin, showing the curves and angulations of the dress. It had to be silver sequin, because what Christmas dress didn't sparkle? Embedded underneath the front of the dress were two red baubles, placed precisely. Miss Mirage was a comedy queen, her jokes and on-stage banter enough to make the deepest sadness lighten. Her revealing her baubles at the end of the night would be the ultimate way to end a drag show.

It wasn't long before David had the dress on and was strutting up and down the unit, overly excited about flashing his baubles. The minute he stepped into his dress, he became Miss Mirage—confidence filled to the brim. Once he'd keep still, I marked where any adjustments were needed and David sat down in his usual spot.

"The dress is insane. Thanks again, Liam. See, I told you—king of drag fashion right here." He looked at me with intensity, each blink of his magnified as I tried to keep my cool—as I tried not to lead him on.

"Do you know what, maybe I am." I laughed as I mocked his remark, looking down to the illustrations I'd been working on. David noticed the sketches and grabbed the book, swiping through page after page, and watched the graphite come to life.

"You're crazy talented. You know that, right? These designs are worthy of having their own stage, their own platform. You're going to make these, aren't you?" he asked, continuing to gaze at the drawings. I blushed and remained silent, struggling to say something after his compliment, because when it came down to both my looks and fashion, in my eyes I'd never be good enough.

"That's what Tamsin always says." I looked down shyly, avoiding acknowledging his compliment, without seeming rude.

"Speaking of Tamsin, where is she? She's always

here, every time I come anyway. She's nearly here as much as you are."

"No, I gave her the rest of the week off. Tess' Christening is this weekend and it's been a year since her mum died."

"A year already?" David shuffled closer, remaining in his seat. His eyes wandered along with his hand that met my chest. Our knees knocked together accidentally as his body inched closer to mine. In just one minute, we'd gone from talking about fashion, talking about Tamsin and her mum, to a silence created by sexual tension—a sexual tension that he'd fashioned and I'd not asked for.

His lips met mine, and for a while, mine moved in harmony with his. His touch felt as it had in the past. Exciting. It turned me on, but it wasn't enough to sweep me off my feet. I wasn't head over heels in love with him. He was a friend—a damn good friend. It had been weeks since I'd had sex, so I couldn't blame myself for kissing back, but I also didn't want to lead him on.

"David." I pulled away from his kiss, leaving him with a look of confusion. "I can't do this anymore, I'm sorry."

"Don't be silly." He pushed himself on top of me, his lips meeting mine once more as his fingers began unfastening the buttons on my shirt.

"David. Stop." I pushed away once more, this time with anger lacing the words from my mouth.

He listened.

He placed himself back onto his seat, further than he'd perched himself all day.

"I thought you wanted it. We've not had sex... in months. I thought you getting rid of Tamsin was..."

"Giving Tamsin the week off wasn't a ploy to get into your pants. I don't always think about sex, you know?"

The look of confusion changed instantaneously, now shrouded with anger. Bitterness.

"Well, something's changed in a matter of months because you could barely keep your hands off me before." He was pissed off, like it didn't matter that I'd created a stunning dress for him. It was forgotten about. He didn't want the dress. He'd come for sex—expensive sex. "Actually, let me rephrase. You could barely keep your hands off anyone. Your reputation precedes you, Liam, and you aren't doing yourself any favours."

Something was happening. I couldn't summon a witty response like I normally would. I couldn't argue back or plead my case because he was correct. I was a slag. Well, I had been. I didn't want to be, though. I wanted more than sex, but it seemed all the men I liked wanted sex and nothing more.

"I know." Defeat spilled from my mouth and I had no way to control it.

"Can you get Tamsin to send the dress to me once the adjustments have been made?" I nodded as David gathered his things and left the building. The lights flickered above as the door slammed behind him and I couldn't help but stare into space and mentally torture myself.

Should I settle instead of holding out for the right guy?

Was I attempting to be with the wrong type of guy? That would have explained the string of one-night-stands and the excuses that followed them. My mind consumed me, thoughts attacking each breath I took like the lions had in my dream. Despite the rockiness of my childhood—a victim of a broken home and a broken relationship—in that moment, I'd never felt worse.

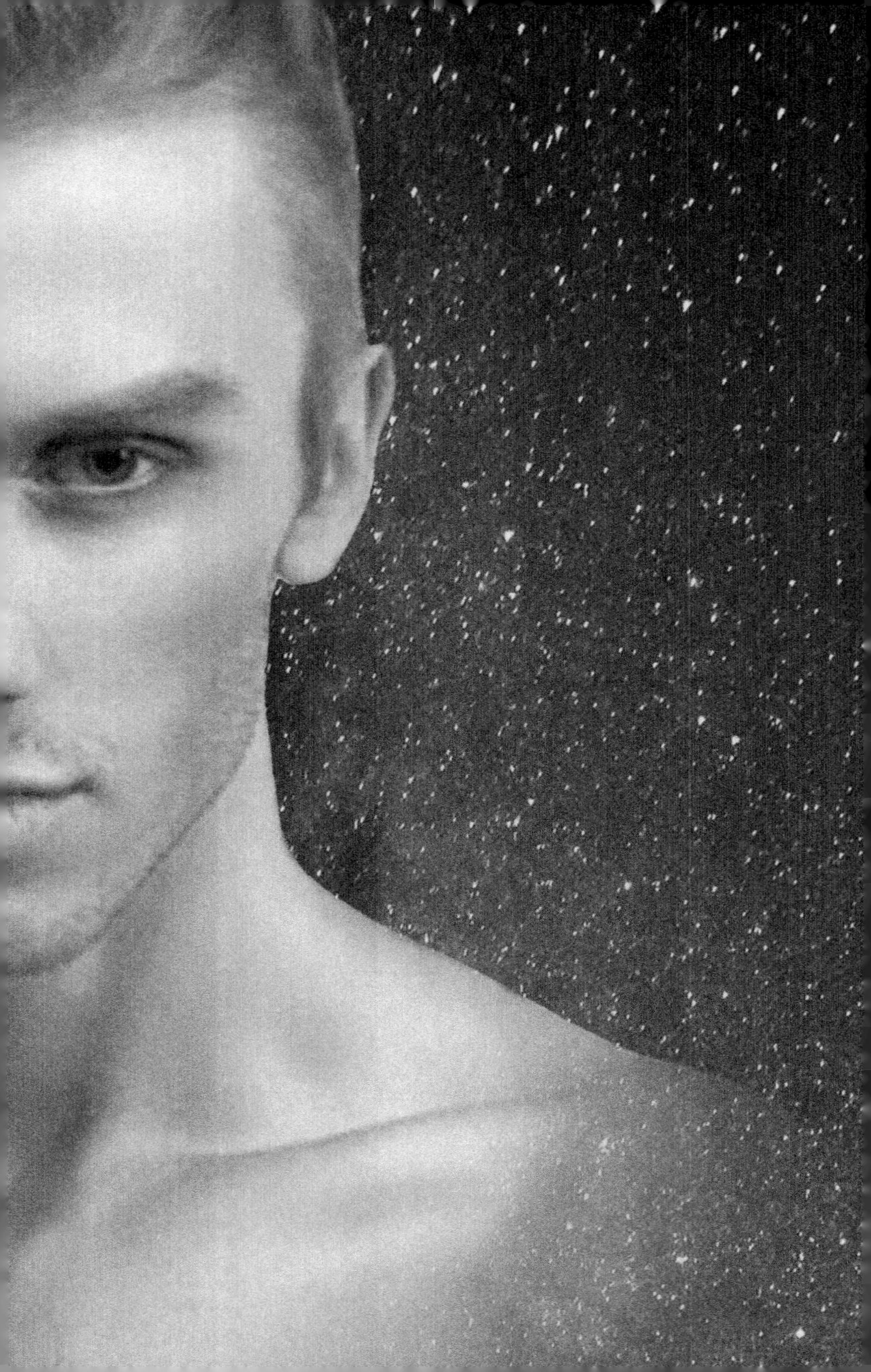

CHAPTER THREE

Tamsin had dragged me to a church of all places, and what for? Little Tess. She must've wanted me burnt at the stake. Ever since primary school, I seemed to get the flu every time a carol service or nativity came around just to avoid going. I wasn't religious and neither was Tamsin for that matter. It was Callum's fault—him and his perfect mother, Jackie. Callum had sweet talked Tamsin into christening Tess but it had taken some persuading, as she was just as stubborn as me. I knew I'd find a reason to dislike that smooth talking, hung, sexy Adonis.

Damn, I was jealous.

Tamsin had landed firmly on her feet—gorgeous daughter, shaggable fiancé and a good job. I guessed I was the one to be thanked for the latter, but still. I just had my job, which was fast becoming the be all and end all of my life, especially after ruling out the men I used to sleep with in what little free time I did have.

"I hate you," I muttered underneath my breath.

"No, you don't." Tamsin nudged me while Tess lay silently on her chest. Tess was wearing a dress just below knee height, gold detailing stitched throughout and entwined with white as pure as snow. The gold still managed to find a way to glisten under the dull lighting within the church. There wasn't a stray piece of thread or splodge of sick to be seen. "You love me more than you love Jade. Admit it," she continued, whispering under her breath as the vicar stepped towards us. I looked to Jade, who was picking her nose, licking away at her finger to reap the treasures she'd found.

Absolutely disgusting.

Everyone always said Jade and I were two peas in a pod and I'd never understood it. That was until Mum had shown me a picture of myself at the age of six, wearing her dress and flashing. Since seeing the picture, I'd realised we had more in common than I'd thought and told Jade to stop lifting her dress and flashing her knickers more than I told her I loved her. We were practically the same person.

"At this moment in time, I think you're right," I admitted, looking back at Jade as she wiped the remains on her dress. She really was a delight.

If it wasn't for the constant cues from the vicar, I would have been snoring loudly, and the acoustics within the church would have made matters worse.

As I sat in a daydream-like haze, I was snapped back to reality with the monotonous noise that was the vicar.

"I baptise you in the name of the Father, and of the Son and of the Holy Spirit. Amen."

He said Amen. We're nearly done!

Jackie had tears falling from her face in glee, and Richard stood next to her with the biggest smile on his face since the first time he'd set eyes on his granddaughter. Tamsin held onto Tess as if someone was about to steal her—there was no love that could ever be greater. I was happy for all of them, despite my mind wandering in boredom. Mental images of wiping Tessa's head dry clouded my vision, and my mouth lifted at one side.

"And now, will you join me in a prayer?"

Urgh.

I didn't know why he asked. We had to. I scanned the hollow church as I stood at the front with the counterfeit smile I wore for Tamsin. I hardly recognised anyone, mostly because what Tamsin lacked in people, Callum made up for. The majority of them had their heads bowed as they listened to the dull hum of the vicar's voice. I caught a glimpse of a few men I found to be attractive and imagined them taking me home. The downside was doubled. For one, I'd sworn I'd turn over a new leaf, and I was already starting to feel better not having the hurt and pain from wearing my heart on my sleeve. I was numb and lonely but not in pain. Secondly, these wild thoughts were to stay in my vivid imagination. These men just looked after themselves, like

Callum did. They didn't bat for my team. My eyes caught those of a male sat amongst the crowd. Eyes as clear as crystal, both lips full of colour and the bottom lip full and voluptuous. I pictured biting it just a little, underneath his spell. He looked back at me. He could have been looking because I was an important part of Tessa's life, but I didn't want him to look at me for that reason. I wanted him to be thinking of ways he could make me moan. Once his eyes looked away, I lowered my head in despair. Horny and one-hundred percent going to Hell.

I knew there was at least one reason I liked Jackie. She knew how to throw a bloody good party—free bar, the good kind of music from the last few decades and enough food to feed a small village. That was without mentioning Callum's family, all of them with a jaw line even I desired—perfect enough to look at as I drank prosecco by the bottle. I could feel the music thudding on the table as Callum rocked Tess on the dance floor, surrounded by love.

"You not getting up to dance? It's the *YMCA*. Why aren't you dancing? Is everything okay?" Tamsin swung by the lonely table where I had taken up residence.

"I'm just tired. I think working those extra hours while you've had some time off and Ima Cuming's merchandise order is catching up on me," I lied. It wasn't my work fatigue getting me down. It was envy brewing in my mind as I watched everyone seem so happy. It was as if time slowed as I watched everyone around me. Not one person was sat by themselves. An old couple danced with huge grins, children ran across the dance floor holding hands and even the staff behind the bar were laughing in couples. I was jealous of all the happiness around me because I truly wasn't.

I wanted what Tamsin had, because I wasn't sure how long I'd be able to be the third wheel or how long she'd be happy for it to stay that way. Family time was precious and I didn't want to invade it like a foreign dictator.

"Are you sure?" Tamsin asked, looking bothered.

"Positive. I tell you what, I'm gonna go to the loo and then I'll come dance, okay?" I had no choice in the matter. I was dancing whether I liked it or not. I hurried to down my last glass of prosecco from a bottle that shouldn't have been downed so quick, and made my way to the toilet.

I splashed my face with water from the sink in an attempt to cool myself down, but instead I looked as if I'd been christened. With a piece of blue paper towel, I looked in the mirror and dabbed my skin, trying desperately not to smudge my bronzer. While attempting to not create flaws in my pore-less skin, I caught sight of a tall guy in a crisp white shirt. His tie was loosened and his shirt unbuttoned slightly, revealing his bare skin underneath while he used the urinal. I shouldn't have been looking. If accidentally glancing up in P.E. at high school was bad enough, then looking at a guy in the toilets was much worse. I rubbed my chest, which started to ache at the thought of Dale and the memories I'd placed to the back of my mind. I wasn't about to make the same mistake again. I was about to look away when his eyes caught mine in the reflection, and he smiled.

What's just happened?

Hastily, my eyes dropped to the sink and I nervously started to wash my hands. He was the guy from the church. The man with the biteable lips and the clearest of eyes—the colour of dark topaz.

From my experience, guys didn't normally smile. I was expecting the head nod, macho fist bump or high-five I usually had to endure, but not a smile. Especially in the toilets. His shoes clicked on the floor, louder and louder as he approached the sink next to me, so I smiled back. It would have been rude not to—he did smile at me, after all.

"Hey. You're Tessa's godfather, right?" he asked, and I nodded nervously. I could feel the material of his trousers brushing against mine. Just stood next to him, I felt electric and yet he probably had no clue.

It was all in my head. He was just a drunk, friendly guy.

"Yeah. I'm Liam."

"Matt." He finished drying his hands and held his left hand out to shake mine. My right hand moved to his automatically without thinking, and we exchanged an awkward laugh as I changed hands. He was a lefty.

I wanted to run my hands through his dark black hair that was the perfect mess. His tongue slid across his lips as he wet them and his eyes didn't leave mine. I was deep in thought, picturing his kiss on mine. In my mind, he was kissing me. Just seconds later, my mind was still spiralling as he took a step forward and pressed his lips against mine. My eyes were seeing exactly what my mind was. They were in sync. My senses amplified, taken completely off guard as his whole body pressed against me, and fuck it was good. My hand dropped to his, stroking each and every one of his fingers as he took the breath from my lungs—a breath I needed and relied on, but somehow unimportant with him so close to me.

I could hear people outside the toilet door, their voices billowing over the music. I should have cared. I shouldn't have been kissing someone I'd only just met, but the blame didn't entirely fall on me. In the moment, the only thing that mattered was Matt and me. The toilet door opened and Matt pulled me into a cubicle, slamming the door shut behind us. His body pressed me against the cold of the door, and his hand crept over my mouth with pressure. Enough pressure that I didn't want to speak but moan.

"Be quiet," he whispered, as his mouth met mine once more and began to wander down my neck. My whole body trembled with my mouth poised to release a groan of pleasure, all from his touch. More people came into the bathroom, each time making Matt flinch and seem uneasy.

On the occasion I opened my eyes slightly, in-between the lust that filled the cubicle, I could see the worry on his face. Each time someone spoke, his lips would tremble with worry.

"I can't do this. I'm sorry," Matt said softly as he pulled away, still squirming.

"What? Why?" I asked, reaching for his hand. The confidence I usually possessed remained distorted as he controlled me and the situation we'd found ourselves in, but I wasn't about to let him leave me stood in a cubicle, lonely and aroused.

"I mean, not here. You're gorgeous. I've not been able to stop looking at you all day and I really want to finish what we've started... but there's too many people and my parents are here," he whispered, holding me close. His breath on my ear worked me up even more.

"They don't know you're gay, do they?"

"No. Nobody knows. Please don't tell anyone about this," he begged.

Damn, I wanted him so bad.

"I won't. It's not for me to tell. Look, just message me. Here's my number." I pulled a Wrighteous business card from my leather *Prada* wallet and handed it to him. His tongue wrapped around mine once more while we waited for silence to consume the entire toilet, just so he could leave. I tucked in my shirt that had been untucked and messed up in the midst of the excitement, and then searched for Tamsin on the dance floor. For the first time that day, I had a sincere smile on my face. I wasn't doomed after all.

"You were ages. Where were you? Did you pull?" Tamsin joked as I waved a little hello to Tess.

If only she knew...

"Are you serious?" I laughed sarcastically. "No. There was some drunk guy in the toilet who wouldn't stop talking to me. I couldn't get away," I blatantly lied as my eyes met Matt's across the dance floor. He acknowledged me for a moment until three people approached him with drinks.

"Yeah, Callum's family are big drinkers." Tamsin laughed, bopping Tess up and down.

Matt smiled at a woman as two people I assumed to be his parents sat by his side. His gaze flashed back to mine until it was broken by a kiss. A kiss that was reciprocated. An envious kiss on my part.

"You're telling me!" My mouth was left wide open in shock. Only minutes before it had been our lips touching. We'd panted in excitement and it had left us both with the taste of satisfaction. She'd ruined that. They both had.

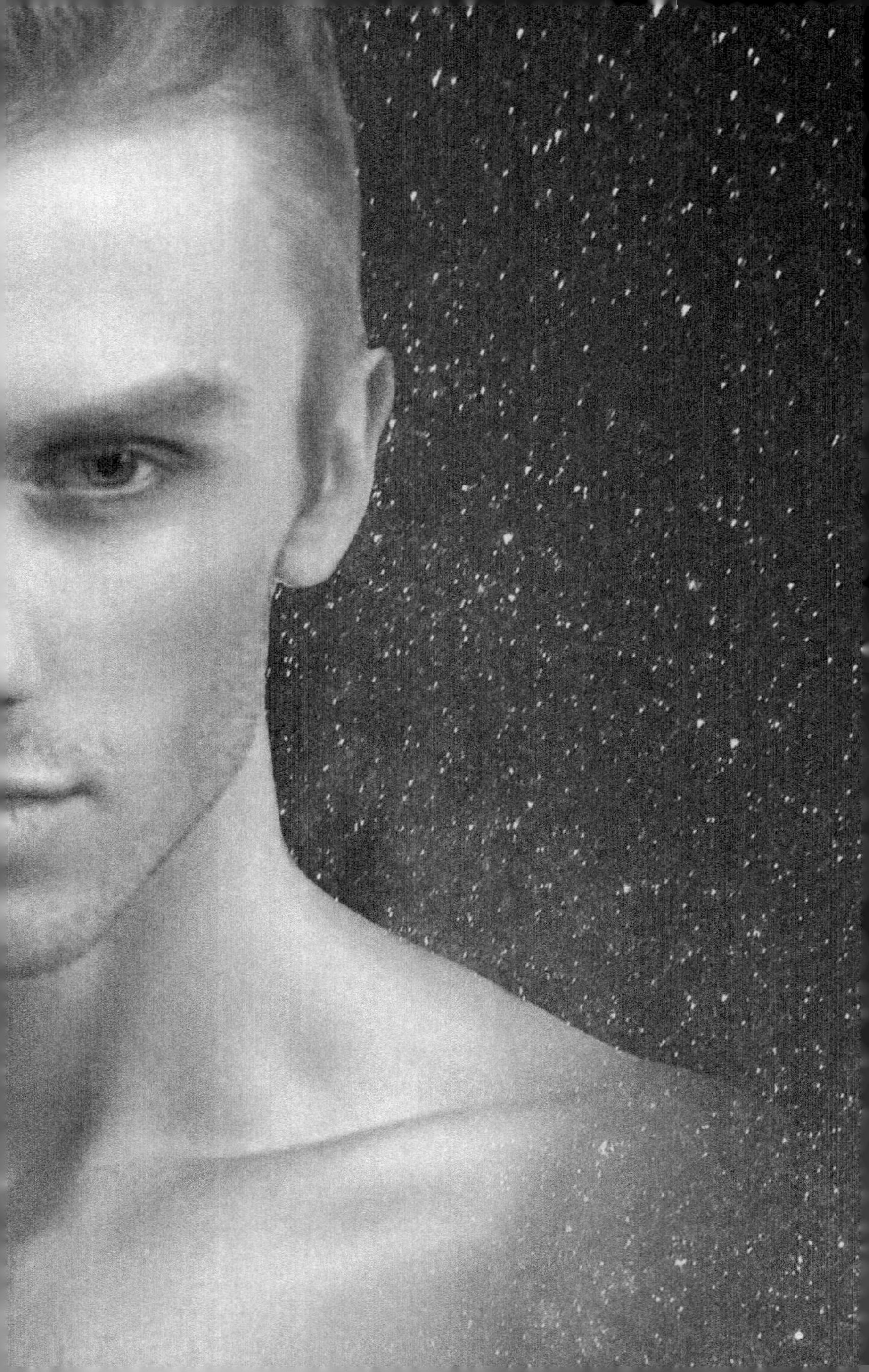

CHAPTER FOUR

My head was spinning just like the room, but in the opposite direction. Occasionally, I'd find myself thinking back to being sat on the lonely table, watching Matt being molested by his girlfriend. The drunk in me wanted to confront him and ask what the hell he was playing at, but I wasn't about to ruin Tess' day. Tamsin's day. Despite not wanting to make a scene, I'd drunk more than I could handle. I'd not consumed that much alcohol since graduation, where I'd thought it was appropriate to straddle any and all attractive men.

Maybe I had made the christening about me.

That thought whirled as my brain fought off the intoxication, vomit rising from my stomach to the bin Tamsin had kindly placed next to the sofa.

"You'll sleep with me, Callum. Won't you?" I slurred once I'd finished throwing up, both Callum and

Tamsin gawking at me. I wiped the sick from around my mouth and tapped the sofa as a way to lure Callum to me. It didn't work.

"You're even funnier when you're drunk," Callum laughed at me as I continued to wipe the saliva from around my mouth.

"I'm putting Tess up to bed now. Sleep tight and be quiet, Gayboy." Tamsin placed a kiss on my forehead, my temperature burning away underneath the red of her lipstick. "Oh, and don't get any sick on the sofa," Tamsin said sternly as she trotted off upstairs. She was a parent, practically turning into my mum or hers with the stuff she came out with. Stuff like 'Turn the bathroom light off when you're done. We're not at Blackpool Illuminations' and she'd reminisce about the good old days at university. She was the same age as me, and already she possessed the power to become irritable at everything. There was no way I'd win an argument with her anymore. Even though she drove me up the wall, I still couldn't get enough of her.

As I lay on the sofa, drowning under the heaviest duvet in the world, I thought about Matt—his spontaneity, his force as he pulled me into the cubicle and his soft lips as they wrapped around mine. It meant something; it had to. No guy could kiss that well and not mean it, especially a drunk guy.

So I did what any average, sane, rational human would do.

I stalked social media to find him.

He was quite easy to find. Jackie had already uploaded pictures and tagged her closest friends and family. There Matt was, on my screen. A picture of him in a blue shirt taken as he stood underneath the exotic backdrop of palm trees. I tried my best to ignore his girlfriend, clinging to him as if he was a piece of meat. I swiped down and started to read his profile.

Matthew Nightingale, aged twenty, University of Manchester studying astrophysics. His girlfriend on the other hand didn't go to university, not according to her profile, which I accidentally-on-purpose clicked on to understand my competition.

Charlotte Price, aged nineteen, worked as a receptionist for a veterinarian practice. She had a cracking pair of tits—pity they were going to waste in the hands of Matt.

Matt kissed too well to appreciate boobs like those, didn't he?

She had to be his beard—a cover, disguising his sexuality because his parents didn't know. I continued looking at the fine specimen of Charlotte, almost feeling guilty for hating her before even meeting her. Poor girl.

Or maybe he's curious?

I didn't know what was going through his head, but I did know that no guy had ever made me feel the way he did, not even my previous boyfriend. No man had ever swept me off my feet, holding an intense power over me that I could almost physically feel. We'd only had approximately ten minutes together and I longed for more.

"Morning, sunshine!" Tamsin pulled the duvet from me with force, leading me to fall off the sofa. "How's your head?"

"No complaints," I croaked.

"You need to stop hanging around with drag queens. You're starting to sound more and more like them each day."

"Speaking of drag queens, I have so much I need to do later. I didn't plan on getting that drunk." I groaned, remembering the mess that sat in the unit and the amount of work piling high. The thought of all of that made my head thump continuously, even without the hangover that plagued my system. "Do you have any paracetamol?"

"Yeah, sure," Tamsin said, heading over to her bag. I looked at her in confusion as she held out a bottle of Calpol with a plastic syringe. "It works the same, just have extra. Besides, this tastes so nice. It's way better than swallowing tablets."

"What have you become?" I laughed at Tamsin, who was still trying to convince me that taking Calpol was a good idea. It turned out to taste pretty damn good.

"Shh, you. Just because I'm always prepared. Anyway, what time are we heading to the unit today?

Just so I can let Jaqueline and Richard know when they are having Tessa."

"Not for at least an hour. I need coffee—lots and lots of coffee."

I stared across the unit. The light from the few windows seemed to highlight the floor covered in packing material, an ocean of boxes and bubblewrap left from days before. Under normal circumstances, I wouldn't have let it get so messy, but with having the christening and no Tamsin to help out, all of the mess from *Ima Cuming's Up and Cuming Tour* was left strewn across the floor.

"We need to get this tidied. I can't have Coco seeing this when she comes later."

"Yes, Sir," Tamsin chirped as she began clearing the boxes in a flash. Being Tamsin's boss could have been weird, a recipe for disaster, especially as we were best friends. Not for us, though. We had our own strengths and we played to them. Whenever one of us was in need, the other would come running. Based on the state of the unit, I was in need, and cleaning had never been listed as one of Tamsin's strengths, but I was desperate. Coco had performed in some of the biggest venues in the UK and around the world, so securing an order from Coco Pop would've given me the exposure I needed and the funds to take a risk. A risk that had sat at the back of my mind just waiting for the right time. A dream itching to be fulfilled. I'd had streaks of success and I wasn't about to let it end––hungover or not, I had to succeed.

The following hours seemed to rush past us as we cleaned nearly every inch of the unit, including the mess that was Tamsin's desk.

"I'll get it," Tamsin shouted as she ran to the phone, which was now visible on the desk while I waited for the arrival of Coco.

"They hung up. That's weird," she said with a giggle each time she popped a bubble within the bubblewrap she refused to put in the bin. She was still a child at heart, no matter how much growing up she'd done.

Just seconds later, Coco stepped through the unit door––ebony skin and dressed all in gold, her outfit was nearly as loud as her personality.

"Coco, welcome. How are you? Do you want a drink?" I asked nervously as Tamsin listened in, ready at the drop of a hat to make her a coffee.

"Liam, thanks for meeting me. A rum and coke would be perfect. That was a hellish drive. Note to self. Do not drive in drag again," Coco said, as if she oozed confidence from her pores, enough to intimidate my usual spark. It was Coco Pop, after all.

"I'm on it." Tamsin grabbed her bag and was out of the door without instruction.

"From London, was it?" I tried to make small talk,

anything to pass the time until we were to speak about her dress. The dress, I could talk about for days.

"Mmm Hmm. Glad I'm not going back until next week. I'm performing in Manchester tomorrow night but I've got some meet and greets this evening. Anyway, onto business. The order enquiry my PA made with Tamsin has changed a bit..."

Fuck. That's that order down the drain. Did she have to come all this way to tell me?

"How so?" I asked, trying not to rage punch her in the face.

"I'm gonna need two outfits, not one. But there's a catch..." A slight grin grew on her face, her teeth pressed together. "I only want to pay for one."

"Oh, erm. I'm afraid I just can't do that. I have a business, overheads to pay..." I stumbled at her request. She was practically a celebrity in the eyes of the drag world, but I didn't have the time, nor the money to put orders on hold and make her a dress for free.

"What if I told you that I'm appearing in a well-known televised drag competition?" she said smugly.

"You're joking?" My mouth hung agape in shock. It was a no brainer. "Deal! What are you thinking for the second outfit?" I made the decision without hesitation, no need to think of the costs or logistics behind the order. She was going to be on television wearing an outfit created by me. That was about as close as Wright-eous was getting to fame any time soon. The drag show was a huge platform for drag and fashion. Fashion had to be either cheap or well known to sell.

"I'm thinking a red pant suit. It has to be a shiny material, but no sequins." She was a drag queen who knew exactly what she wanted.

"Perfect, so like a PVC, pleather, bondage type material? I can do that. Let's take some more measurements." I pulled my tape measure from around my neck to size the famous queen up. She was curvy, and it wasn't hip pads giving her shape. She was a big queen and her fans loved her fashion just as much as her one-liners.

"Girl, you already know me so well." Coco snapped her fingers and bobbed her head from side to side with sass. I always did my research on my clients, and I knew exactly what she needed, but one thing I'd learnt since starting this business—drag queens were kinky. Just mentioning the word bondage would have been enough to win her over.

"Thanks for the rum, you two. I needed it. Liam, we'll speak soon. Don't keep me waiting too long now," Coco said as she strutted out the door, her car keys swinging from the keyring hanging off her finger. Thankfully, she'd only had the one drink to take the edge off and not managed anymore, leaving Tamsin and I with nearly a full bottle of rum to celebrate with.

"I won't. Take care," I replied, looking over to

Tamsin. A girlish scream leapt from my mouth the minute the unit door was closed. "Wrighteous is gonna be on TV. Can you believe it?"

"Amazing!" Her voice twanged with glee. "You totally deserve it. I've told you so many times. Your eye for design is something else," Tamsin said, pouring another rum for both of us.

"I know. I just hope I'll be spotted once people see what I can do," I said, taking a sip from the crystal glass I'd received as a present from Mum and Stuart when I'd purchased the unit.

"Your time will come, I just know it. Look, you've only got a call with Drew later. I'll tell him you're sick and that you'll call him tomorrow. Go nurse that hangover and take the rest of the day to take in what's just happened. You're always here. Have a day off." She was right; I was always working, but I had no clue what I'd do with a day off––I used to have a routine. Scroll on my phone, get a kebab, go for drinks and slip into a stranger's bed before the day was out. I'd barely seen my family over the past few weeks. In fact, the christening was the first time I'd seen Jade awake in over a week as she'd always been in bed before I'd arrived home. I needed to slow down, otherwise there'd be nothing left of me to put into Coco's outfit, and that had to be perfect. The rest of my career depended on that.

The autumn sun was nowhere near ready to set, but with Tamsin's instruction I drove straight home and walked through the front door––no going on a dating app to find my next prescription of love, and no texting David for a quick, desperate fix. No texting him at all for that matter. We'd not spoken since he'd stormed out after I'd denied him all of me. I missed him as he'd became one of my closest friends, but the stubborn in me just couldn't forgive him for thinking I'd get my dick out at just a lick of his lips.

"Well, this is a nice surprise. What're you doing home so early?" Mum said, bemused as I walked through into the kitchen as she topped up her pot of tea.

"Tamsin's cleared my afternoon because I'm hungover. Pop a tea bag in for me? I'm gasping for a brew," I said, grabbing a biscuit out of the ceramic jar on the kitchen side.

"Nothing new there then, you're always hungover. Oh, wasn't Tess' christening beautiful? Sorry we didn't go to the party afterwards. You didn't mind, did you?"

"Don't be silly, it's fine. I made friends." I smiled at the thought of Matt. What I didn't tell her? I'd likely made an enemy out of his girlfriend.

"I don't doubt that for a second, sweetie."

"I'm off upstairs to sleep for a bit before tea. What are we having?" I grabbed my cup of tea, brewed to perfection.

"Bacon, new potatoes and peas," she said warmly. My favourite—I could always rely on Mum's cooking. Nothing could beat her homemade meals, despite the times I'd chosen a kebab over them.

"Can't wait!" With my brew in hand, I promptly

made my way to my room, too hungover to even pop my head in to see Jade.

Just a nap, then family time.

I lay in bed in a daze, staring at the glow-in-the-dark star stickers that should have been peeled off years before. Each time I'd look up to them, I'd remember the good times I'd stored safely away, but the bad would always creep forward, out of the place in my mind I'd tried to lock them away in. I'd remember the years without Dad, and the days when Mum had suffered. All those memories from stupid star stickers that should have been taken down but hadn't because the ceiling was too high. It was too much effort for stickers. For me, they weren't just stickers at all.

My door crept open slightly as Jade poked her head into the room.

"What ya doing?" Her voice was enough to melt anyone's heart. I may have been biased, but she couldn't have gotten cuter.

"I've been trying to sleep. What about you?"

"I miss you," she said, ignoring my question and clumsily running towards my bed. By the age of seven, I thought she would have found her feet.

"Miss you too, cutie. What've you done today?"

"I played with my toys and my rabbit's head fell off." Her dramatic laugh echoed below the high ceiling. She'd spend hours playing with her Sylvanian Families. The amount of money I'd spent on her on those toys alone could, no doubt, have paid for a years worth of rent at my unit. "Where've you been?" she asked simply.

"I was at work with Tamsin this morning..."

"Oh. Is Tamsin your girlfriend?" she interrupted inquisitively, her face blushing a shade of rose with embarrassment.

"Haha, no."

"Who is your girlfriend then?"

Impossible. An impossible question to answer but one I'd expected for a long time. Her tiny mind was absorbing everything around her. She was at an age where she questioned everything.

I couldn't answer her without opening a can of worms, and I wasn't going to lie to her—she needed to know. I'd spent a lot of my life thinking there was something wrong with me, hiding away from a world that was in no shape or form ready for me, but I knew better than that now.

"I don't have a girlfriend, no. I don't have a boyfriend either, but maybe one day." I watched her process what I'd said for a second. Just a second.

"Oh," she said obliviously.

"Would you be happy for me if I got a boyfriend?" For one second more I watched her think about what I'd said. Her golden blonde hair fell in front of her face, so I swept it to one side before she could answer.

"Yep, but who would be my boyfriend if you have one?"

"I don't know but I think you're a little too young to

worry about boyfriends. Besides, one day you'll find someone that makes you really happy and you'll know you want to spend the rest of your life with them." I smiled at her innocence and she returned it, resting her hand on mine. Her hands were as soft as silk. I dreaded the day she would come home with a broken heart. She lay back onto my pillow next to me, not ready to move any time soon.

"How much do you love me?" I asked in our usual way.

"I love you like twenty thousand and thirty hundred."

"Wow. That's a lot," I spoke as Jade snuggled into my arm, entirely unaware of how those words made me feel. "I love you more, though."

Her words were jumbled, but that didn't matter. I knew exactly how she felt. We may have had different dads, but there was a bond between us and it had never faltered. Unbreakable. The love between a big brother and little sister. I wasn't about to test the unbreakable bond, nor continue to ignore how precious my time with her was. It was all about to change.

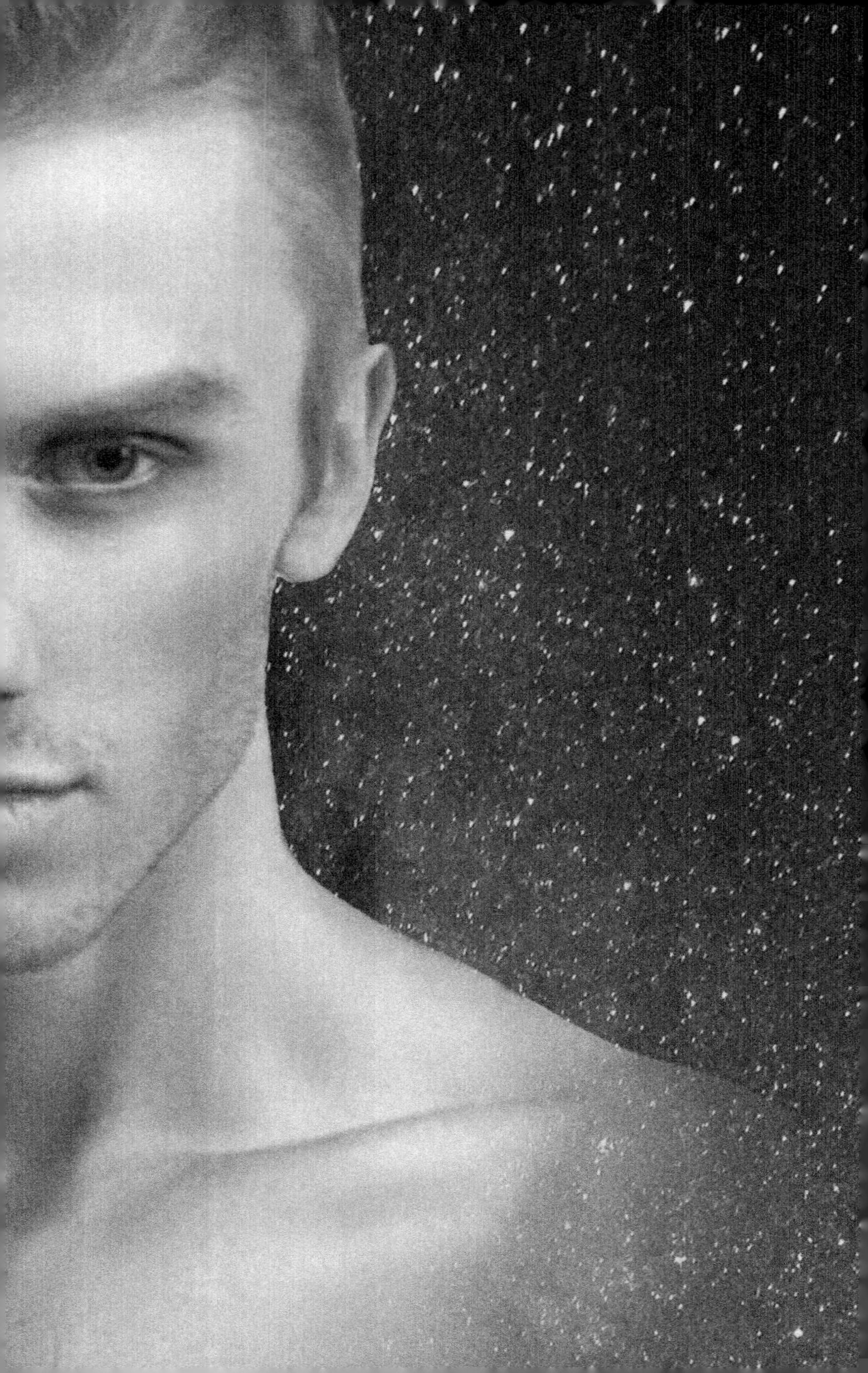

CHAPTER FIVE

The following morning I was hangover free, the smell of freshly cooked pancakes assuring me of the matter. In my normal routine, I opened my phone first, glancing at a message. My perfect stranger.

Matt Nightingale
12th November 2019

[06:12]

Hey, it's Matt from the christening. I tried calling your work number yesterday but Tamsin answered so I panicked and hung up. You haven't told her, have you? Anyway, why don't you have your mobile number on your damn business card? Hope you don't mind me messaging you here, but I want to talk and I realise I have some explaining to do.

He was the person that had called the unit and hung up.

He was right. He did have some explaining to do. I wanted to know if that kiss had meant anything, or if it had just been a release his girlfriend wasn't giving him. I needed to know if I was just in the right place at the right time, if he'd have kissed any willing guy.

Did he have to justify his actions to me—his perfect stranger?

He'd acted on impulse. He'd swept me off my feet so effortlessly. I was a nobody to him and I should've just been happy it was me standing in that bathroom instead of anyone else. Technically, he had some explaining to do to his girlfriend. Until then, I definitely wanted to hear him out.

We'd exchanged phone numbers just a few messages in, and that evening I found myself sat waiting nervously in a coffee shop at Manchester Piccadilly, waiting for a man who had unknowingly touched me in all the right ways within minutes of meeting him. A man I could tell had a lot to offer, but who came with secrets and baggage. I wrapped my hands around a warm cup of coffee—Americano with sugar-free gingerbread syrup to be precise. Tamsin had taught me well enough to steer clear of those dreaded lattes. I'd learnt that excess milk would make me fat from the countless times Mum had done *Slimming World*. Pastries with their flaky goodness, on the other hand, were an acceptable reason to put on weight.

There he was. He walked in nervously, looking around the coffee shop, his head dropping to his phone multiple times. I held my hand up slightly so he'd notice me where I was hidden, nestled in a secluded alcove. I wasn't stupid. I knew he must've sneaked off for this, and that he wouldn't want to be seen with me. I was okay with that. That's what I thought, anyway.

"Hey. It's good to see you," he said with a nervous smile, his mouth twitching slightly.

"You too. I got you a coffee. I know how being a student can leave you on a tight budget," I said, my mouth moving quicker than my brain.

FUCK. I shouldn't have said that.

"How do you know I'm a student?" he asked with intrigue as he sat down, immediately quaffing the drink in front of him. His thumb ran across his lips, wetted by the coffee, and then pushed back the dark hair from his face, continuing to wait for an answer.

Think, Liam. Think.

"You told me at the christening, in the toilets. Do you not remember? I'm clearly not as memorable as I'd hoped." I crossed my fingers underneath the table, hoping I'd pulled it off and not come across as a stalker.

"Oh, really? Well, this is the thing, Liam. It's really cringe me saying this, but I can't stop thinking about you."

Marry me.

"Why do I sense there's a but coming?" I gazed at him but his eyes nervously wandered around the room. He was clearly battling with himself—fighting the fact that he felt like he shouldn't be sat with me.

"I don't want there to be a but, but there is. It's complicated but I have a girlfriend. We've been dating a few months, but it's not working. I think we both know it and we're holding onto hope, but I'm not sure I can do that anymore since meeting you. I also live in Manchester for uni, and she works about an hour from here," Matt said, and his fingers tapped the table as he squirmed. His posture held such confidence, and you wouldn't have known it from his rugged exterior, but he was vulnerable. "That's without mentioning the fact that... I'm bisexual. I'm not sure she's fully okay with that."

At least he'd told her about his sexuality and he wasn't entirely in the closet. I'd never been with a bisexual guy before, but his sexuality didn't bother me. Did it turn me on more? Probably. I liked a guy with a rough edge. Maybe that was why I found myself broken both physically and mentally after every experience. I pictured him slamming me up against the cubicle once more, playing out the memory like a movie, but this time the credits didn't roll straight after the kiss.

"So, what are you saying?" I said, taking another sip of my coffee as I mentally undressed him. I stroked the hairs on his chest that were still vivid in my mind from the first night I'd met him, and felt his breath on my bare skin.

"I'm saying that those few minutes we spent together can't be forgotten, and that's got to mean something, right?"

"I guess," I said casually, but inside I was jumping for joy.

"If I were to break up with Charl, things would still be complicated..." He paused as my mind played games.

If.

"You see, I'm actually Callum's cousin." Should that have bothered me? I didn't know how Tamsin would react. "Oh, and to top it all off, my very Christian parents have no clue that I like men and would probably disown me if they found out. That's why it's complicated. I guess I'm holding onto Charl because she's my safety net. If my parents were to even doubt my sexuality, having her would make them believe I'm straight." I continued to listen to him, my voice mute so I heard every word. "I'm always careful. I'd never, ever kiss a guy on a night out just in case someone were to see me or it was posted on social media, but with you... it was different. I couldn't not kiss you. I couldn't keep my hands off you. In fact, it's hard not to right now." He spoke quietly, rambling to fill the silence I'd created. Not once did he break eye contact. This was serious.

"Okay, that's rough but I've been there. Not the whole being Callum's cousin or being Christian parts, but I had to come out once. I know how hard it is.

Personally, I think dumping your girlfriend is a big jump to take after knowing me for a matter of minutes, so why don't we just... get to know each other? Let's see if we're compatible before you turn your life upside down. I don't want you to do that for nothing." My knee grazed his under the table and rocked up and down. His leg twitched in response as if it craved my touch as much as I wanted his, but it had to stop. This time, I was thinking with my heart firmly held in my chest and not on my sleeve. This time I was thinking with my brain and not my dick.

"Yeah, okay. You're right. I guess if we're gonna be friends, we better get to know each other."

We drowned in each other's company in the coffee shop for about an hour before downing the remains of our second coffees and heading home. He'd told me things I already knew since stalking his social media, but the less he knew about that, the better. He loved space just as much as I did, but his parents weren't overly keen on his degree choice, since astrology kind of diminished the idea that there was a God. He told me that he spent a lot of time at Jodrell Bank, an observatory tucked away in the countryside of Cheshire, the night skies perfect for stargazing. I'd been there a few times. As a child, I'd begged Mum to take me so I could learn about space and see the stars up close. One time, we went to a stargazing event in the freezing cold, but Mum had queued with me for hours just so I could get a look through a professional telescope for the first time.

Maybe stars were more than giant balls of gas. Maybe wishes upon stars did come true? I hadn't wished on many recently, but I was sure as hell about to. Fate was calling, and all my stars were pointing to Matt.

A whole day had passed, and I'd slept the easiest I had in a long time. I found myself not preoccupied by thoughts of work, but instead about Matt—the way I'd controlled the situation and established ground rules. I must've had some willpower to not hold his hand as he grazed mine just walking in the street. To not go in for a kiss goodbye as we'd parted ways, even though our lips had already met. To not send him countless nude pictures in response to a clearly flirtatious message that got me riled up in the right way. The old Liam wouldn't have hesitated and I was proud of not being my usual slutty self.

"So, what did you do over the weekend then, Mr Slow Reply?" Tamsin mocked, and rightfully so as normally I'd have been glued to my phone.

"I was... kind of on a date," I said, grinning like the Cheshire Cat.

"Ooh, a date? Wait. A one-night-stand is not a date. We've been through this." In her defence, we had debated that subject long and hard.

"Ha. No. A proper date. No sex. Not even a kiss," I said, eager for her reaction.

"You've got to be kidding. I don't believe you. Who with?"

Callum's fit cousin who has a girlfriend.

"I can't tell you. Not yet, anyway."

"That's not fair. Don't you remember when I first started seeing Callum? You wouldn't rest until you had all the juicy gossip. What's different about me knowing who your little love affair is with?"

It was an affair she couldn't know about; that was the difference. There was too much at stake. She'd met a straight man and they'd happened to work at the same place. Matt, on the other hand, stood to lose his friends and family for talking about his sexuality. No, I had to lie and luckily I was a terrific liar. Tamsin should have lied if she'd wanted to keep her and Callum secret at first.

"Ugh, fine. It's with Drew's assistant. You know, Drew P Cox?"

"Oh, really? You see, the other day I called and asked to speak to Drew's assistant, but got straight through to Drew himself. He doesn't have an assistant."

FUCK.

"He doesn't anymore. He sacked him because of our love affair. Quite the scandal to be honest," I lied confidently again without a thought.

"Cut the crap, Liam. You're really not good at lying. Don't you remember playing Pineapple? You suck at lying. What's going on?"

There was no chance in Hell that I'd make it

through the day if I didn't tell her. I should've remembered that Tamsin knew me better than anyone else.

"Ugh. Okay. If I tell you, you have to swear not to tell anyone. Not even Callum. I mean it."

"I swear," she said bluntly. I knew she'd keep it a secret with anyone else, but I didn't know what kind of relationship she and Callum had. I didn't know if she burst through the door when she arrived home and told him everything about her day.

"There wasn't a drunk guy talking to me at the christening in the toilets... I kissed someone. That's why I was so long. Don't be mad." I flinched as she moved her hand, but only to prompt me to speak more. "Oh, and that someone turned out to be Callum's cousin. I wouldn't have kissed him if I'd known." I continued to wait for a swift punch from Tamsin, who was the definition of small but mighty.

"Shut up! I want all the details, but before that... You aren't very smart at times, are you? I mean, who did you think it was going to be? Literally the only people that attended were our closest friends and family. Of course it was going to be a relative." She had a point, but even so, I'd had no choice in the matter. Matt had kissed me whether I liked it or not. "Also, why would I be mad? Was it Matt?"

"How..." Before I could answer her first question, she went straight in and snatched the trophy. Ever since Tess had been born it was like she had some mind-reading super power that all mums were gifted with the second they give birth. As a child, I'd always tried to sneak biscuits from the kitchen and Mum had always known. It was clear—mums knew everything.

"Two reasons. Callum has had his suspicions about him for a long time and the second? I saw the way you were looking at him that night. You really like him, don't you?"

"I think I do, but it's confusing. This isn't me, Tams. I can take it and leave it usually, but not with him. I want more."

Matt was a delicious apple growing on a tree full of forbidden fruit. Maybe that was why I wanted to pick him off. Maybe knowing he had a girlfriend made me like him that little bit more than I should. He was the ripest, brightest apple on that tree but he still felt out of reach. God, I wanted to take a bite out of him so bad.

"Does his girlfriend know?" Tamsin asked casually, seeming entirely unfazed by the news.

"Not yet. That's why we didn't kiss. We met up to talk and we've decided we're going to get to know each other first to see if it's worth pursuing."

"I was going to say I'm happy you used your mouth before your penis, but I'm sure you'd find too much joy in me saying that, so instead, I'm just going to say I'm really proud of you." Tamsin smiled with her eyes. It was our deep and meaningful conversations that were a rarity, combined with the laughter and mutual love that made up our friendship.

"Love you," I said in return before ordering us both to get on with work.

Ever since high school, being taught by Miss Chan, I'd known I wanted to design fashion. Fashion that would walk the runways of the world, or maybe even appear in a high street store or two. Drag wasn't the fashion I wanted to do, nor had I set out to do it. It had sort of fallen into my lap when Miss Mirage had asked me to do her anniversary dress and then I couldn't stop the orders from coming in. Only a real idiot would've turned them away. I wasn't getting any closer to that dream while designing fashion for drag queens—that was part of the problem, but also the solution. Dressing drag queens was making me thousands each month, a lot of which I'd managed to save. So I was going to put my money where my mouth was.

"I'm going to block off three days a week from the diary. The first day will be a day off. After spending time with Jade the other day, I realised just how much I bloody miss her," I said as Tamsin scribbled notes in her diary.

"Good decision, boss," she jested, and waited to find out what the other two days would entail.

"The other two days will be blocked off for me to design fashion—couture fashion not for drag queens. I don't want any appointments on those days, nor will I be working on any of their pieces. It will be solely for me to work on that dream I've had. I need to start doing things for me and start working on the types of fashion that I love," I said as Tamsin continued to make notes, although this time a look of concern had grown on her face.

"Will that not mean you'll lose money, as the drag pieces you'll be booking in will have a longer lead time? Losing three days is going to cut your revenue in half." She was right, it would, but it was also about time Wrighteous became more exclusive.

"Yes, but I have savings to prop up the business until I can get sales on the couture pieces. We can just bump up the prices a little and choose who we want to work with. A more exclusive feel for the client."

"Are you sure that's gonna work? I know you're working with some big names at the moment, but don't forget about the queens who are just starting out—the queens who got you to where you are now. They won't be able to afford you."

"It has to work," I said, listening to her every word. Those small-time drag queens did help me, but I had aspirations, too. I couldn't just sit around waiting for them. I'd get complacent and I knew I'd lose all the passion I had. I needed to do this for me. Business was about taking calculated risks and with this one, the pros outweighed the cons, so I had nothing to lose.

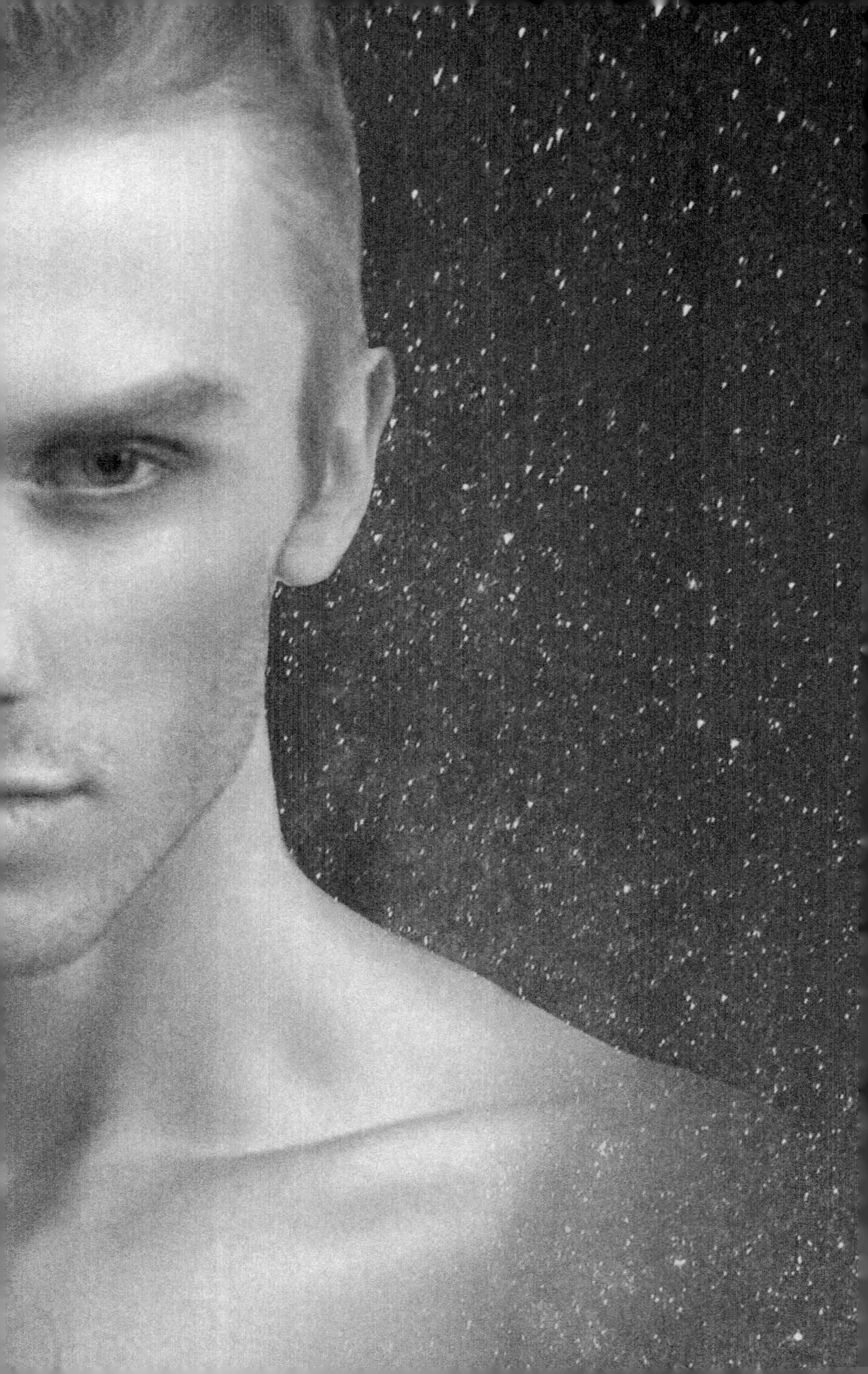

CHAPTER SIX

"Hey, I'm here. Where are you?" I said into my phone waiting for Matt to respond. He was late and had been the past two dates we'd been on. I, for once, was early.

"I'm nearly there, just a few minutes away. See you in a bit, okay?"

"Okay." I hung up and stood in a lobby of sorts, waiting for Matt to arrive. The ceiling was at least three storeys high with huge light fixtures displayed in the centre. It was as if the architects had built the whole thing to showcase them alone. Although Matt and I were meeting as friends, it felt as though we were both sneaking around. Each time I saw him, nerves filled me, something that didn't happen often, but I knew why. This time, there could have been a different end game. This time, if things worked out, I could step away from the lonely table and not look back. I'd have what Tamsin had—love—the one thing that seemed to be missing in my life. Until then, nobody could find out about us, not yet. So for each date, we found different places to meet. The first place was the train station coffee shop, busy but secluded. The second was a bar in the rough part of the city, which I hoped never to return to. Our third date had brought me outside a hotel at least forty storeys high. He had been insistent that we were coming here.

I should have been at home spending time with my family, especially as Jade was the reason I'd decided to take more time off, but this was only short term. One day wouldn't hurt.

"Hi, are you okay?" His cheeky grin alone was enough to make me melt. Just the sight of him had me weak at the knees, practically ready to collapse in the streets of Manchester.

"Yeah, I'm good, are you?" My voice wobbled. I didn't know what to expect from our third date. He was still with Charlotte and as much as I'd have liked him to lead me into one of the stunning suites at the hotel, he didn't and rightfully so. Instead, we checked in at a small side reception and took a lift up to the twenty-third floor. There was a bar and restaurant combined, displaying a three hundred and sixty degree view of the city of Manchester.

"Welcome, gentlemen," a waitress greeted as we stepped out of the lift. She was wearing a sleek and slightly revealing dress and looked pristine, with not a stray thread in sight. She walked us over to our table that sat up close to one of the windows after Matt had checked us in using his last name.

Nightingale.

The waitress smiled, handing each of us a menu.

"Your glass of Prosecco is included, and you can look out over these gorgeous views. My name is Stacey, so if there's anything I can do before your afternoon tea arrives, just give me a wave." The waitress's voice became a hum as I looked out across the city. I couldn't believe I'd never been to this place before. I felt on top of the world, even more so looking across at Matt.

"Thanks, Stacey." Matt smiled at her as if he'd known her forever, and the waitress delicately strolled away to greet some more guests.

Matt seemed relaxed, not looking around the room as often as he had on our previous encounters. His eyes took a quick sweep of the floor before his foot met the inner seam of my right leg and began to graze up and down, higher and higher with each movement. I wanted to enjoy the views, but the electricity between Matt and I clouded my vision. I looked out of the windows, but I didn't see anything. All I saw was Matt.

"Isn't this nice?" His words were coated with seduction, whether that was his intention or not.

"Mmm hmm," I hummed, trying desperately to distract myself. "All this food looks amazing. Thanks for bringing me here." I picked up the menu and nestled my blushing face behind it.

"You're welcome. I thought it was only fair after

taking you to that very dicey part of town last time." He laughed as he reached for my leg under the table. His touch made me flinch at first, almost making me spill my Prosecco. He reached for his glass, as the other hand rested on my thigh. I'd have been lying if I told him I wanted him to move it.

"To us." He held up his glass and I followed, desperately trying to stop myself from getting aroused. We were in public, but that hadn't stopped him during our first encounter in the toilets at the christening. I knew we couldn't repeat what we'd done at the christening, not yet, but I couldn't deny I wanted more.

Just a few hours later, we left the hotel after Matt insisted on paying. I wasn't going to complain as I was slowly seeing my savings diminishing as my work at Wrighteous slowed down.

I pulled my black faux fur coat tighter as I walked into the autumn wind with Matt. The minute I stepped out into the cold, my head started to spin.

"God, I feel a bit tipsy." We stood together outside the hotel, as close as we'd been in the cubicle the first day we'd met.

"Do you? I guess I do, too." He pushed a lock of my light hair away from my forehead, and I let him. I didn't flinch that time. I craved his touch; I didn't care where or how or what. I wanted him. "So, what now?" he questioned, his eyes somehow sparkling under the dark clouds above us, and not once did he look away from me.

"I don't know, but I'm bloody freezing, so anywhere warm."

"I could... get us a room if you want?"

Yes.

I wanted his warmth all over me, his bare skin pressed on mine. Seeing him had become a form of torture, and was testing my self-control because I knew I couldn't have what I wanted.

"You know we can't, Matt. I'm not about to willingly let you cheat on Charlotte." I turned away and he grabbed my arm to pull me closer.

"I know, you're right. Over our past few dates, I've noticed you have a habit of being right and it's starting to get to me. This time, can you not be wrong? Can you let me be right? Can you let me do something I don't think is stupid at all? Can you not resist temptation just this once and allow this to happen? We both know it's going to happen." His words were whispered, and with each one we shifted closer together. People swarmed us yet that didn't matter. I could feel his breath on my face, his lips creeping toward mine in what seemed like slow motion, as if time had stopped to allow me to make a decision. Was I going to give in to myself like I always did?

His lips touched mine for just a second.

"Matt. I said no." My eyebrows pointed as I pulled out of his embrace. My raised voice caught the attention of a few people.

"Okay. I'm sorry. I just..."

"I know... I know how you feel because I feel it, too, but I'm not doing this. It's crossing the line. We agreed to get to know each other before we made a decision. If you've made a decision and can see something with me, then you know what you have to do," I interrupted in frustration, still stood in the cold looking at him in anger for clouding my judgement for just a second too long. He didn't say anything, his eyes fixated on me with a look of sadness. "I'm off. Let me know when it's done, if it ever is." I walked away and restrained myself from looking back, because I knew if I had, I would have changed my mind.

Nearly two weeks had passed, and naturally, I drowned myself in work, using my days off to catch up on work that had fallen behind quicker than I'd imagined. Those days I'd allocated for family, but instead I'd always ended up with Matt.

MATT
2ND DECEMBER 2019

[12:58]

HEY! I'VE JUST GOT OUT OF A LECTURE. ARE YOU OK? I'M SORRY I'VE NOT TOLD HER YET, BUT I PROMISE I WILL. PLEASE BELIEVE ME? X

I still believed him, but my patience was wearing

thin. I should have been spending time with him instead of holding onto empty promises.

[13:10]

Hey, it's fine. Don't worry. Sorry I've not messaged back recently. Work's been mega busy. I'm not gonna lie, this is starting to get to me. I know I said I was gonna be okay with all this, but I don't know how much longer I can handle waiting. Keep me updated? Hope uni went okay? x

The past year had flown by, with Christmas fast approaching. So much had happened—Tamsin had Tess, I'd bought the unit and had increased profit month on month. It had been the perfect year, but I had one final wish: I wanted the perfect Christmas. I wanted mistletoe kisses, hot-water bottle cuddling and festive market drinking with someone special. I wanted it to be Matt, I really did, but I needed him to act instead of setting the scene for what could be. Actions spoke louder than words, after all. What I didn't realise, at the time, was my selfish wish for the perfect Christmas was going to ruin someone else's. It was going to be a Christmas to remember.

"Tams, can you get that?"

The phone rang continuously. If my business hadn't depended on it, I would have turned the damn thing off at the mains just to get some peace. It had been three weeks since I'd decided to focus on my dream, and within a week we'd been drowning in work. No matter how many times I'd said no, drag queens always came back insisting we take their order. Two weeks later, being pulled down into the pits of Hell, I eagerly awaited a response to the job vacancy I'd put out.

I knew that creating a portfolio wasn't going to happen over-night, despite the many evenings I'd spend working on a garment until the crack of dawn. I hadn't sold a piece yet, and interaction on social media was comparable to tumbleweed rolling around in the empty desert. I didn't have the audience, but I couldn't give up. I had to give it the time it deserved so I'd put an advert out to hire a fashion assistant to ease the rising pressure that was beginning to bubble.

"Who was that? Any enquiries about the job yet?"

"Not yet, sorry. It was Drew again. He wants to know if his dress is going to be ready for the twentieth so he can wear it at his Christmas Extravaganza?"

"It'll be ready. It has to be. If I die before it's finished, my dying wish will be for you to finish the damn thing." I laughed, imagining for just a second that she knew how to use a sewing machine.

"You'll have more chance of me going to the dentist!" I laughed with her, gritting my teeth in pain as I straightened my back that ached from the non-stop work.

"Have you checked the job advertisement online? Any responses there?" I waited, pressing my lips with my tongue in concentration as I threaded the sewing machine.

"Only three. The applicants are Julie Evans, Joanna Chan and Ruth Sampson. Shall I review the applicants we have and close it down?"

"Yes please. In fact, just invite them all for an interview, but make it soon. We need someone desperately."

Within days, Tamsin had managed to schedule interviews, sort interview questions, answer calls and make countless cups of coffee. Matt, on the other hand, still hadn't broken up with Charl. I knew that breaking up with someone wasn't an easy task, but knowing I was waiting for him on the other side should have made it easier. I hadn't a clue what was holding him back. I sat typing out message after message in between interviews, deleting them every time. Nothing I typed could tell him how I felt without me coming off sounding like a dick, and I didn't want to ruin something that hadn't even become a something.

"Hello." A familiar face stepped through the front entrance—as beautiful as the day I'd last seen her, her fashion better than it ever had been, still sporting those revealing tops.

"Shut. Up. It can't be Miss Chan?" I gasped as she walked into the unit.

Joanna Chan.

It almost felt naughty knowing my past teacher's full name.

"Liam, I thought it was you I saw while I was researching Wrighteous. My, you've certainly shot up," she said with the same grace she'd carried in high school.

"I guess I have, yeah. I can't believe this... I haven't seen you in almost ten years. What have you been up to?" I placed my hand out to shake hers. Joanna's palm was sweaty, and I felt a nervous shake as she tried to mask it with fake confidence. I hadn't seen her since the start of year eight. When she'd left, I'd had one less person fighting my corner—fighting for the unique and wonderfully weird.

"Oh gosh, where do I start? Well, I went on to teach textiles at another school, as you can see from my CV, then I moved on to a college doing the same thing, but I left just before summer. I loved teaching textiles, but it was my time to leave, with all the politics and the increasing demands for teachers to work outside of their hours. I spent most of my time at home working instead of with my wife. In my nearly sixteen years of teaching, I'd never known it to be more about stats and crowd control instead of making a difference and actually teaching the children." I gawked at her, taking in each word, thinking of a million more questions to ask her.

"You got married? When?" I said, focused entirely on something I shouldn't have been. Once again, I was in awe of the woman who had inspired me so much as a child.

"We got married a few years ago. The minute same sex marriage was legalised, we started saving. The rest is history now, I guess."

Minutes quickly turned into an hour and a half of catching up and reminiscing. I told her about my family, not forgetting to mention the bundle of joy that was Jade, with no mention of Matt—not even the text that I'd glanced at under the table. He'd done it. He and Charlotte were no more, but his texts came with a demand. He wanted to see me, and who was I to say no?

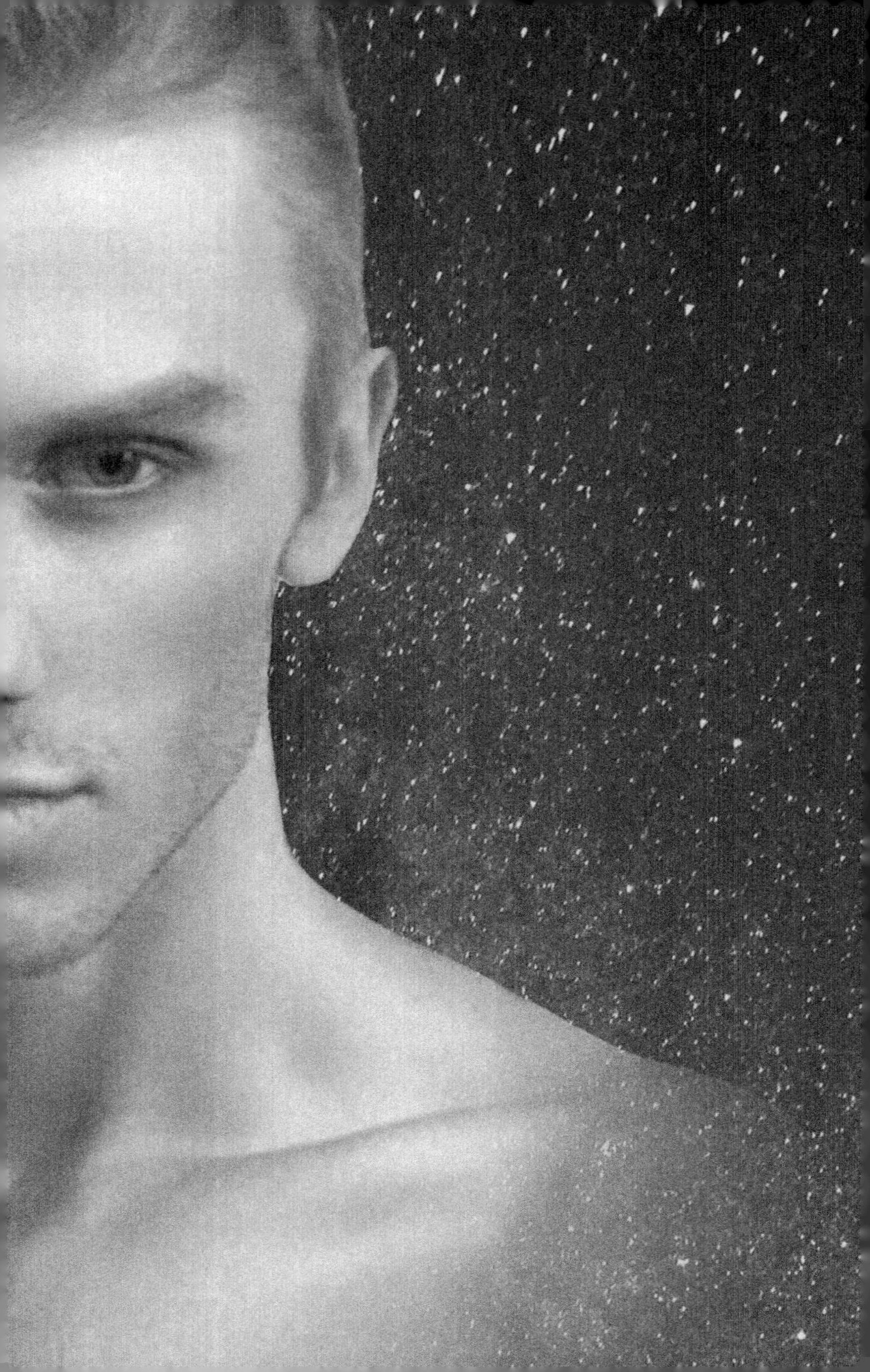

CHAPTER SEVEN

Matt and I had been on dates, but they hadn't really been dates. They'd been encounters, friends meeting, because he'd had a girlfriend. That was until he'd broken up with Charl. It had been years since I'd been on a proper date—since the first year of university to be precise. My emotions battled, shaken with nerves but overcome with excitement. I was excited not to feel guilty about our touch lingering for a second too long, but entirely nervous. I was all in, and I wanted to believe Matt was all in, too, after just breaking up with Charl, but at that moment, something was telling me different. Deep down, my gut feeling was telling me to run from what could be a catastrophic mess. Maybe it was instinct to run instead of getting close to someone. Maybe I was trying to safeguard myself. Normally, I'd have listened, but not this time. Instead, I summoned Tamsin.

"Thanks for coming so late, Tams."

"It's fine. What couldn't wait?" she asked, looking flustered just twenty minutes after I'd called her. Even with Tess strung over her shoulder, she still had chance to pop her head in the living room to wave hello to my family.

"Matt broke up with Charl. He's picking me up tomorrow morning and I'm scared and I don't know what to wear," I said, walking up the stairs, panicking as much as Tamsin had the first night she'd met Callum.

"You do realise you've worn clothes around him before? You can just wear anything. I think you were both already past the point of impressing each other when he pounced on you at the christening."

She had a point.

"But this is real. It's a date and I don't do dates, Tams. I fuck and run." I pulled a dozen different outfit combinations from my wardrobe and hung them from my curtain pole.

"And this time is different because?"

"I really like him. We've spent the past few weeks trying to resist temptation and now we don't have to, and that makes me nervous. There's so much uncertainty. What if I sleep with him and he doesn't like me? What if I don't sleep with him and he holds it against me? What if I'm just not ready to settle down? Am I really ready to commit to one guy?" I sat on the bed, looking to Tamsin and then to the outfits.

"Here, hold Tess," Tamsin said, passing her over to

me. Tess' face was filled with intrigue as she looked at all of me, her eyes wide and absorbing everything. Once she realised she was no longer in her mum's arms, she howled a delicate cry. "Look, Liam. Only you'll know if you're ready. I haven't slept with a fraction of the men you have, but you'll know if Matt is right for you. The electricity between you could be that of a hundred men you've slept with, and being nervous is a good sign. It means you care about him. It means you care what he thinks." Tamsin swept each outfit from one side of the curtain pole to the other, glancing at each as she spoke. She then pulled out two outfits and placed them on my wardrobe handles. "Whatever you decide, I'll be here... waiting, okay?"

"Okay. We're having too many of these heart-to-hearts for my liking recently. It needs to stop," I jested and looked down at Tess who'd finally stopped crying once I bounced her up and down on my knee. "Doesn't it, Tess?" I turned my attention to her and she threw me a small smile. I wasn't even sure she recognised my voice, never mind what I was saying. Tamsin looked down at her and then sat next to me, stroking Tessa's hair.

"Agreed. We used to be fun."

Tamsin left me with two outfit choices, which should have made it easy to decide. Instead, it took me just minutes before Matt pulled up outside my house. I dressed myself in an oversized white tee and black jeans, and eagerly put on a new pair of *Alexander McQueens* while I made him wait outside—all black with silver studs and a thick, white sole. I'd been saving them for a special occasion.

"Well, don't you look nice?" Matt said from the window of a black Mercedes, which was affordable for no ordinary student. His parents had money just like Callum's did. I stepped into the car as gracefully as I could and looked him up and down. His pecs bulged from a white muscle-fit shirt that was paired with a green bomber jacket. I took every part of him in before replying.

"Thanks. I know. You look gorgeous, too." I tossed him a wink and tried to downplay my nerves. His black hair had been lined with wax, styled up in a quiff instead of in its normal tidy mess. I knew from the effort he'd made that the date meant as much to him as it did for me. "So, where are we going?"

"Before I tell you, first things first," he said, leaning in and wrapping a kiss around my lips. It took me a second to reciprocate before placing my hand on his lap. I'd spent weeks dreaming about the moment we'd be able to kiss again, and it was happening quicker than I'd anticipated. I wanted more; in fact, I'd have had him in the car there and then, but I didn't think my mum or the neighbours would have appreciated seeing my bare arse pressed up against the window. Before he pulled away from me, his teeth lightly held onto my bottom lip, tightening his grip as he pulled away. "Fuck. You're so hot," he said, as confident and happy as I'd ever seen him. "So, now you can ask again."

"Where are we going?" I cleared my throat.

"You said you loved things about space, so that's where we're going. We're going to space."

It wasn't long before we arrived, enduring Matt's erratic breaking as he navigated the country roads leading to *Jodrell Bank*. We approached a sign even before we got to the car park that read 'radio quiet zone, switch off mobile phones', something that, as a kid, I hadn't noticed. If he were going to murder me and didn't want me to call for help, this would have been the place.

"Matt! Fancy seeing you here today. How are you?" A middle-aged lady shuffled from behind the desk and spread her arms wide to give Matt a hug.

"Ahhh! Come here, Suzie. I'm good, are you? This is Liam."

"Liam. I've heard so much about you." She placed her hands on my shoulders, looked at me for a short minute and then embraced me, too. She was more of a hugger than my mum.

"I've not got my badge but I've got my card. Are we alright to go through?" Matt asked, about to get his wallet out.

"Yes, of course. Don't worry about scanning your card. I'll mark you down on my fire safety sheet. Just sign out with me later, okay?" she said, poised to scribble on a sheet of paper attached to a clipboard.

"Will do. Thanks, lovely," he chirped.

Lovely. She had to know he was bisexual. No 'straight' man says lovely.

"You two have fun!"

We sat ourselves in a small cafe just across from the star pavilion. Matt went and got the coffees; he didn't need to ask what I wanted. Naturally, he stood chatting to the staff for a few minutes, and I was left on my own without my phone to play on.

"Cheers," I said when he re-joined me, offering me my coffee. "So how long has Suzie known that you like men?" I asked, and a small smile grew on Matt's face.

"Since I started working here, pretty much. Every morning when I came in she'd always be so friendly. We would stand there talking for ages. I even had to start leaving for work earlier just to factor in my chat with her. She's my confidant, one person who is an outsider to my life. She'd probably slap me for saying this, but I kind of see her as a mother figure. I can tell her stuff that I can't tell my friends or family because they're too involved with me. With her, it doesn't matter what I tell her—she listens and gets it, and then we both get on with our day. She's the only one here who knows." He wrapped his hands around his coffee and took a mouthful without checking the temperature, as if he had an asbestos mouth.

"So she's the only one... who knows about me?

What if you're seen with me?" I asked, concerned his cover would be blown.

"I've told them you're my friend from school. Don't worry. It's okay."

"Okay," I said, trying my best to smile and not look disappointed. I knew I wasn't going to be put on a pedestal straight away, and I guessed I was there with him, so I couldn't be too unhappy he'd not shouted from the rooftops about me. It was different. "So how did the break up go? Not nice?"

"It was actually alright, you know. She agreed we weren't really working. She cried and I cried over upsetting her. What wasn't nice was my parents finding out. They told me I was an idiot for ruining things with such a wonderful girl." He looked through the window off into the distance behind me as though he was reflecting on his life. "Have you ever felt that you just aren't good enough? Like, no matter how much love you give someone, you're fighting a losing battle and they are always going to find something wrong—something to disapprove of?" His smiled faded and darkness grew over his face. The relationship he'd fought to hold onto with his parents was hurting him, just like I'd been hurt.

"I haven't for a long time. My dad left around ten years ago, which just so happened to be after I told my parents I was gay. Before telling them, Dad and I had a great relationship, aside from coercing me to enjoy all of the gender stereotypes you could think of—football, action movies, beer, the lot. But… I could live with that.

The minute I came out, things changed. Hate grew over my dad's eyes, and no matter what I said—what Mum said—nothing would make it go away... aside from the drink."

"I'm sorry, Liam. You knew quite early then?" he asked as though he was only just coming to terms with himself.

"I guess so. I remember not fitting in, wanting different things to the rest of the boys in my class. I'd be sat watching movies with my parents, being the hormone ravaged teenager I was, getting aroused at the car sex scene in Titanic. I guessed that part was normal, aside from the fact I was fantasising about Leo, not Kate." I had to pinch myself to pull away from the thought, picturing the iconic hand run down the misted up window.

"Wow. You know, I've never watched Titanic."

"You're kidding me?"

"Nope, not kidding. Maybe we can watch it together soon?" he said as I nodded, mouth full of the last dregs of coffee. "Anyway, I have a surprise."

After guiding me for a few minutes, ordering me to keep my eyes shut the whole time, Matt sat me down in an auditorium and stood behind the podium placed centre stage.

"Told you. Space."

"Oh my god. This wasn't here the last time I came."

"Nope, it's brand new, and I managed to convince some very important people to let us have free rein in here in between the school trips that are scheduled in. So, what will it be? Life on Mars? The Big Bang? The Milky Way?" Matt asked, flicking through a selection of light shows to display above us.

"I'll let you choose. After all, you're the professional."

The lights faded into darkness and he quickly found his way to me, pulling out some peanut M&M's that he'd learnt were my favourite.

Damn, he was good.

I sat looking up, in awe of the display, fascinated by each and every fact spoken by Brian Cox. When the first film finished, Matt wrestled with his jacket, taking it off due to the screen radiating so much heat.

"This is amazing. Another one?" I asked politely, wiggling in the slightly reclined chair to get more comfortable.

"Sure."

Another display started to play above, and this time Matt snuggled closer than before. His fingers grazed my arm that rested on the armrest next to his, and I could feel his breath on my neck as I looked at the spectacle above. Although I couldn't see him, I knew he wasn't watching the lights above. I felt the slightest touch of his lips as they pressed on my neck, sending shivers down my spine in entirely the right way. His tongue flicked, too, as he kissed just under my jaw.

I loved sitting there, exploring space, lost in the beauty that was the universe, but I definitely wanted to explore Matt more. My head turned to his, and although I couldn't see him, I knew exactly where to kiss. It wasn't long before Matt stood above me, his shadow looking broader than it had seemed in daylight. His arms pressed on my shoulders, pushing me deeper into the seat. I was pinned down and I should have been submissive but I couldn't help but reach out to his torso, to feel him some more. I'd missed out on three weeks of touching him like this, of him touching me, so we had some catching up to do. His teeth held my bottom lip in place again, pulling gently.

It drove me crazy—crazy for him.

In an instant, the lights flicked on as the show finished, and the door was pushed open. Matt jumped off me and fell into his seat in a breathless mess, fastening up one of his buttons that had come undone in all the excitement.

"Hello?" A man spoke from the top of the auditorium. I slid further down in my chair, covering my mouth to conceal the panting. "Oh, hi, Matt. Are you okay?"

"Hey, Steve. Yeah, I booked this room out until the next school trip arrives."

"Sorry. My mistake." The door shut behind him and Matt and I sighed with relief.

"Fuck, that was close," I said, holding onto his thigh.

"It was, makes it more exciting, though."

. . .

In the car, I couldn't pull myself out of a flashback on repeat—Matt and I under the stars. He'd not even dropped me off yet, and it was safe to say he'd left a lasting impression. My instincts had changed; I didn't want to run. In fact, I couldn't get enough of him.

"What are you doing for Christmas?" Matt asked, forcing me out of the uncontrollable image of him on top of me.

"Oh. I'm not sure. Christmas Day is usually presents in the morning and an early Christmas lunch and then I tend to go to Tamsin's later on in the afternoon when they have theirs. You?"

"That sounds great. Erm... Christmas Eve, I'll be going to Midnight Mass with my parents and then the usual Christmas Day—copious amounts of food and alcohol to cope with being around the extended family. It would be nice to see you, though. I've been thinking, and well... maybe I could try to sneak off to see you for a bit?"

"Are you serious?" I couldn't help but smile wider than I ever had.

I could be having the perfect Christmas, after all.

"Definitely. I'll try, at least."

Christmas Day was set to be the best yet and nothing was going to get in the way of that.

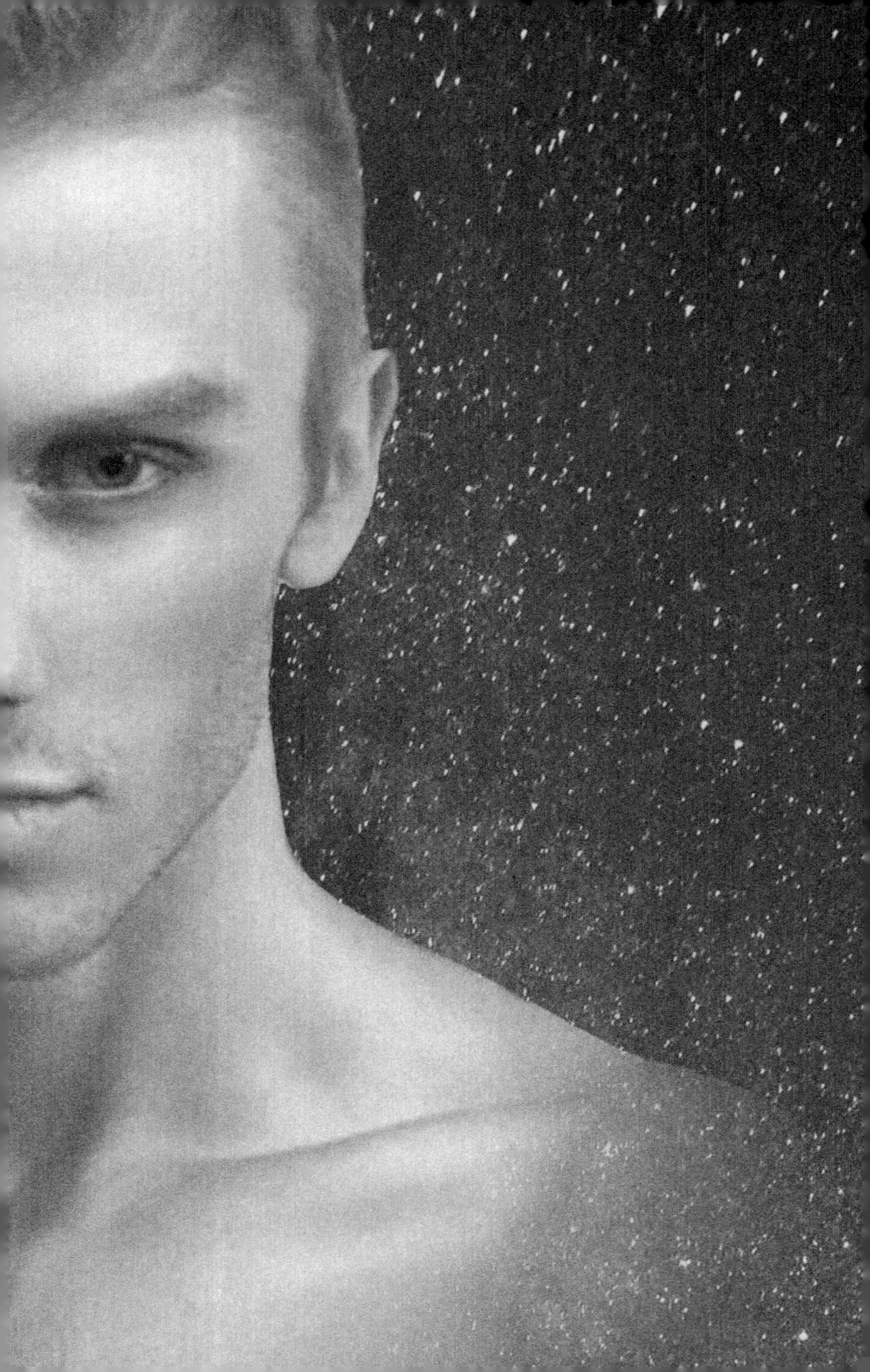

CHAPTER EIGHT

My primary school was exactly as I remembered it, with only a fresh coat of grey paint to try to cover the aged building. It still had the same games marked on the concrete, like snakes and ladders and hopscotch. I'd fallen on them more times than I could remember. The school held magical memories that came alive once I stepped onto the playground. Memories of running around without a care in the world—not one single responsibility, other than the occasional nagging to hang my coat up on the correct hanger, which was clearly labelled with my name and photo.

What was better? My friends had had no idea about my sexuality at that point; I wasn't even sure I had. We'd played, laughed, cried, and role-played. I'd been a normal child with normal friends.

I stood just inside the playground, next to the

green metal gate where Tamsin and I had met our parents. Each day, after being dismissed by Mrs Marsh, we'd hopped, skipped, galloped, run and to the dismay of our mums, one time we'd even crawled. Tamsin's mum, Theresa, always went ballistic after seeing the state of Tamsin's trousers. Memories flooded my mind as if Theresa were back with us. I could hear her vividly saying, "Tamsin, look at the state of you. This will be the third pair of trousers you've gone through in a month. Next time your antics with Liam cause another pair of trousers to be ruined, I'll be sending the bill to Diane." I could even picture my mum nodding back. At the time, it was a threat we took very seriously. There was no way my mum could afford pants for the both of us. It was only looking back I realised they'd often used each other as a threat, and it had worked. There was no way in hell you'd find Tamsin arguing with my mum, nor me with Theresa.

A smile grew on my face as I relived the memories of Tamsin's mum. It had already been a year without her in my life. Day to day, it didn't seem real, but coming to my school some twelve years later, I couldn't help but long for some time with her. Being here on the last day of term would have been too much for Tamsin, so I was glad I'd come alone to surprise Jade. I couldn't wait for her to see me. I'd never been to pick her up before, nor had I been to parents evening or the ballet recitals the teachers had the year ones and twos do.

From what my mum had told me, it was basically a lot of children on stage falling over.

In reality, I'd been focusing on my business and neglecting everyone around me, and I knew if Tamsin's mum had still been with us, she would have been the first to kick me up the backside to re-align my priorities. I knew that now, and I had to make it up to Jade.

"Okay, class, let's see if it's your turn to be collected." The side door to the classroom swung open as a petite teacher stood by the entrance. Small but mighty, she exuded an authority it seemed impossible for her to embody.

I tapped my feet impatiently as the teacher dismissed the children one by one after waving enthusiastically to each of their parents. Of course Jade had to be one of the last, her teacher having to shout her name twice to snap her out of a daydream and back into reality. She wandered out, dragging her purple backpack on the floor and then looked up to where I assumed Mum always stood. It took her a second to glance my way and after a double take, her eyes filled and her smile brightened.

"Liam," she sobbed. "Miss, that's my big brother." Her voice was filled with raw emotion as she tugged on the teacher's cardigan to grab her attention.

"So you're the famous brother Jade doesn't stop talking about," the teacher said after prompting a teaching assistant to take over dismissing the children.

"That's me," I said, laughing and kneeling down to

Jade's height to squeeze her as tight as I could without causing suffocation.

"Well, it's lovely to meet you. She has some Christmas things she's made in that bag of hers. I hope you have a lovely Christmas. You too, Jade." She looked down at Jade, who smiled through her tears as they carried on streaming from her eyes.

"You came to pick me up. Where's Mummy?" Jade sniffed.

"She's at home. I thought I'd come and surprise you. Were you surprised?"

"Yes." laughter abruptly erupted from her as she swung her backpack by her side.

"Good. Did you have a good day?"

"I did but Candice took all my pens off me when I was making you a card," she said, pulling a sad face, frowning like she was reliving it in her mind.

"Oh no. That's not good. Did you tell your teacher?"

"No. I threw my water bottle at her." A cackle spontaneously leapt from her mouth. She was definitely my sister; there was no denying that.

What I would have done to be her age again. I'd met some awful people in my life. I just wished I had the courage such a tiny person possessed. If only it was acceptable for adults to behave like children—to casually throw your bottle at someone for not being very nice. Now, that type of adulthood I would sign up to.

"Well, good news. I have so much fun planned for

us this evening that you'll forget about that silly Candice."

Some children want hot chocolate in the winter. They want to snuggle up and watch films or play on their games in the comfort of their bedrooms. Not my sister. She loved being outside and going for walks, but most of all, she loved ice cream. It didn't matter that it was December because *the ice cream stays frozen longer when it's winter, just like how snowmen don't melt.*

I flicked through my phone as Jade wolfed down her ice cream, eager for her next surprise. It had been nearly a year since we'd spent spontaneous quality time with each other, just the two of us. Did time make love grow stronger? Probably, but when it came to us, there was no chance of us loving each other more than we already did.

"Was that nice?"

"Mmmh, I love mint choc chip ice cream," she squeaked, wiping the bright green remains on her forearm and licking it afterwards.

"Good. Are you ready to go meet Santa?"

"Santa, really? We're going to the North Pole?" She jumped with excitement, somehow managing to keep down the mint chocolate chip ice cream and not vomit.

"No, he's close by visiting some very good boys and girls. Are you excited?" I asked, grabbing her hand as we headed towards the temporary grotto in the town centre.

"Yes, but who will make the toys if he's here?"

"The elves, silly." I laughed at her innocence. She was a clever girl, but not in the conventional sense, a little like myself. She had the concentration of a fish, allowing her to get entirely lost in her imagination. I was in no position to bring her back to reality, because in my eyes, children weren't children for long enough.

With a small gift from Santa, Jade trotted in front of me as we browsed the Christmas market. I purchased some reindeer food in line with a tradition we'd started a few years back. On Christmas Eve, Jade and I would sprinkle it on our front lawn, which would glisten for weeks after due to the amount of glitter the food contained. We then visited a stall to purchase hot chocolate reindeer cones as the perfect festive treat on the morning of Christmas. Her smiles and laughter were as infectious as the music that poured from the speakers, with the people around us looking at her as she skipped with glee. Christmas was about being with family and friends. Yes, I wanted the perfect Christmas. I wanted Matt under the mistletoe; I needed us to see each other. But really, my Christmas wouldn't have been the same without Jade.

I stopped at a personalised tree ornament stall, in awe of all the hand painted designs. I stood waiting for twenty minutes as three tree decorations were personalised for me. One for my family, the second for Tamsin, which included the latest addition to their family, and a third one for Matt with our names on. I knew he couldn't put it on his tree, not at his flat or at his family home, but I hoped one day he'd be able to. I wished that one day it would take pride of place on his tree—our tree. Mostly, I wanted to mark our first Christmas together with sentiment. I couldn't wait to give it to him.

Once we'd found ourselves back in the warmth as my mum refused to turn down the central heating, Jade jumped onto Stuart. He was covered in a thick tar-like oil. The more he made contact with Jade, the more I winced at the marks covering her uniform, knowing full well mum would have a fit when she saw it. Another school uniform ruined, just like mine when I was her age.

"Stuart, your hands," she cried out as she magicked a tea towel out of nowhere.

"Sorry, love. There's no hope with that car. We're gonna have to take it to a garage. I can't sort it," he said as he attempted to wipe his hands clean.

"What's up with the car?" I asked, and I didn't know why, because I wouldn't have the foggiest clue what he meant. I didn't know the first thing about cars, aside from the fact I had to put the right fuel in. Once you make that mistake, you don't make it again.

"There's loads of oil leaking from the front. At first I thought it was the gaskets but there's too much oil for them to be worn. It's an old car, but we haven't really budgeted for a new one"

"Especially before Christmas. Either way, we'll sort it," Diane said as she undressed Jade, removing her scum covered clothes. Jade then proceeded to march back to Stuart wearing just her knickers.

"So, did you have a good time, sweetie? What did you guys get up to?" Stuart asked his daughter as I scrolled through my phone, with Jade's voice acting as a distant hum. I knew what I had to do. I browsed the internet and looked at multiple car sale websites, thinking I'd let myself in for an impossible task, when in fact, every car I came across was ten times better than their ninety-nine plate *Skoda Octavia*. I logged onto my online banking, swiftly checking my savings balance to see what I could realistically afford. Then I found it.

Vauxhall Zafira, five doors, 11 plate, low milage, £2,700.

That was about all I could understand from the advert.

Reserve.

"Right, I've been struggling with what to get you both for Christmas, and it's just been settled. I've bought you a new car. It's a Vauxhall, looks quite big, too," I said, sending a screenshot of the car to their phones. Mum started crying in an instant, and well, Stuart seemed speechless.

"You've bought us this? Are you serious? We can't accept this." Stuart looked down at his phone and Mum nodded, wiping away a tear that was puddled under her eye.

"Well, it's tough because I've bought it. We can go and pick it up as soon as you need it. That car out there has seen the end of its days, and it looks awful parked next to my gorgeous Mini on the driveway. It's about time I did something for you both and I'm not having you worry about money over Christmas, so it's sorted." Warmth filled me. The amount they'd done for me, the amount Stuart did for Mum, not mentioning the fact that he worked countless hours bringing home just a little more than a few pounds an hour. I had no idea how they survived on Stuart's minimum wage income. There was never a day without a plate of hot food on the table. It didn't matter that my savings had taken a dent. I could earn more money; I had my business. What I'd given them was worth more than money. I'd given them a worry-free Christmas.

"Thank you so much, son," Stuart said with his hands on my shoulders, and then moved in to hug me. He wasn't the affectionate type, and for the first time in seven years, he'd called me his son. Although it was factually incorrect, he'd been more of a dad to me in those seven years than my biological father ever had.

I wondered if my real dad ever thought about me—ever wondered how I was doing.

"Thanks, Dad," I said, still being strangled unintentionally by his broad shoulders that wrapped around my neck like a tie. Mum was creating puddles around the house after our exchange. I could tell it meant everything to her. Did I miss my dad? Sure, I did. There was still so many questions I needed to find the answers to—answers I knew I couldn't get from Mum, as the minute I mentioned him, she would put up her walls as a way of coping. I understood why. I told my parents about my sexuality and her life was turned upside down because of my dad's actions. She'd effectively had to choose between her husband and her son, something I could never imagine doing. Although I'd sometimes sit and stew, asking him questions in my mind, I had to remember that my dad wasn't around. Instead, I had my step-dad, my adorable sister and my mum. I was so glad Mum had chosen me.

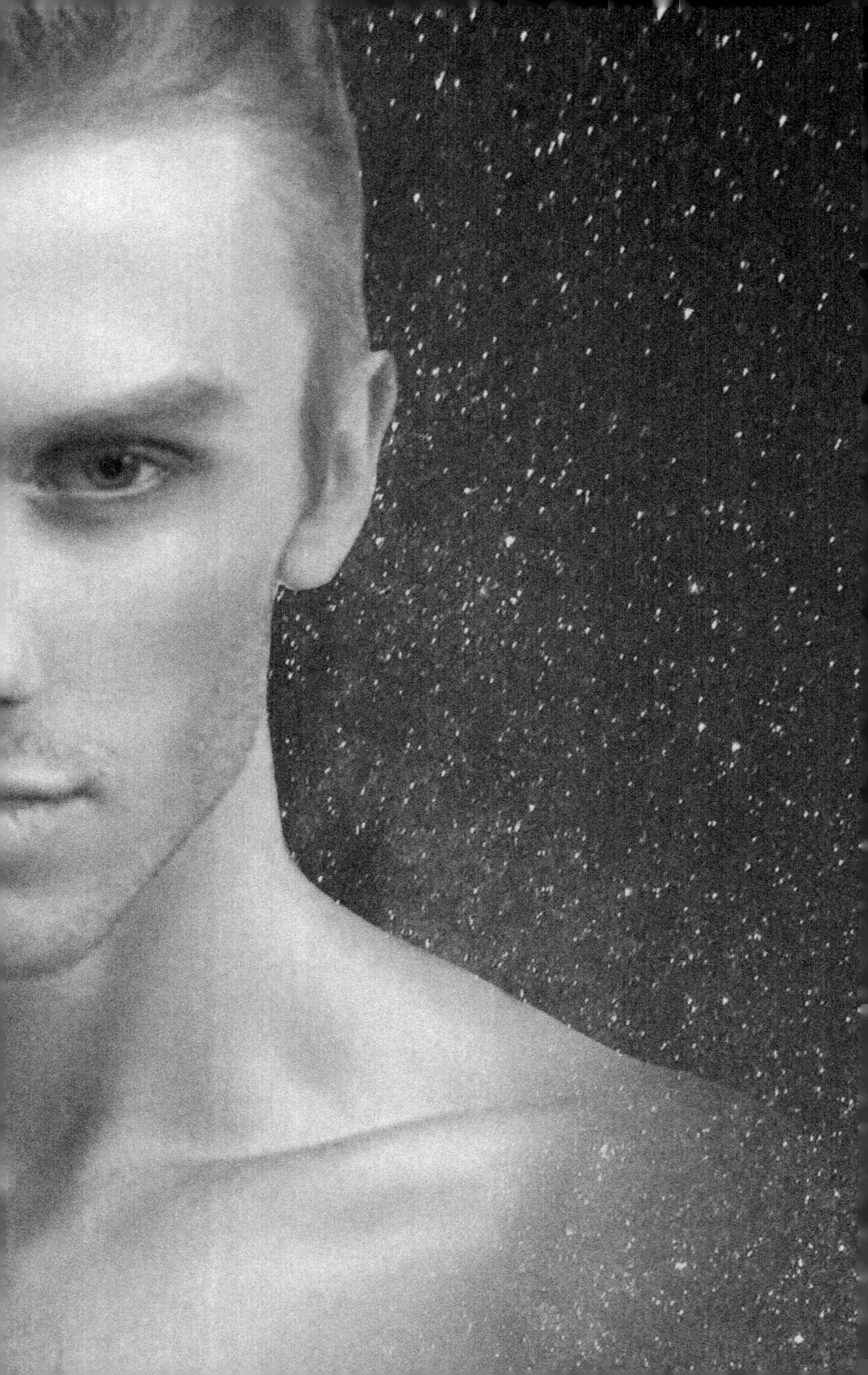

CHAPTER NINE

Christmas was only a few days away, and I couldn't wait. Joanna, our newest addition, was settling in to the Wrighteous family, often putting me to shame with all her experience. She'd already shown me tricks to get patterns created quicker and I could count the days she'd been with us on my hands. Tamsin had to bring little Tess with her to work as Callum was swamped with work at the hotel, and his parents were getting some Christmas sun in Barbados before returning home just in time for the festivities. Jackie and Richard had decided they deserved a big holiday after sacrificing the other three they'd normally go on in order to move up to Cheshire to be closer to Tess. If anything, Tess' cute giggle filled the unit with even more Christmas joy. Occasionally the giggle was ruined by an excruciatingly painful cry, which I tried to look past.

The drag orders had all been finished for Christmas and I was finishing up a garment for my portfolio while Tamsin and Joanna tidied the office space, ready to close up for a few days over Christmas.

"You excited to finish for Christmas, Tams?" I asked, trying carefully not to prick my finger with a needle.

"You know I love it here, but I'll be excited for a lie in when Daddy can wake up and look after you. Won't I? Yes," she answered my question, also talking to Tess at the same time to stop her from crying.

"What about you, Joanna?" I said laughing, trying not to call her Miss Chan, something I'd made a habit of since she'd started working for me.

"We're heading up to Scotland to see my in-laws as normal. We go every year like clockwork. What about you?"

"Well, I'm so glad you asked," I said, looking pleased with myself. "I'm going to go and stay at Matt's flat because all the other students are going home for Christmas. It's going to be just me and him with lots of..."

"Whoa, too much information," Joanna interrupted before I could finish.

"I was going to say films. Bloody hell." I laughed, throwing a wink to Tamsin. "And lots and lots of colouring, too," I whispered mischievously to Tess.

"Ew. *Sex And The City* code, you've got to stop. Soon, she'll know exactly what you mean and I'm not going to be the one to explain to her teacher why Tessa is terrified of colouring," Tamsin said in an angry tone laced with a smirk. A small part of me wanted to accept it as a challenge, but I knew I'd live to regret that day.

"Pft, and you say I'm the drama queen."

We walked through the automatic doors into his student accommodation, the lobby area resembling the hotel where we'd had our third date. I signed in with reception as Matt stood proudly by my side.

"This place is huge, and fancy," I said, arm in arm with Matt.

"It's great, isn't it? The common room is down there with a games room, and the best thing is, we've got it all to ourselves. Not like we'll have time for any of that, though." He nudged me playfully, his hand now stroking the bottom of my back.

"I guess not." I smiled back flirtatiously. Matt was so easy to be around. Natural. He didn't always talk about himself and I tried to limit the amount I spoke about myself. He was always smiling, and for the short period of time I'd known him, I knew I could speak to him about anything. It didn't matter that we were miles apart and didn't see each other for days, because when we did see each other, we made the most of it. That being said, I was relieved we were spending the night in, instead of gallivanting from place to place like some sort of operative mission so nobody would see us together. As much as sneaking around was fun and exciting, it was a spark our relationship didn't need. I wanted him, every inch of him, and I wanted everyone to know that.

Matt swung open his heavy door, which crashed into me on its way back to the frame. He threw his keys onto his white oak desk, which matched the clean white aesthetic of the room. It was a small apartment but Matt had everything he'd need to hibernate and not see people for at least a week.

There wasn't a poster strung up with blu tack in sight— no blue residue clinging to the walls, unlike my room at university. Instead, one wall was entirely covered in frames, all different shapes and sizes, all filled with different pictures. Some of friends and family, some of the starry night sky and space. He kicked off his shoes and placed them in his wardrobe as I glanced around his room some more. The inside of his wardrobe door was blu-tacked to the heavens, covered in posters. Covered in Madonna. Eighties pop Madonna, cowboy hat Madonna, even a throwback to when she tongued Britney. It was all there. Showcased in the middle of the posters, a piece of paper with a signature.

"Wow, this is awesome. I was beginning to think you were a neat freak having loads of frames and no posters," I said, pulling off my shoes, sat on the edge of his double bed that lay exactly opposite his front door.

"Ha, no. It's against the rules. I wouldn't dare get blu tack marks on these walls."

"What's that?" I asked, pointing to the piece of paper held in its own plastic wallet.

"Oh, that's my pride and joy. That's Madonna's autograph. I met her while I was on holiday with my parents in Australia."

"Shut up. You're kidding. Why didn't you lead with this? As if you've met Madonna. The only thing better would have been if you'd met Zac Efron, then *I* would've pounced on you in those toilets." I laughed.

"You love him that much?"

"It's weird because obviously he's a treat to look at, but even before then I'd sit at home and watch *High School Musical* at least twice a week because it installed happy in me. That film and Tamsin were the things that got me through some really dark days. Overcoming the pain I felt that might not have been there if I wasn't gay. It's just a bonus that he's gone from being a twink to the Adonis he is now."

"I get it. Madonna is that person to me that Zac Efron is to you. I can put my headphones in and drown in her music. Most of her songs help me forget that I'm different, and the ones that don't, make me feel like it's okay to be different."

"I couldn't agree more." My eyes locked with his and for a short minute we gazed at each other. There was nothingness around us; that's how it seemed. "I have a present for you, by the way. It's not much, but I wanted you to have something that marks our first

Christmas together." I pulled out the tree ornament with our names proudly positioned together.

"That's gorgeous. Oh, Liam, I feel bad I've not got you anything." His head dropped for a second and then lifted as he turned and pulled the piece of paper away from the blu-tack that held it to the inside of his wardrobe.

"Take this."

"What? Are you crazy?"

"Crazy for you, absolutely. Now you'll always know that within a month of us knowing each other, you already mean more to me than my saviour. The one person who reassures me that one day the world will be better." I couldn't say anything to him as he placed the signature in my hands, fresh from its protection. I ran my fingers across the wrinkles of the paper with the gentlest of touches. I placed the signature on top of his wardrobe and without hesitation, I pulled him closer by the waist. Our torsos met at the same time as our lips, both trembling in anticipation for each other.

I couldn't pull myself away, my senses wild for him—craving his next touch, wanting another taste, another growl of pleasure. If we were going through the honeymoon phase of our relationship, I didn't want it to end.

I'd only ever felt this way about someone once before, but even then there weren't sparks like this. Despite that, they still managed to shatter my already broken heart. My heart broken from tearing apart our family, for being the reason my dad abused mum. A shattered heart from disappointment after always fighting for validation. I'd slept around for all those reasons before; I needed validation that I was good enough, and a night of pleasure with someone I didn't know gave me that, for a short while anyway. Things were already different with Matt. Yes, we couldn't keep our hands off each other, but gazing deep into his eyes in the confines of his apartment gave me all the validation I needed.

With just a single look.

With every word that came from his mouth, reassurance that I was enough.

Our bare skin met with the duvet draped over us, making it as dark as it could be. Matt loved darkness; I'd learnt that over the past couple of dates—at the auditorium, the dingy bar and under the covers. The darkness hid him from the world, hiding his sins—those sins that didn't deserve to be sins. He didn't deserve pain just for being attracted to men. Attracted to me. The darkness was his safe place. I was his safe place. We were so caught up in the midst of each other's love, we almost missed a knock on the door.

"Just ignore it." Matt's breath on my neck convinced me that was best. I'd waited far too long for us to be interrupted. It was happening. No more anticipation.

"Uhhhh," I moaned, hearing another knock to the door, this time louder and more repetitive.

"Am I that good?" he jested, kissing down my chest.

"Yes, but go answer the door so you can get your arse back to bed. We have unfinished business."

"Fineeee." He grabbed a towel large enough to wrap around himself, taming his excitement, and made his way to the door. I lay in bed, hidden under the covers, breathless and hungry for him to return.

"Mum," Matt said abruptly. "What're you doing here?"

I covered my mouth in panic, trying not to stir the cover that lay on top of me. It was at that moment I knew we wouldn't be finishing what we'd started. I knew that I'd be stuck with anticipation for at least a few more days before we'd get our next chance. Most of all, I knew all of that was our best case scenario.

"Put some clothes on, Matthew," she ordered before answering his question. "Can't your own mother surprise you? Besides, I need to apologise. I know I was hard on you about breaking up with Charlotte. Your father told me so. I was disappointed. She was a lovely girl." His mother spoke, her accent similar to her sister, Jackie's.

"She was lovely. It just wasn't working," Matt said, his voice sounding uncomfortable, as though searching for justification he didn't even need.

"Anyway, I'm sorry. I've got your father waiting in the car. We're taking you for a meal to..." She paused for a split second. "Is there a girl under there?"

Shit.

My whole body went tense as Matt denied the accusation.

"There is, isn't there?" she said. I could hear footsteps approaching closer.

"No, Mum, there isn't. I promise." Matt's voice screeched with nerves. I knew what was coming, so my hands slowly slid over my crotch to prepare for what was about to happen.

"You know I can't stand liars, Matthew." In anger on his mum's part, the duvet was flung into the air, revealing me.

Not a girl.

I lay there, naked, my hands just about covering my modesty.

His mum screamed in shock, her hands shaking with rage.

"See, I wasn't lying." Matt's response was almost inappropriate for the situation, but he wasn't wrong. I could finally see the despair on his face.

"You think you're funny, don't you? I'm so disgusted in you. After everything we've done for you, you repay us this way." She inhaled deeply. "You are a disgrace."

I sat in silence but I didn't want to. I wanted to hold Matt as he was verbally attacked. I needed to tell his narrow-minded mother to shut the fuck up. He wasn't a disgrace at all. If anything, after her response, he owed her nothing at all.

"Mum, I'm sorry." He pleaded with her, trying to

slow her retreat from the bedroom. His eyes were dry but I could tell his body ached with pain.

"I am no longer your mother. You don't deserve me." The door slammed behind her.

Matt's body went limp as he believed every word she'd said. His eyes were no longer dry, instead a flaming red colour and set to burst. I agonised for him after hearing those words, but there was nothing I could say to make this go away. She'd come round to the idea of him being gay; she had to. Until then, I had to be there, to listen to him. To hold him.

"I'm sorry, Matt. That was awful," I said, putting my trousers back on. His fists were clenched but he was silent—deadly silent and emotionally drained. "Is there anything I can do?" I slipped my top over my chest and went to approach him.

"Just leave," he whispered, walking through to the kitchen sink. There were very few signs of life.

"What?"

"Just fucking leave, Liam." Anger grew on his face and made his voice deafening. Even more manly than he'd ever seemed before, but not the man I'd grown to love. In a state of fury, he launched a glass across the room. It smashed against the wall, shattering along with the hope that I'd be able to comfort him. I had to leave.

The sound of that glass smashing resonated deep inside me, sending shivers down my spine as I walked back to my car. It was ironic that my dad finding out about my sexuality had resulted in smashed crockery in just the same way.

I'm gay.

Although he didn't have to say those words to his mum, it was awful to think that just two words could tear a family apart, turning relationships sour, and leaving cracks in your life. His life had been turned upside-down for good. Both of ours had.

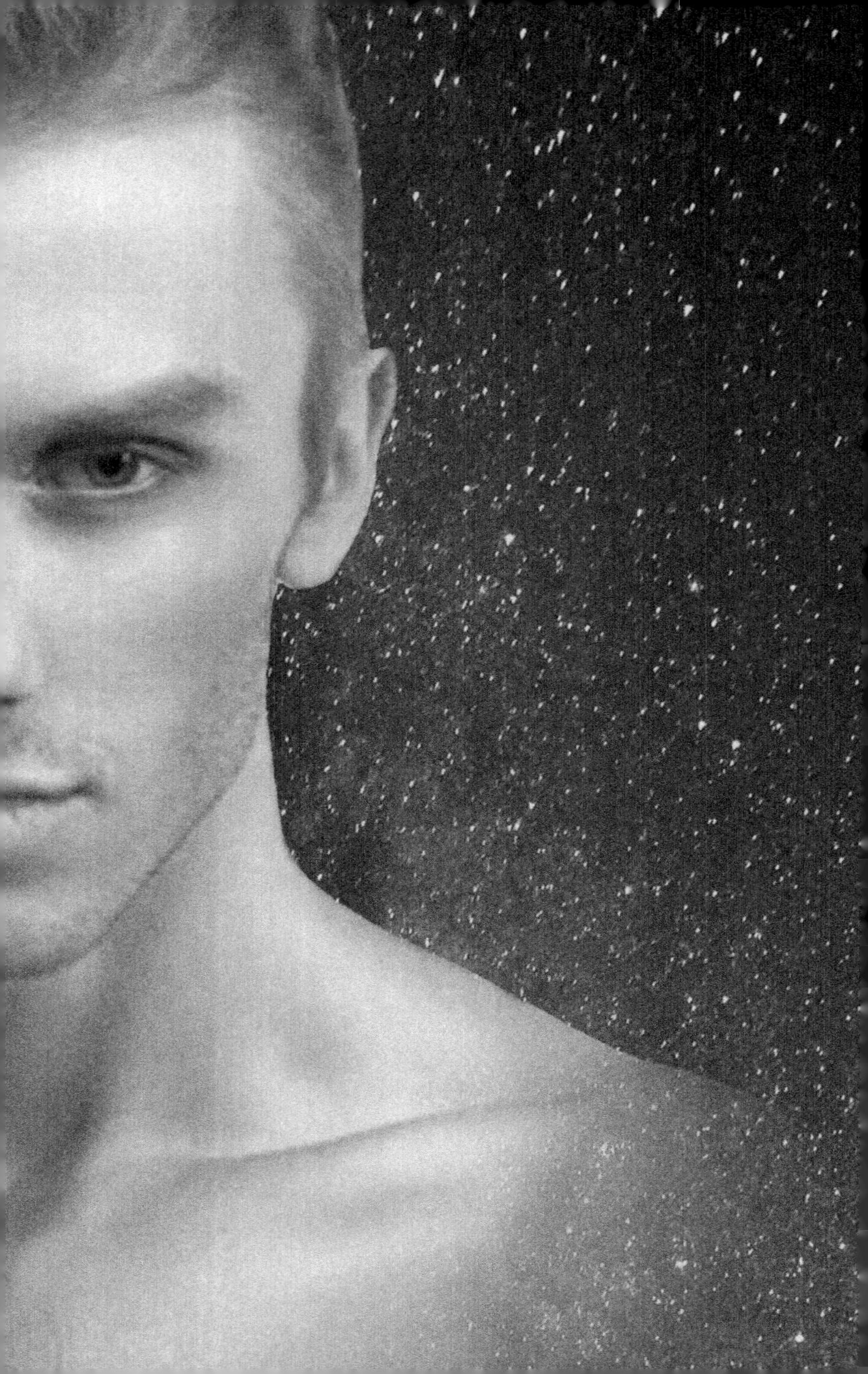

CHAPTER TEN

TEN YEARS BEFORE

I didn't want to go home, not after the night before. Not ever. Not after listening to my dad scream at my mum with no consideration for our neighbours, not even for his crying son upstairs.

Did I want him to react this way? Not at all.

Would I have taken back the two words I'd said to them if I could have done? Every. Single. Time.

I didn't want cracks to appear in our walls. In the past, we'd been like no other family—parties, family gatherings with what little family my dad had, and even days out when we could. That morning, I woke not only to hostility leaving metaphorical cracks in my relationship with Dad but also physical fist shaped holes in our poorly plastered walls. I tried to ignore it. I tried to pretend that I hadn't heard a word he'd said last night, because what else was I supposed to do?

"Morning, Dad. I made you a tea. Two sugars, just

how you like it," I said, carrying a large mug filled to the brim in from the kitchen. By the time it had arrived with Dad it was barely half full.

He could have said anything, thrown me a smile even, but instead there was silence. Nothing. He didn't acknowledge that I was there and I deserved it. His eyes looked worn, like he'd sat up for hours reading a newspaper, allowing himself to be lost in someone else's words instead of consumed by mine.

I could have bugged him to speak to me like I normally would have, but I knew that wouldn't be sensible. I knew I had to go to school in an attempt to distract myself from the reality of the hate that surrounded me.

"Tamsin, this is your wake up call. Come in," I said beneath the crackles of the walkie-talkie.

"Ugh. No, sorry, Tamsin isn't here. Please stop calling." Her distinct voice echoed through. She had never been a morning person.

"If you aren't up and dressed in twenty minutes, I'll be coming over and dragging you to school naked."

"Fine. God sake, Liam. Will you ever stop being part of the lie-in police?" she questioned with slight anger, her lips dry and untouched by her new-found love for coffee. That was her mum's fault; neither of them could get enough of it.

"Never."

. . .

Just like any normal school day, Tamsin and I found ourselves dragging our heels to school. If I had a choice between staying within the four walls of my house where I'd be ignored by my dad or going to school where I'd be beaten up by a stranger, school marginally had the edge. Dale had laid into me not even twenty-four hours before, so I was hopeful he'd had enough violence for one week. At least I didn't have P.E. to worry about.

"Is it time to go home yet?" Tamsin said, taking a slurp of coffee from the travel flask she'd purchased with her pocket money just weeks before.

"Nope. Today's not a bad day for lessons, though. We have double science, computing after break and then maths and languages after lunch," I said, reeling off our timetable from the scrunched up piece of paper that sat in my blazer pocket.

"You've just described Hell," Tamsin quipped.

I fielded remarks from my form tutor as she accused me of looking tired, and I lied about the bruise on my neck that crept just above my collar, left as a reminder of Dale's hate, as she questioned it during registration. Once that was done, I fought my way through the packed corridors to find Tamsin on the way to science. It killed me not having her in my registration group, but it was only thirty minutes of the day, and I had her sat right next to me for a whole two hours that morning.

"Boo!" I jumped up behind her, flinching as she swung her arm around to attack me.

"You frightened me, Gayboy," she said, a little under

her breath so no one could hear.

The class was just as loud as it was in the corridors, with students sharing their gossip from the evening before. Tamsin and I didn't have much to say. She knew about my eventful night—most of it, anyway. I scanned the room as Tamsin hid her coffee-filled flask in her bag before it could be confiscated by our science teacher. As soon as Mr Tomos entered the class, the students were brought slowly to silence.

"Okay, class. Settle down," he said, placing his brown leather satchel under his desk and straightening his tie. "You are my favourite class, and do you know why? You're the best behaved and today I want it to be no different because we're learning about the reproductive system." The electronic whiteboard flashed on as he continued. "Who can tell me an anatomical name for a female reproductive organ?" The class went eerily quiet; nobody wanted to embarrass themselves. I knew, but there was no way I was raising my hand with Dale giving me a death stare from across the room. "Well, you have a uterus, fallopian tubes, ovaries and a vagina."

"I don't have a vagina, sir," a boy at the back of the class remarked, raising a small amount of laughter throughout the classroom.

"Now now, Sam. I said female. Are you a woman?" He shook his head as his smile faded. "I didn't think so. Okay, what about an anatomical name for a male's reproductive organ?"

"Willy." The class erupted with laughter as Dale

made the childish remark.

"No, that's not right," Mr Tomos quickly stated, throwing a stern look in his direction. He didn't care, though.

"Why don't you ask Liam what the answer is? He loves willy." Dale's words were lined with venom and they hurt. It was as if they ran through my blood, infecting me, inducing an anger I couldn't control.

"I won't tolerate that, Dale. Outside." Mr Tomos' stern words were now laced with anger. Dale wasn't going to listen. It was clear he had a vendetta against me, and I wasn't going to escape it without admitting the truth. Admitting defeat to his bullying.

"It's true, though, isn't it?" If looks were enough to kill, I'd be dead on the ground all prepped for Tamsin to bury me. But they weren't, and I had to react. I had two options: fight or flight. I could run out of the class, go on pretending like I was at home, or I could do something else.

"Fine. It's true." I pushed back my stool and stood up, towering just slightly above the tall science desks. "I'm gay. Make fun all you want."

The words escaped my mouth as I fought for freedom from judgement, from both my class mates and myself. What had started happening so quickly had turned into a slow haze, the people around me just shapes as I openly told the class my deepest secret. A secret that shouldn't have needed to be told.

It wasn't until a clap from Tamsin brought me back

into the room.

Tamsin was clapping. For me. A nerdy student at the front of the class started to clap, too, and I hadn't spoken one word to her in my life. Mr Tomos followed, and slowly, so did the whole class. Everyone but Dale and his friends, anyone short of braincells. For the first time, my sexuality didn't seem like such a burden. I'd defeated Dale and won over my class, something I'd never thought I'd do. I knew I was going to be the talking point of the school by lunch time, but if only a few idiots out of the whole student body didn't like my sexuality, that was something I'd be able to live with. School felt safer than ever before, and the next time I got a beating from Dale, I hoped it wouldn't just be Tamsin and the teachers who had my back. All that was left was to feel safe at home.

It had been a whole three months after coming out to my entire class—an impulsive decision that could have made my life a living hell, but instead made it easier. Three months of hell at home, but three months of heaven at school. Within days, popular girls who'd never given me the time of day wanted to speak to me. I still had to take a beating from Dale and his friends once in a while, but mostly, my school life had shifted and my peers wanted to be friends with me. I was in fashion, the latest must-have accessory. It was fun at first, but I couldn't truly be myself, not like I could be with Tamsin. She was my person and her mum, too. I spent practically every evening at their house so I didn't have to be around my own father because when I was there, it was like I wasn't. He'd started drinking, and not at the times you'd have a bevvy with your mates down the pub. It was constant and he reeked of booze. The pungent stench of whiskey lingered on him all day; I didn't have to get too close to smell it either.

I did miss them.

I missed my dad before I'd told him of my sexuality, before all the cracks had started to show. Most of all, I missed Mum. I felt awful for leaving her with him, especially as I knew they weren't doing okay either. The amount of times I'd awoken in the night to screaming and shouting, where I'd try to muffle the sounds by shoving my head under my pillows. It didn't work. Mum had even started sleeping downstairs, and I might have been young, but to me, it was a clear sign their marriage was over. I just wasn't expecting it to happen so soon.

"Liam, can you go to the school office please?" The class oohed as Miss Chan instructed me, looking sheepish after taking a call on her class phone. I gathered my belongings and dragged myself up the flight of stairs to the office that overlooked the front of the school. I'd only ever been called to the office once before, and it was when my nan had passed away, so I knew it was serious.

Nerves escaped me, written all over my face as I turned the door knob to enter the office. The usual receptionist sat there, along with another lady, her hair in a long blonde bob and dressed in a pencil skirt and matching blazer.

"Liam, come and have a seat in my office," Mrs Tillett said in a soft voice, entirely different from the stern bellowing that would normally echo across the hall during assemblies. "This is Olivia. She's going to join us today."

"Hi, Liam." Olivia smiled sympathetically, like she'd already delivered some bad news. I gave a weak smile and took my seat, unable to control my body as it continued to shake.

"Liam, we wanted to let you know that your mum is in hospital." Mrs Tillett spoke slowly, or that's how it seemed, as I jumped up out of my seat in a hurried panic.

"It's okay, Liam. She'll be fine. Take your seat please," Olivia interrupted.

"She is going to be okay, but I'm afraid Jed, your father, has been arrested due to an accusation of domestic abuse. Olivia works for Social Services in the Duty Team, and she's here to discuss what's going to happen next. Liam, your mum is going to be fine, but today, our priority is making sure you are safe." My headteacher spoke, but I couldn't register anything else. I could just hear her words, words I so desperately didn't want to hear.

"First of all, your mum gave us permission to be here today. She mentioned that you don't have much family, but you spend a lot of time with a close family friend, Tamsin and her mum, is that right?" I nodded as I tried to focus on the questions Olivia asked instead of the whirlwind of thoughts that were starting to cloud my brain.

"That's good then. I'll make some phone calls soon to see if I can arrange for Theresa to pick you up. Now, I've got to ask you a few more questions, if that's okay?" Olivia asked and I nodded. She continued to reel off questions, asking me about my life, but her questions were left open. I couldn't just say yes or no. I couldn't nod. I had to talk.

It was hard to focus, occasionally being brought back to the room after staring through the window with the repetitive hum of my name.

"We're all done. Do you think you'll be okay to go back to class? Tamsin will be with you, yes?" Mrs Tillett asked as her finger ran over the master timetable that was stuck to her wall.

"Uhh hmm."

"I'm going to come and visit you and Diane soon, when she's back from the hospital, but before I go, is there anything we should know? Anything you want to talk about?" Olivia probed gently. I looked down at my left wrist, which was covered in bruises from Dale after he'd pinned me to the ground the last time I'd taken a beating from him. I pulled the arm of my blazer over my wrist and shook my head. I knew that school had seen the bruises. I knew that they'd jump to conclusions if I mentioned it to them. My dad wouldn't do that to me—he wouldn't hurt me.

He didn't hurt mum, did he?

"Okay, well I just want to re-assure you that you are safe. Your dad is in custody and the police are pursuing a DVPN. That's a Domestic Violence Protection Notice, which will mean your dad won't be able to return home for a while. I'll talk more in detail about this with you and your mum when she's feeling better, but if you have any questions in the meantime, both myself and the school are here for you. We will speak soon, Liam." Olivia held out her hand and I shook it limply, her eyes darting to the bruises on my wrist.

I left the office with feelings of worry and anxiety. Most of all, I was left with guilt pitted at the bottom of my stomach knowing I'd not been around for Mum. I'd barely seen her, all because I selfishly wanted to escape the tension that had filled the house because of me.

For the first time since the first week in high school, Theresa came to the school gates to walk Tamsin and me to her house. As always, Tess couldn't do enough for me. As hard as she tried, no matter what film she sat us in front of, no matter the amounts of hot chocolate and marshmallows, I couldn't clear my mind of the image of my mum lying in a hospital bed fighting for breath.

Alone.

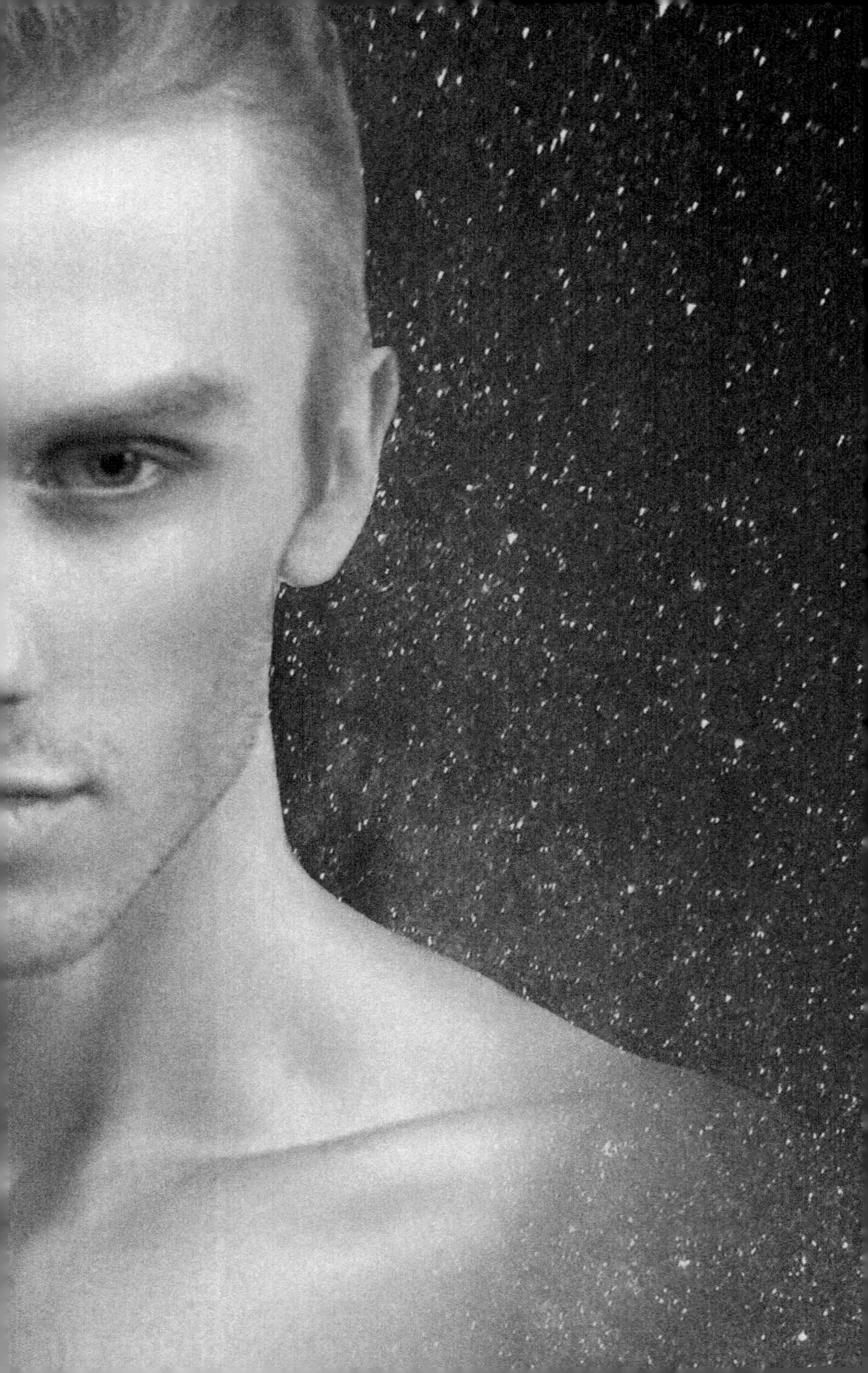

CHAPTER ELEVEN

The next few days crept upon me—days without speaking to Matt even though I desperately tried to reach out to him in his moment of need, days right up until I sat there on Christmas morning with not even so much as a text message from him. I guessed the only thing missing that year would have been Matt. All I wanted was to share something special with him, but it was clear by now I wasn't going to hear from him. That didn't stop me from trying to enjoy the holiday, though. Christmas was one of my favourite times of year. I looked forward to it as a day with family and friends, to consume questionable amounts of alcohol and relax, that was until the actual day when it somehow seemed more stressful than I ever remembered. Firstly, I had to wake up at home at stupid o'clock in the morning with Jade, a tradition that I'd foolishly started with her, followed by the never ending table of food with Mum and Stuart. If there was anything my mum could do better than anyone it was to put on a serious Christmas feast. The second half of my day consisted of traveling over to Tamsin's and starting all over again, and this year it seemed even more exciting as baby Tess was there, too. Tamsin had actually asked me to come on Christmas Day this year; I didn't have to invite myself like I usually would have. I couldn't wait for Tamsin to see the new dress I'd made for my favourite goddaughter—a sparkly pink, floral creation of mine, made so it sat just above the knee, perfect for crawling. What more could a baby need?

Tap tap tap.

"No thank you, not today," I grumbled as Jade tapped my forehead.

Without any consideration for my need to sleep, Jade screamed down my ear, "IT'S CHRISTMASSS." It was at that point I knew I had no chance of getting back to sleep, but one more try wouldn't hurt.

"Did we not tell you, Jade? It's cancelled," I said with a smirk.

"Liar. Mummy says we can go downstairs and open presents but you have to come, too."

I got up without complaining and we skipped down the stairs together. As much as I liked my sleep, there was nothing I loved more at Christmas than to see Jade's face brighten at every present she opened, whether that be an expensive iPad or a small slime ball. I wished to be her age again. Once Jade was finished, I rushed to open the presents I'd received from Mum and Stuart. I pulled apart the wrapping paper with no care to reveal the most luxurious candles, which were far too expensive for their own good. I'd have never been able to justify buying them for myself, despite the fact that one single candle was enough to fill a room with scent—lighting that candle would've effectively been burning money away. I then opened my stocking fillers, along with a beautiful frame of a star constellation print, beautifully encasing the night sky as it sat on the last time Mum and I had been to Jodrell Bank together.

"Mum, it's beautiful. Thank you. Thank you, Stuart." I held onto the frame, studying the stars and how they aligned. To some, they were huge balls of gas burning in the night sky. To Jade, the frame just had loads of dots and lines and held no magic at all. To me, it made sense. How the stars aligned and were placed in the night sky so precisely. How they'd hide away to those who didn't care or weren't looking properly. To me, they were hope. Not hope of a new life on a different planet, but if something so natural could be so beautiful, then maybe each and every person had the chance to be something beautiful, too.

"It's the least we could do after you bought us that car. We love it, so thank you, too." Mum sat on the arm of the couch next to Stuart, both smiling as bright as the sun. Mum was always filled with joy during Christmas, but at once, her smile started to fade.

"What's up, Mum?" I asked, popping down the framed print carefully.

"It's just, you have your life together, especially with your business. I'm so proud of you but soon you'll have a boyfriend and you'll eventually move out. This could be our last Christmas together as a family," Mum said as Stuart pulled her tighter, practically on top of his lap as he held her, not once making a joke about how emotional she was.

"Mum, don't be silly. Even if I did move out, do you really think I'd miss Christmas morning here? Seeing Jade's face light up, your Christmas food and Stuart shouting at the television for no reason. Nope, that's all too good to miss." I hadn't told them about Matt. I was going to tell them during the festivities, though there wasn't anything to tell after being ghosted. "I love you guys. You aren't getting rid of me that easily."

"And here I was, hoping we'd get a quiet Christmas next year," Stuart teased, with Mum slapping him lightly on the arm.

"Ha. Even if I were to give you a quiet Christmas, you do realise Jade lives here? She's a mini me, and she's going to give you Hell." I picked up Jade and spun her around. She was getting heavier by the day. I'd have her small forever if I could, a cute ball of love, simplicity and sass—a combination that couldn't be greater.

"At least we'll have quiet when he goes to Tamsin's later," Mum giggled, trying to join in on teasing me, but she never quite had the knack for it. Never as good as Stuart, anyway.

"You're right, and I'll be heading over there soon so don't miss me too much, okay?"

"Happy Christmas," I screeched as I walked in to Tamsin and Callum's house after texting to give them fair warning, holding gift bags containing presents. I winced at the memory of last year, yelling "bitches" and then profusely apologising to Jackie as she straightened the decorations in the hallway. Luckily, she saw the funny side, but I wasn't about to make the same mistake again.

"Liam, welcome." Jackie took my coat as if it were her house and led me into the lounge where everyone was sat. "Merry Christmas, bitches," she spoke softly and leant in with a huge smile as if she'd been planning it for the past year and she'd pulled it off.

"Someone's in a good mood." I laughed, setting myself down next to Tamsin on the floor, with Tess crawling around already wearing the Christmas dress I'd wrapped and dropped off earlier in the week.

"She's either in a good mood or it's the fact she's hit the Port a little too early this year." Tamsin looked at Callum and threw him a sarcastic smile.

The house had already filled with the luscious smell of Christmas dinner. My mouth watered, one hundred percent ready to feast on Jackie's pigs in blankets.

They were as delectable as I remembered. We all sat around the dining room table full to the brim with festive food.

"That was gorgeous, thanks, love," Richard said to Jackie as he unbuttoned his belt with no shame.

"You've got the right idea. I think I'm gonna have to go put on my maternity pants," Tamsin said, pulling at her jeans that gave her no give whatsoever.

"Maternity pants? Oh my, is this your way of telling us you're pregnant again?" Jackie said with excitement as Callum's face mirrored Tamsin's in horror.

"God no. Tessa is plenty enough, thank you. I barely have a minute to myself as it is, aside from being at work. Nope, I'm definitely not ready for another." Tamsin shook her head and got up to get her maternity pants before we went to gather in the lounge for presents.

Christmas was a distraction—an annual distraction that I was in desperate need of, especially this year. As I sat amongst Tamsin and her family, with Tess sat on Callum's knee as he swung her back and forth like some sort of rollercoaster ride, I couldn't help but be devoured by my thoughts. Thoughts of being alone, even though I wanted my friends to be enough—the family I didn't ask for, but they weren't enough. I was surrounded by couples, surrounded by love, and that shouldn't have been a bad thing. Darkness crept up on me as those thoughts wandered, taunting me with my dwindling savings balance and lack of sales on the product range I'd given my all to over the past month or so.

It's still early days. Snap out of it.

I tried to convince myself that we'd recover and that in a few months the risk would pay off, but deep down I knew it was going to be a struggle. I knew if I wasn't to do something soon, the only thing left standing of my business would be me. I'd only just hired Joanna and I couldn't let her or Tamsin lose their jobs. Tamsin was fortunate to have Callum's income, and I knew Jackie and Richard wouldn't let them starve. For once in Tamsin's life nothing was going wrong. They were happy and I couldn't be the reason for that to change. There was no way I'd go back to designing fashion in my bedroom.

"Liam, you made Tess this beautiful dress. You didn't have to get her anything else." Callum sat with Tess between his legs, holding a huge box that was neatly wrapped in pink glistening wrapping paper.

"I can't not spoil my goddaughter, can I? I wonder what it is?" I directed the second question to Tess who sat making excited squeaks as her gentle hands bashed against the wrapping paper.

"Sand," Callum spoke with Tess squeaking above him. She probably had no clue what was going on, but I knew how much she loved going to sensory play with Jackie.

"Yeah, Liam, you shouldn't have." Tamsin glared at

me. I could tell she was already picturing the mess that sand would make in her mind. "Maybe you should open your presents now." I didn't know whether to be scared about opening my presents as she continued to frown at me, occasionally looking at Tess already sat in the sand.

"It's a diary. Thank you," I said, holding the leather bound diary, wondering why she'd bought me one when she knew full well I used my phone for everything.

"Well, it's for the unit, and it's partly a gift for me because it's super pretty and we needed a new one. So the real gift to you is actually a more organised version of me. Merry Christmas." She grinned, finding herself hilarious.

"You're a dick. Pardon the language, but you are." I threw a grin back to her. I guessed it was payback. Not only had I bought sand for Tess knowing how much they valued a clean house, but in University I'd bought Tamsin a Dictaphone so someone else could listen to her moan and whine for a change. I guessed I deserved the diary.

"You know, if someone didn't know you two, they'd think you were the married couple," Callum said as there was a knock at the front door—he had a point. With all of the banter, exchanging presents and laughing at another Christmas themed jock strap to match last year's, I started to perk up. I forgot entirely about being alone, and about my business that seemed to be sinking quicker than the Titanic. This Christmas was turning out to be perfect.

"Matthew, what are you doing here?" Jackie answered the door as her nephew stood in the cold. I caught a glimpse of the falling snow through a gap in the closed curtain and a winter wind rushed through into the lounge from the open door. Was this the Christmas miracle I'd wished for all this time? Or was it a looming disaster set to ruin Christmas for everyone? As Tamsin flicked on the film *The Nightmare Before Christmas*, I hoped it wasn't the latter.

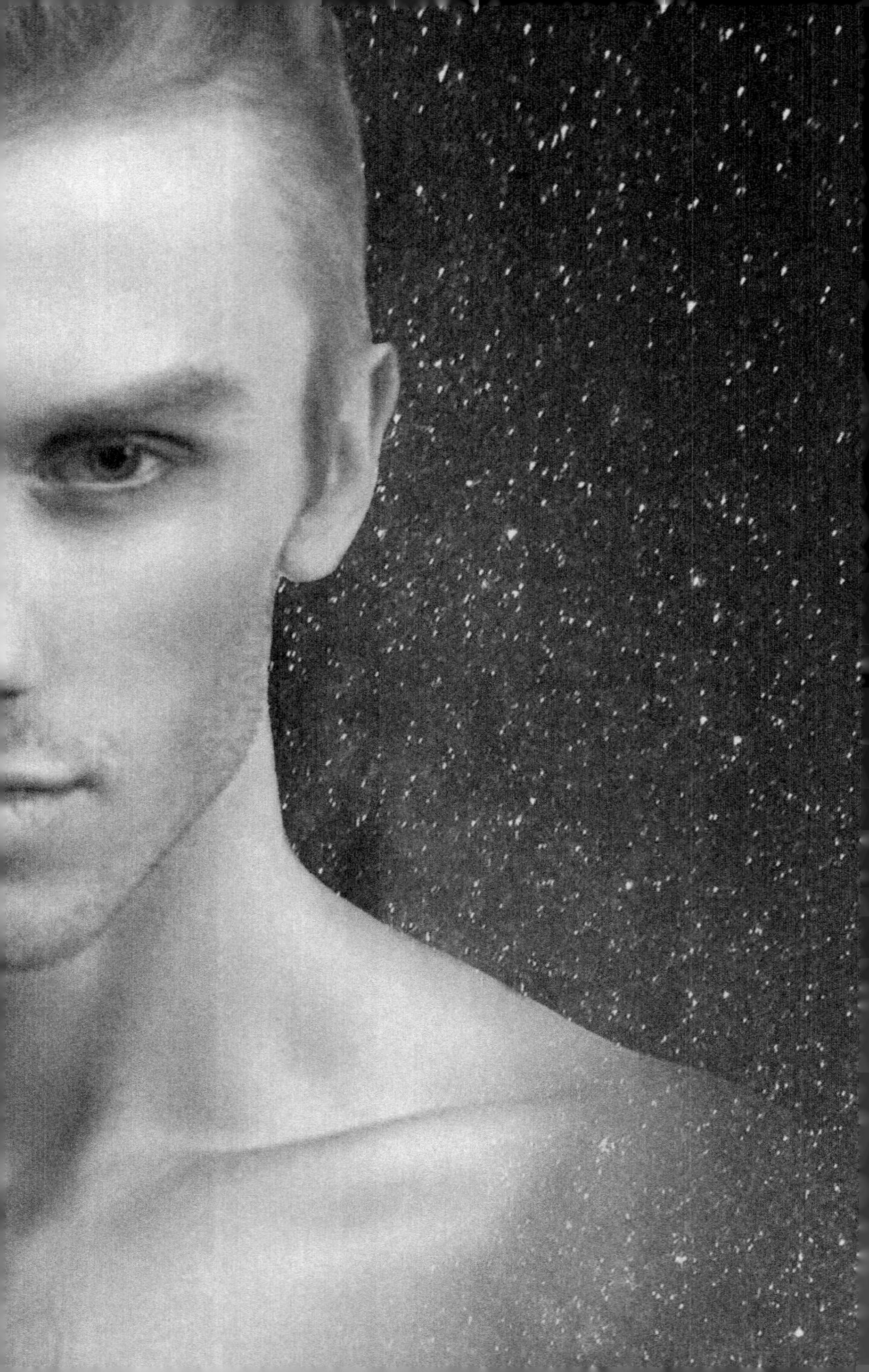

CHAPTER TWELVE

Matt stood beneath the door frame, his broad shoulders practically filling the space between. His eyes dropped to the floor. The spark that had once ignited the personality I'd grown to love was no longer there. Defeat swept across his face, as did his wet hair from the snow that made it look like he'd swum there. I sat on the floor waiting for his eyes to lock with mine, but he avoided them at all costs—he avoided me.

"She won't look at me, talk to me, acknowledge I'm there," he choked, his hands rested in his pockets and his face treading the ground. I wanted to get up and hold him, but I didn't. After not hearing from him since he'd kicked me out of his flat, how could I have been sure that's what he wanted? So I stayed there, on the floor. Helpless.

"What's going on?" Callum asked, entirely clueless

of our situation. Unaware Matt had been caught by his Mum in bed with me. Unknowing of the aftermath.

"I can't be around my family, knowing they are judging me for something I can't control. I don't know what to do?" he asked rhetorically and barely answered Callum's question, with not one person wanting to speak. There was an awkwardness, no one knowing what to say or do. He was hurting, understandable as my mind traced back to the harsh words his mother had no trouble saying.

"Look, you sit down and make yourself comfortable and I'll make you a stiff drink," Jackie reassured, heading to the alcohol cabinet to pour him a whiskey. He took a large sip, shaking his head a little as he was filled by the warm sensation of the spirit running down his throat, and then sat on the floor in between Callum and I.

"I'm sorry for just turning up. I didn't know where else to go." I could smell the whiskey as he spoke, its scent wrapping around the air.

"Don't be silly. I'm always here for you. Now, tell me what's gone on?" Jackie said, taking another gulp of Port as she placed herself next to Richard on the sofa.

"You mean my mum hasn't told you?"

"Told me what, Matthew?"

"That I like men and women? I'm bisexual—and she found out." He looked at Jackie as she shook her head. "Of course she hasn't told you. She wouldn't want to tarnish the family name with such a disappointment.

Maybe she meant every word she said." His sadness quickly turned to anger, just as angry as he had been when he'd launched the glass at the wall and kicked me out of his apartment.

"What did she say?" Callum asked softly, bouncing Tess on his knee as she was fascinated by the television.

"She said I wasn't her son anymore. She said I didn't deserve her." There was another silence that filled the room, this time broken by gentle sobs from Matt as he relived the memory. His eyes were raw, like he'd spent the past couple of days attempting to live with the pain his mum had caused.

"My sister said that?" Jackie said in dismay.

"How did she find out?" Tamsin looked in our direction, asking Matt but also looking at me for answers—staring, a look of disappointment that a mother would give her child for lying to her.

"She came to my apartment when I had a guy over." Matt finally gave me a passing look, no longer than a second. His eyes looked softer than usual, sagged with exhaustion that the past week must have brought him.

Hiding who I was, pretending to be someone I wasn't and putting on a brave face made me physically and mentally worn out. Most people opened their arms out wide to catch me as I fell, but the minority let me fall. Those falls were easier to remember than the good. Luckily, I had Tamsin, a constant in my life, always there to pick me up time and time again, and I sure as hell was going to try to pick Matt up as many times as it took. Nobody should have to go through pain alone, especially when the pain is inflicted at no fault of their own. I wasn't going to give up, not after just one measly speed bump on our road. No matter how many speed bumps, we were going to be together.

"That probably wasn't the best way for her to find out, but I'm sure she's shocked. She'll come around, Matthew, I'm sure of it. In the meantime, you can stay with Richard and me until things blow over, and if it's okay with Callum and Tamsin, you can stay here tonight. I'll speak to your mum over the next day or two, okay?" Jackie said calmly, taking control of the entire situation, with Tamsin and Callum nodding in agreement that he should stay the night because it was Christmas. Nobody should feel alone at Christmas.

"Thank you," Matt said, out of sorts, seeming overwhelmed by the kindness he'd been graced with in his time of need. His hand fell to the floor, inches away from mine. I didn't know if he craved my touch as much I did his, but that didn't stop me wrapping my hand around his and squeezing tightly. Tamsin's disappointed look merged into a smile and my eyes fell back into Matt's. He wasn't speaking to me but his eyes told me more than his words ever could.

"Wait..." Jackie paused as she examined our hands encased in each other's. "Are you two an item? Were you the guy, Liam?"

"Shut up. Liam, are you with Matt?" Tamsin piped up, pretending to be shocked, her drama classes not paying off one bit. It was either Tamsin's poor acting or my cheesy grin that told the whole room that something was going on between us. I wasn't sure if we were still together at that point but I sure as hell wasn't letting go of him for the rest of the night.

Laughter is the best medicine.

That's what Tamsin always used to say, right up until her Mum passed away. It had been what got me through my break up at university and what still got me through each and every day as I lived with that fact that my sexuality had driven a wedge between my family.

She'd always make inappropriate jokes or tickle me, anything to make me laugh if I was feeling down. As much as I hated being cheered up that way, it worked and so I'd do the same for her. I hated when Tamsin was right—laughter absolutely was the best medicine. I could see the laughter in the room infecting Matt. Just a few hours before, he'd been drenched and defeated, looking for a lifeline and fighting for survival. In just a few hours he'd returned to the man I'd started to fall in love with. We were laughing, playing games, and as much as he didn't have much of an appetite, he'd still managed to eat something. Tess had been put upstairs in her nursery to sleep, and Jackie and Richard had made their way up to the spare room. Before that, Jackie had kissed my cheek and told me to look after Matt, so that's what I was going to do. She'd drunk more than I'd ever seen. She even had trouble getting up the stairs unassisted. No matter how drunk she was, she still had enough love in her to reassure Matt that things would be okay.

"Right, I think it's time we went to bed, too," Tamsin said, standing up and making the decision for Callum who was mesmerised by the television.

"Borrrrrinnnnnng," I mocked her, now nestled in between the cushions on the sofa. I never knew why I always sat on the floor when their sofa was so comfy.

"I'm not as young and energetic these days. We can't all get our energy from a can or bottle as Matt does, can we?"

"Hey! Don't bring me into this," Matt said, defending his love for mango flavoured energy drinks.

"She has a point, Matt. You drink them far too often. You're going to have no stomach left by the time you're thirty. It'll have rotted away," I said, rubbing his hand as we sat practically in each other's laps.

"Blah blah blah. I don't smoke, so energy drinks are my substituted pleasure for ruining my body."

"Fine, I'll allow it. I couldn't bear you smoking so it's a fair compromise. Where are we sleeping?" I never could stand the smell of smoke. I'd always end up gagging if the smell of smoke caught me off guard, and I'd end up throwing up if I tried to prepare for the smell—almost as if my brain was teaching me a lesson for trying to re-wire it and putting me in my place.

"Sofa bed, if that's okay? I'll pull it out for you both

now," Tamsin said, folding a throw and placing it neatly on the arm of the sofa.

I'd got myself ready for bed and brushed my teeth in just a few minutes, then found myself lying next to Matt. His body instantly warmed the cold cover that fell flat above us, and even though there were a few inches between us, I could feel the heat radiating off him. We faced each other, communicating solely with looks. The Christmas tree lit the lounge dimly so I could just make out his teeth pulling at his bottom lip, followed by his tongue running along them. The last time we'd found ourselves together in bed, we were unable to keep our hands off each other, until his mother had ruined the moment. In bed for a second time, we found ourselves hesitant to kiss, to touch. I didn't want to be the first to make a move, not knowing how he'd react.

He was there because he wanted to be rescued.

Of course, that didn't stop my mind from wandering, picturing him all over me––his breath caressing my neck, his hands running from the top of my body to the bottom. The thought aroused me so much, I unintentionally shuffled closer and pressed my excitement against him. He didn't hesitate much longer. Our lips wrapped around each other's, barely parting while we caught our breath, hard to breathe through the passion.

For the first time in a long time, sex wasn't just about pleasure, nor was it about validation. It was pure passion, love and lust, unable to get closer to each other even if we tried. We had to be quiet with everyone sleeping upstairs, but thankfully the sturdy sofa bed didn't make much noise. Did I want our first time to be in my best friend's house on a sofa bed? No. Did that take away the magic? Absolutely not. I wouldn't have changed it for the world. I lay breathless, feeling euphoric, my senses wild as Matt wrapped the used condom in some tissue he'd tactically brought from the bathroom.

"That was incredible," Matt said as he shuffled back towards me.

"It really was." I turned and kissed him, still half-mast from feeling his pleasure.

"You know that was the first time I've—had sex with a guy," Matt said lightly, running his fingers along my side, still looking as good as the day I met him, despite his messy hair.

"Really? And was I—okay?" I hesitated, trying to find the right word.

"Do you really have to ask that? You heard me trying to be quiet. Fuck, just thinking about it is turning me on again."

"Oh god. I don't think I could cope," I whispered, laughing as I caressed the side of his face. "Night, babe. Merry Christmas." I placed one last kiss on him before I turned over to sleep.

"Merry Christmas, Liam. I love you."

My whole body tingled as each word echoed through my mind. He loved me. Was it that I was there in his time of need? Was it the pleasure that forced the words out of him? I didn't care, because he'd said those three words I'd once doubted I'd ever hear again. That night, I slept with the biggest smile on my face, wrapped in his arms, and dreamed sweet dreams entirely because of him. It turned out I'd had the perfect Christmas I'd dreamed of, after all.

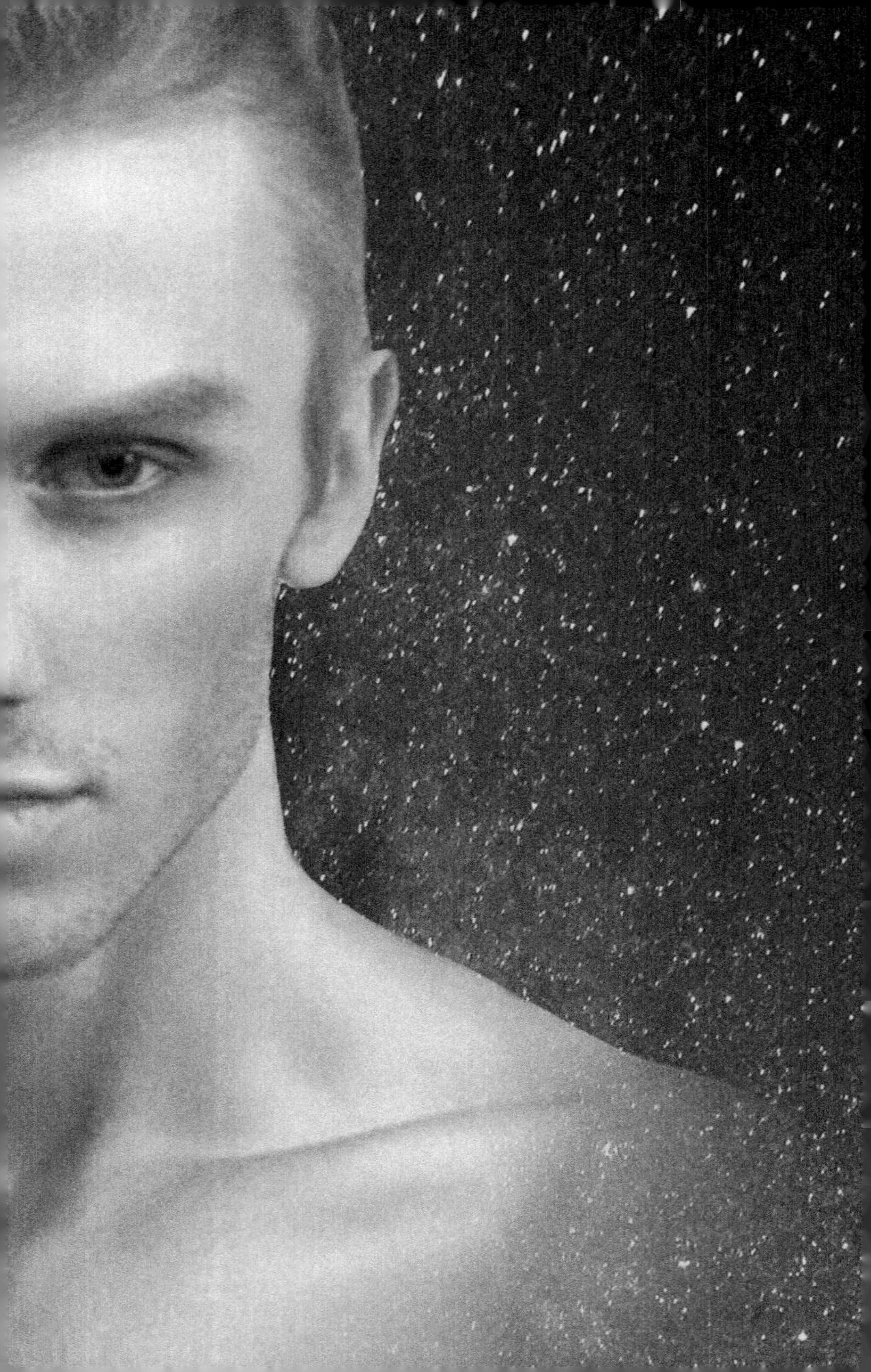

CHAPTER THIRTEEN

The tinsel from the trees had fallen and the festive flickering of lights switched off, with the weather seeming bleaker than over the holidays. There were no more kisses in the snow, but hiding under umbrellas to escape the constant rain that seemed like it would never end. People carried on being their rude selves as though the Christmas season was their only excuse to be happy. Christmas was over and daily life had resumed. Maybe that was why everyone was so miserable; I knew it was getting me down.

I'd spent more time faced with my balance sheet and my accountant than I had creating fashion masterpieces. The more I looked at the financials, the more I felt Wrighteous slipping out of my hands, despite having a firm grasp around it. The loan from the bank was helping us short term, to pay for bills and wages, but it was going to make us pay long term. The loan was a plaster, a temporary fix to a much bigger problem that I didn't have the answers to, no matter how deep I dug for them.

"Surprise!" Matt entered with a huge grin on his face, carrying a very large bottle of Prosecco and a beautiful bouquet of flowers. Flowers you could tell had been put together and tied with love by a florist—not the type of bouquets you'd get from a twenty-four hour garage. Since Christmas evening, we'd never been stronger, and despite the pain he was going through from effectively losing his parents, he was still there for me. We had a relationship I'd never thought I'd fall into, a connection stronger than any I'd had before.

"What are you doing here? I thought you were back at uni today. Don't you have some late lectures?" I asked, running over to him while my arms flailed in excitement.

"I did have, but a few lectures are worth missing if I get to see my favourite, especially as you should be taking a day off today to see Jade." His teeth glistened as his smile grew big enough to fill the unit. I was supposed to have spent time with Jade. I guessed coming to the unit while she was at school wasn't breaking any promises, but time ran away with itself and it was already close to five. Somehow, I'd found myself at the unit even after Tamsin and Joanna had left for the day. "Besides, I have news," Matt spoke once more, restless as excitement took over his body.

"Go on." I took the flowers from his hand, kissed

him on his cold cheek, and walked towards the storage cupboard to fetch a vase.

"My dad came to see me today."

"No way. Seriously? Are you okay?" I asked, promptly placing the flowers next to the vase, eager for his response.

"Yep. He said he was sorry. He said it was a lot to take in and although he still doesn't understand, he will try to and that he's still there for me." A smile was still bright on his face.

"Oh, babe, that's amazing. How do you feel? What about your mum? Have you seen her?" I asked as his smile lost an inch.

"I feel good, relieved I guess. No, he said she was having more trouble understanding than he was. I get it. It's not acceptable in their society or whatever, but the world is uniquely diverse. I just wish she'd love me for who I am." His arms swung around a little as his words were glazed with passion, wanting the acceptance he deserved for just being himself. For just being human.

"I know, babe. I hope she'll come around soon. It's great your dad came to you, though. It must've taken balls to effectively admit he was wrong. He must love you to pieces," I said, trying to reassure him, coaching the smile to stay on his face as he thought of his mother.

As I reassured him, my thoughts became dark, thinking of how lucky Matt had been to have so many people around him accept him, thinking of how he'd been comforted by the love of his father. That was something I'd never had as I battled the thoughts of trying to get my dad to accept me. He didn't have a religion getting in his way; it was just his pre-historic views of the world.

I wondered how I'd change my dad's mind, teach him a new way of the world, one with glitter and rainbows. I was older now; I had life experience. I owned a business for damn sakes, a failing one, but nonetheless a business. I wondered if I could just see him, whether I'd be able to mould his mind into believing I was more of a son than he could have ever wanted.

"You're right. Shall we go get food? I'm starving," Matt said as he practically whisked me out of the unit, leaving the flowers on the counter, ready to wilt.

"You didn't have to put foundation on, you know?" Matt said, pulling up outside The Country Club just outside of Nantwich.

"I know. I just want to look nice for you." I smiled and he returned one before pressing his lips against mine.

"You always look nice."

We walked up to the front entrance, the entire outside area lit up as bright as Blackpool in October, yet the seating was abandoned as everyone escaped the cold. We were promptly seated in a cosy corner booth close to the entrance. Each time the door opened, a chilling wind rushed in, though the temperature was compensated by the indoor heating sat above the door. I looked the food menu up and down, practically drooling as I gazed at it sensually and stroked the seams of the folded bound menu as if I hadn't eaten before.

"You painted your nails, too?" Matt asked with embarrassment brushed across his face as my nails attracted attention, brightly painted to stand out against anything.

"Yeah, do you like the colour?" I held up my hands, showing off the sky blue nail vanish painted with precision, a lighter blue than my eyes.

"Babe, people are looking."

"So what? The whole point of *coming out* is that we don't have to hide or care about what people think any more."

"Not everyone accepts our sexuality, Liam. We need to be careful. Let's not throw it in people's faces," he said and I sat in silence, unable to find words as I stared at somebody I thought I knew. "What's up, babe?" Matt's hand reached across the table, but mine stayed hidden underneath and I pushed my seat back in an attempt to move further from him. I would have hated to embarrass him more than I already had.

"You're ignoring me? Great. My dad stops ignoring me and my boyfriend starts," he said sarcastically with his hands in the air as he slouched in his chair.

"Oh, so I am your boyfriend now and not a huge embarrassment?"

"Of course you are, Liam. I just don't remember you

being this—camp. I mean, I know I'm bisexual, but I want a boyfriend not a girlfriend." His words stung more than ever.

Camp.

A word that I'd learnt to deal with in the past. An empty word from Dale in school as an attempt to insult me. Matt's tongue was coated in venom, a loaded word that was set to infect me. Poison me. I knew I wasn't masculine. In fact, Tamsin was probably more manly than me, but to hear that from someone I loved... Being camp wasn't a bad thing. It was something entirely out of my control. It made me... me.

"Wow. I literally have no words for you right now. I'm done." I stood up with the chair dragging on the floor underneath me, enough to make everyone glance over if they weren't already.

"No, Liam, wait..."

As quick as that, I was out of the restaurant, being battered by the frozen winds of the countryside, feeling as emotional as I'd been for a long time. Feeling as lonely as I had the night of Tess' christening and as hurt as I had hearing my dad say I wasn't normal. I ran through a few nearby farmer's fields towards a small school I recognised, and called a taxi from there.

I didn't go home. Instead, I went straight to the unit. I could have been with family, but I had room to think at the unit. When I arrived, at long last, I placed the flowers in the vase with some water and plant food before slumping down on one of the sofas. Thoughts swirled in my mind as I looked across the room, seeing the countless mannequins dressed in fashion that had been a waste of time and money.

I pulled out a long piece of floral material and dragged it without care to a nearby sewing machine. Fashion had been a distraction I'd used since I was small. It was my creative outlet, a way to get out all the emotion I'd had pent up inside of me.

A few hours had passed and without thought, the material had been turned into a flowing gown suitable for any drag queen. I held it up against me, looking at my reflection in a group of mirrors. Tears fell down my face as if they were running away from me, fleeing from the emotional pool I'd trapped them in.

Just minutes later, I found myself choked with emotion and putting on the dress along with makeup and a styled wig. I stood in front of the mirror as light crept in through the very few windows. I was tired but I didn't feel it, not with the adrenalin that rushed through my system. I was tired of the thoughts consuming me, but not tired enough to sleep.

I stood in a dress that hugged me in all the right places and wore makeup that cleared any and all imperfections from my skin. My fake eyelashes fluttered as though they were casting a spell and the socks I'd rolled up to act as breasts made my confidence soar.

I felt infinite.

Somehow, embodying a character, a different persona, gave me all the answers I'd been looking for all along, with the determination to find answers to the ones I didn't have.

I needed to save my business and the answer was simple. I needed to stop trying to fulfil a dream, because that's all it was. A dream. Creating drag fashion was providing an identity to an art form, a way for them to express themselves, their brand. I was fuelling an outlet for these unique queens to be themselves and that was once important to me. I was so caught up in working on something I didn't need. I had to go back to basics, make drag for the clients I'd neglected just as much as spending time with my family. These drag queens had become a family.

A look of determination grew on my cosmetically enhanced face as I stood with heels reaching the high heavens. I was going to find Dad. I was going to get the answers that I needed—that I deserved. I was going to convince him that I'd become everything—more of a man than he ever could have imagined. Once I was done convincing Dad, I'd convince Matt of the same thing. We shouldn't have to hide away and be something smaller than we were capable of just because of society. I just hoped those around me would understand. I stood feeling euphoric, a confidence I'd never felt before, but it wasn't going to last.

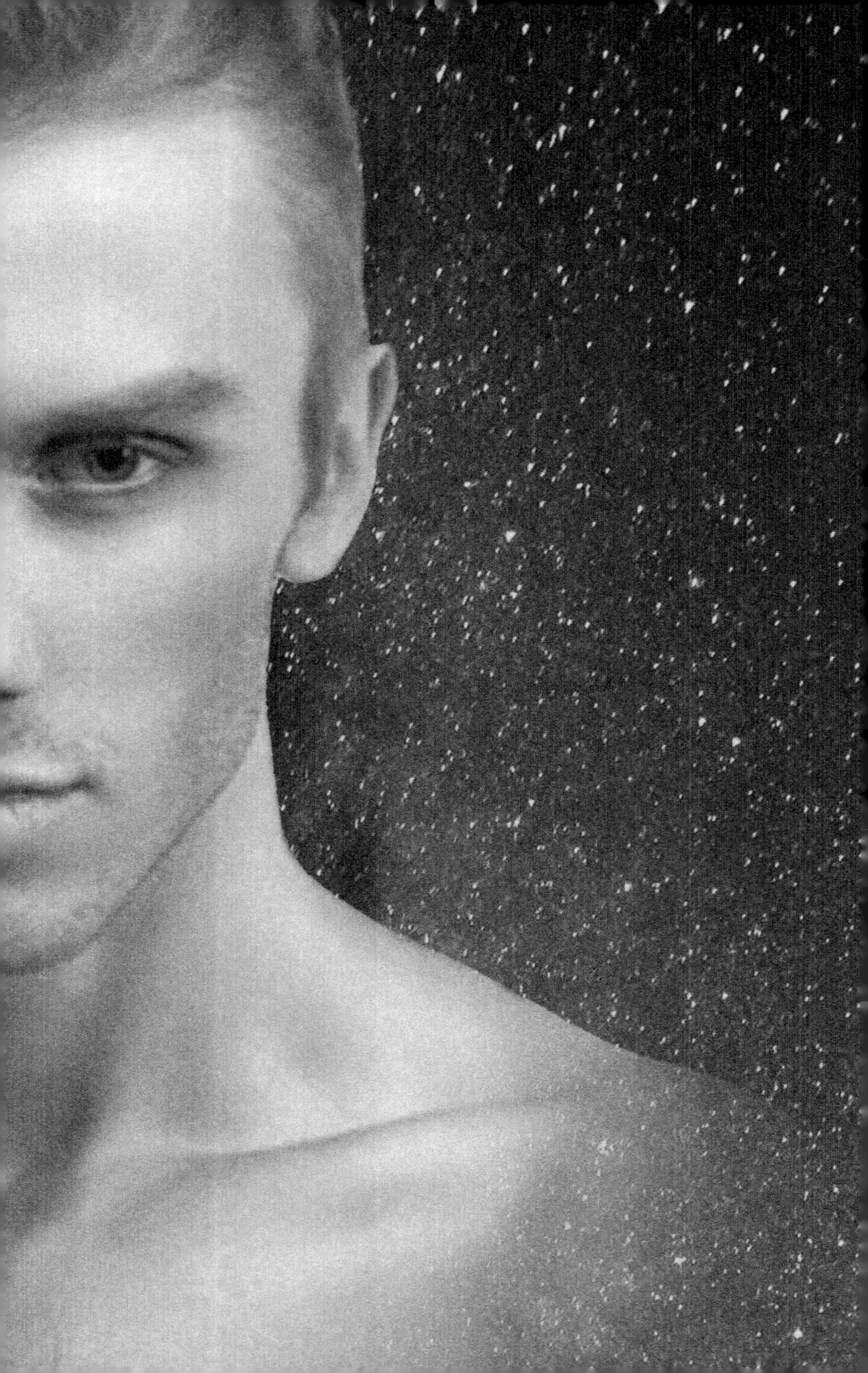

CHAPTER FOURTEEN

"Oh my god, Liam, is that you? You frightened me!" Tamsin entered the unit as I stood at the mirror, practically frozen since the night before.

"Yeah, it's me." I pushed the words out from my chest, trying to disguise the pain in my voice, but my throat wobbled, drier than ever.

"Why are you dressed in drag? Love the hair," she said, complimenting the ginger wig woven with purples and blues that I'd bought the year before at a drag show. As I stood in drag, I realised I could bottle up my worries and thoughts no longer. My tears clung to the cheap mascara and fake eyelashes for dear life. They were a tell-tale sign I had to talk, but even so, it was hard. Instead, I turned around and allowed my tears to tell her everything she needed to know—I needed help. I needed my Tams more than I ever had.

"Oh, Liam. What's wrong?" she said as her eyebrows dropped in concern.

"What isn't?" I huffed with my fists clenched, battling my emotions.

"Let's sit and talk. Have you been here all night?" I was surprised my panda eyes didn't give that away, although I was wearing a thick layer of foundation that must have concealed them well.

"Mmm hmm," I hummed, sniffing unattractively.

"If it's any consolation, you look insane, even with the mascara running down your face."

"Thank you." I wrapped my arms around her as I perched next to her on the sofa. Over the past couple of years it had been me picking up Tamsin and whatever was left of her each time life threw something her way. I'd been surviving fine, thriving even, up until a few months before. Up until I'd had the crazy idea to change a perfectly good business model. Up until I'd met Matt. I had been happy sleeping around. At least with mindless sex, I didn't have all the upset a relationship brought, but I wanted to settle down.

Without Matt, I won't feel love.

Love was painful. I knew that. With that thought, I pulled out my phone as Tamsin sat next to me, and sent a text.

Matt x

7th Jan 2020

[8:17]
Hey. I'm sorry for storming off. I've been thinking and I know I promised you time so I'll change. I'll change for you. I'll try to tone myself down, especially in public, just until you get used to me. That's if you will? xx

"What the hell have you just said? Let me see that." Tamsin grabbed the phone from my hand. Normally I'd have snatched it right back, but I couldn't conjure the energy. "Are you fucking kidding me, Liam? You'll change, will you? You'll stop being yourself, will you? You'll tone yourself down? What the hell does that even mean. Whatever has gone on between you and Matt, I want to know. Now." She repeated my message in anger, each of my words I regretted instantly, even more so after being met with her punches. He meant as much to me as the stars. I'd have given my all for him even if it meant sacrificing something Joanna and Tamsin had drilled into me since school.

Be one-hundred percent Liam. Don't be someone you aren't because the world isn't ready for you.

To avoid another beating, I told her everything. All the angst I'd been feeling and bottling up, how I felt as though I'd never be good enough for Matt.

"You are more than enough. Matt clearly has some issues with himself and his own self-discovery. You are so uniquely Liam. This has never bothered you before, so why now?" she asked me with a soft voice after she listened to me pour out my heart and soul, and she grazed my arm up and down to comfort me.

"I love him, Tams. I'm actively fighting for him to love me, too," I said, trying desperately to not drown in my own tears. All I wanted was for someone to love me for me and it hurt that Matt didn't.

"Look, Matt will come around, and if he doesn't, fuck him! I'm sure Callum would agree, too."

I nodded and changed the subject abruptly, speaking of Wrighteous, because there was nothing more I could say to Tamsin about Matt. It took me a while to tell her about how the business was falling on its knees.

"Why have you kept this from me? We're supposed to be a team?" she asked, only her facial expression signifying her disappointment.

"I've not been thinking straight. I've been so caught up in my relationship with Matt and following a stupid dream I had at university that I've been naive to the problem all along. I'm the problem. I should have listened to you. Drag is the way forward. I know that now and I'm sorry." I unintentionally begged her, down on my metaphorical hands and knees, waiting for her to fix my mess. "Please help me rescue what I've broken?"

"You know I'll help in any way I can." Tamsin quickly grabbed the diary she bought me for Christmas and starting scribbling notes and ideas down. Her work hat was on, but she didn't realise I had more to tell.

"This all looks great. You're so clever. We've also got

Joanna so I'll get her working on some mock designs. We'll call it ready-to-go drag and we'll do it discounted to flush some funds into the business."

"Perfect. We've got this, Gayboy, don't worry. How are you feeling now?" Another punch hit me, this time playfully.

"Better—there is one more thing, though." I paused. "I want to find my dad. Maybe things will be different now that I'm older, just like Matt and his dad?"

"Liam, he hit Diane. He left her with a broken nose and bruises around her eyes for weeks. She was in hospital for a long time. Have you really forgiven him for that?" Confusion swept over Tamsin's face. I knew she'd disagree, especially as she was better for not knowing her own father.

"Of course I've not forgiven him. I don't want to play happy families with him. I'm more than happy with Mum, Stuart and Jade. It's just... I have so many questions––questions only he can answer."

"If you want to find your dad, I'll support you, but I think it will end in tears. You've supported me through everything, and I don't know where I'd be without you, so if you really need to see your dad, I understand. While we're talking about tears, the next time you're in drag, wear this." She reached into her handbag and pulled out a waterproof mascara.

"Thank you," I mouthed to her, the words not coming out of my mouth as I intended.

. . .

For the second time in a short period, I found myself stalking on social media. This time was like no other. Instead of searching for men, I was looking for my dad. My family. People I didn't consider family and hadn't spoken to in more than ten years, only connected by blood. Relatives I probably wouldn't have known about if it hadn't been for going through storage and finding Mum and Dad's old phone book.

Growing up, I'd never had an interest in speaking to Dad, and not once had he reached out after the restraining order had been lifted. Our family was broken, and he didn't want to fix it. I'd have been lying to myself if I said I hadn't wanted him to make amends for all he'd done, but we didn't matter.

It didn't take long at all to find my aunty, someone I'd met once when I was as small as Jade. She wasn't friends with anyone called Jed, and there wasn't one profile picture that resembled my father. He didn't have Facebook, which didn't come as much of a surprise as he was more of a newspaper and TV kind of man.

In a mind-numbing way, I lay in bed that evening scrolling down my Aunty Norma's profile, my arm aching from holding my phone up. Frustration filled me each time the slightest flick of my finger the wrong way would result in having to start scrolling her profile from the start.

I was about to give up when I came across a post with my dad's name in it after scrolling past hundreds of status updates and countless birthdays.

One I didn't expect to read.

I couldn't tear myself away from the screen, looking at the words in black and white.

RIP Jed. My brother xx

I had no time to grieve. My stomach felt as though I'd been punched, the air sucked out of me, winced. I wasn't sure I would have needed time to grieve for him; his actions had hurt our family in the worst of ways, but he was still my dad. My blood. The right to grieve had been taken away from me. His family had taken it from us by not telling us. I hadn't been told my own father had died.

Did Mum know? Had she kept this from me all this time?

I had to ask, otherwise I'd have sat in bed stewing on it all night and I couldn't afford another sleepless night. My eyes were already stinging from being awake for around forty-eight hours.

I slammed into Mum's door and ran into her room. She was sat reading a battered old book she'd read more times than I could remember, with Stuart sat flicking through the channels on the TV in order to avoid adverts.

"Hey, sweetie... What's wrong?" She shuffled back against the headboard, her pillows propping her up, after seeing my look of terror. In a natural reaction, my whole body shook as a way to rid whatever emotion was gathering as I tried to understand.

"Did you know?"

"Know what?" Mum asked. At this point Stuart rose an eyebrow at my unusual behaviour.

"Dad—Jed—died four years ago?"

"What?"

The look on her face told me all I needed to know. She had no idea and promptly jumped out of bed to hold me. I showed her the post on social media, and Stuart sat us both on the edge of the bed to calm down.

"Are you two okay? Do you need anything?" he asked, running his fingers through my mum's hair.

"I'm okay," I said, as Mum stared at the blank space in front of her. He had been a big part of her life for a long time. I encased her hand with mine and tried to get her attention. "At least we're safe now."

Those words snapped her out of whatever trance she was in, and a small smile grew on her face as she turned to me.

"Sweetie, you've always been safe. Your dad would never have hurt you."

"How can you be so sure?"

"We weren't in a happy relationship at all, Liam, and although he started drinking more than he could handle after you told us you were gay, he'd been controlling and aggressive to me for a long while before. I'd became someone I didn't recognise, some sort of ideal nineteen-fifties housewife, and if I stepped a foot out of line like not having tea on the table or decided I wanted an evening with Theresa, I'd have to face the consequences. Your father was the reason Tamsin's mum and

I drifted apart. I was scared of him. You aren't to blame for your father's mess. If anything, you telling us exactly who you were saved us." She spoke with tears puddling in her eyes, yet her voice remained strong as she reassured me.

"Then why did you only call the police that morning he assaulted you if it had been going on for so long?"

"Because, Liam, sometimes it's easier to fight and save somebody else than it is yourself. I knew I had to protect you." Her head bowed in sadness with Stuart wrapping both arms around her.

"I'm so sorry, Mum." I sobbed in her arms, in both of their arms. "I love you so much." For the few moments we all held each other, our world was at peace.

Tamsin was right. It had ended in tears.

I was never going to be accepted by my dad, but my journey to find him had provided answers I never thought I'd uncover. Words that mum had kept locked away so she wouldn't have to relive her pain. I didn't need my dad. I had everything I needed and more right by my side.

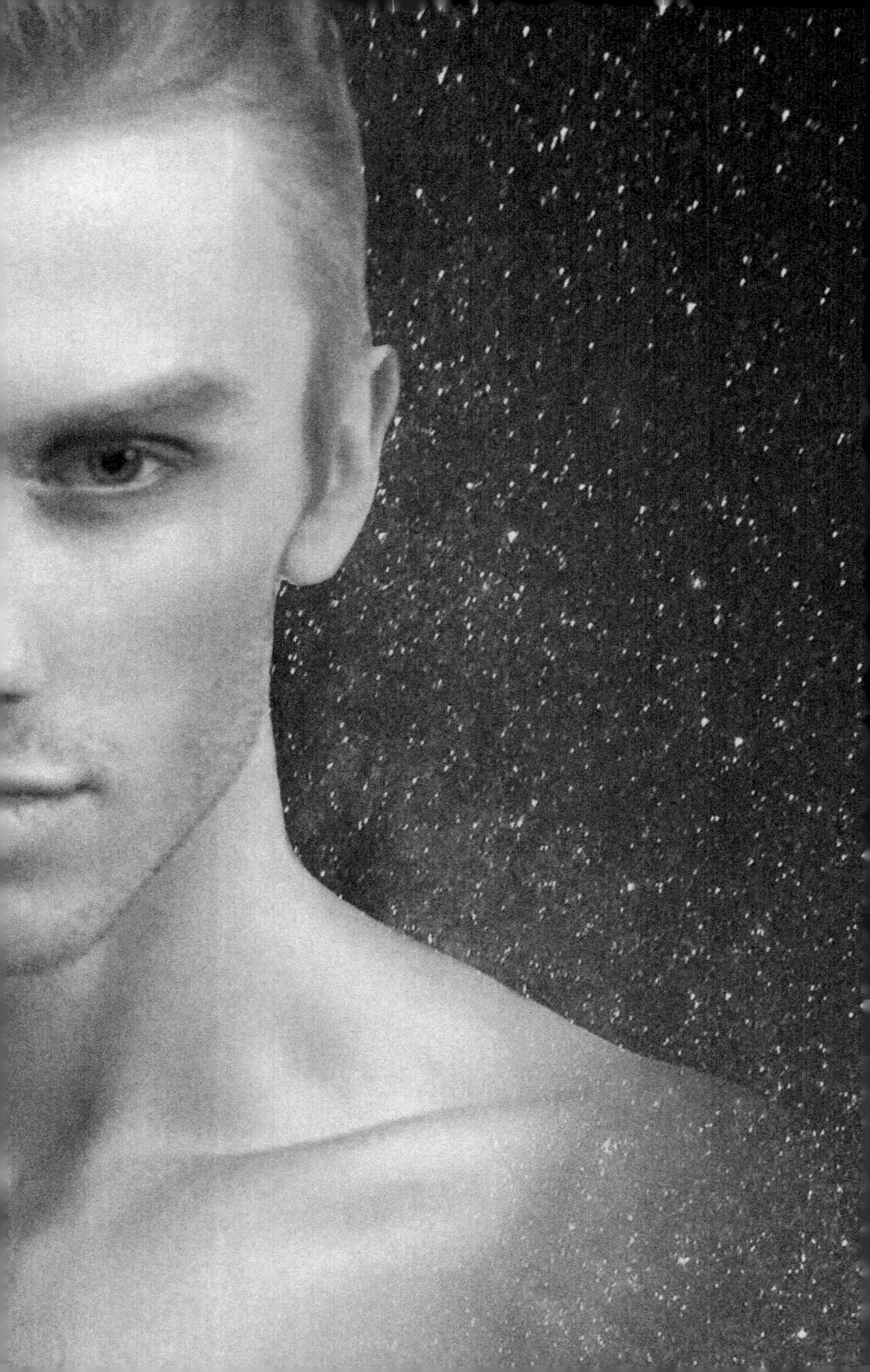

CHAPTER FIFTEEN

The unit was silent, eerily so with neither Joanna, Tamsin or I saying a word. We were all focused, working on saving Wrighteous and all we'd built. It was important to all of us, and not just for the money it paid. Joanna could be creative and not be dictated to by criteria, exams or statistics. For Tamsin, it was a time in her life where she'd fought to regain control of all she was losing. For me, it was my livelihood, my life leading to allow me to be creative as my job. There weren't many as lucky as I was.

I dropped a needle to the floor as I juggled two pieces of fabric while hand stitching details. The sound echoed off the concrete, which resulted in Tamsin looking up swiftly from her desk. She threw me a smile and then continued to post on social media and message previous clients to offer them a one-time discount to lure in some orders. Joanna had her tongue pressed against her top lip as she concentrated while threading a sewing machine, until the silence was broken by the machine. Once the repetitive hum ceased, in an adult like strop, Joanna placed down the garment and sighed.

"I have no idea what I'm doing anymore. I feel like I can be too creative and that shouldn't be a bad thing, but coming from teaching and having to stick to rules and guidelines and a syllabus, it's strange. I'm really finding it hard to put my creative hat on," Joanna said with a flick of her straight black hair.

"You're having a brain fart, and that's fine. I have them all the time. What I tend to do is think of something tangible, like a mermaid or a skyscraper, and try to incorporate those materials or the aesthetic of that physical thing into the fashion. It gets the creative juices flowing."

"You're right. I'll do that." Joanna's face immediately seemed brighter. I could tell her thoughts had already started to wander. Sat in her classes ten years ago, I would never have believed that I'd be giving the wonder that was Joanna Chan advice.

"Right, you lot—take a break, go for a walk or have some lunch. I don't care what you do, just stop working for an hour," I ordered, but naturally, Tamsin carried on working.

"Are you sure?" Joanna asked and stood up without haste, stretching her back that ached from being hunched over.

"Yes, very sure. Tamsin, stop typing!" I yelled, my

voice bouncing from wall to wall as it echoed throughout the unit.

"Urgh, okay bossy. Fine, if you want me to take a break, caffeine me up, baby," she said, gleaming as she spun around on a swivel chair she took far too much joy sitting in.

I made my way to the coffee machine that Tamsin had purchased for us because, in her words, *'she was nothing without the posh coffee she used to have when she worked at Farden's Hotel.'* I offered Joanna one, but was left without an answer as she'd already escaped into the winter air for a brisk walk, eager to keep up her January fitness resolution. Music started to play through the speakers and Tamsin jumped out of her seat and started to dance.

"What are you doing?" I laughed, shouting across the room over the music as her coffee oozed from the machine. She turned the music down to reply but carried on dancing anyway.

"Dancing is like a reset button for your body. Just start moving and you'll feel like new, like you can take on whatever life throws your way. It's something my counsellor taught me. Come on, try it."

I found myself holding a mug of coffee filled to the brim, smoothly dancing across the unit in an attempt not to spill the hot liquid all over me. As she'd said, all my stresses seemed to roll off me like water off a duck's back. Despite using up what little energy I had to dance, it somehow fuelled me with even more. I could have gone for hours.

"You should put on that drag dress again and get all done up. I want to see all of that beauty with no black smears on your cheeks." I didn't need to be told twice and reached for the floral dress and wig once again. In no time at all, I was applying my makeup over the orange corrector I'd used to cover the 5 o'clock shadow that had already appeared on my freshly shaven face. "I would offer to do your makeup for you, but you've always been *way* better at it than me," Tamsin said, sat next to me as she rolled a mascara between her palms.

"You're not as bad at makeup as you think." After battling with my eye makeup, which was, for me, the most unnatural part of applying makeup, I then pressed my freshly painted lips together and blew Tamsin a kiss.

"You are literally the prettiest drag queen I've ever seen."

I gazed at her reflection in the mirror and then focused on myself. I didn't focus on the clarity of my skin, nor my eyes made to look a deeper blue against the ginger wig I'd placed on, but for the first time I wore a smile.

"I do look good, don't I?" A sudden rush of confidence ran through me. Validation was something I'd sought after for a long time, and unconsciously, making sure I looked my best in drag was a form of wanting approval. I studied all of the other drag queens I'd come to know in my mind and realised that drag wasn't all about the look. "Thing is, drag is about more than just some makeup and a wig. Look at David—he isn't the prettiest of drag queens and yet you can't help but fall in love with him. If I've learnt anything from Miss Mirage all those times seeing her in drag, it's that drag is a persona. It's about using everything you've bottled up to fuel yourself to be bigger and better. Drag is the person I wished I could have been all those years back, and if I had been, maybe things would have been different."

A sincere grin grew on Tamsin's face as each word left my mouth.

"You literally have no idea how happy it makes me to hear you say that. Be that person, Liam. Not the person with tear filled eyes and pain inflicting thoughts, but the person you wish you could have been all those years back."

After a while, I danced around the unit to the music Tamsin had resumed. The floral dress billowed underneath me, with Tamsin following behind dancing like an Egyptian. She took out the Polaroid camera we used to take pictures of our clients and occasionally snapped pictures of me, shaking the film as the picture ejected from the bottom.

"Wait. STOP!" Tamsin held a developed picture up, its ink capturing one of my first moments in drag.

"What?"

"What do you call her? Does she have a name?" She looked at the picture as she spoke.

I stood and pondered her question for a while, but I couldn't answer. In such a short space of time, the person I looked at in the mirror had already impacted my life. I couldn't pick any random name, it had to mean something.

"No, not yet. I'll get my thinking cap on." As those words left my mouth, the unit door pushed open. I turned expecting to see Joanna returning from her break, but instead I was greeted by Matt and a shocked expression.

I was wearing a wig. I was wearing makeup. Bloody drag makeup. I was in drag!

I looked down at my outfit before looking up at Matt, stood frozen in the doorway—not moving, not speaking, mouth agape. Tamsin tried to release the awkward air by quickly grabbing her phone and resuming the music, before sitting back down at her desk.

Just a few days before, Matt had insisted I was too camp and stated he wanted a boyfriend and not a girlfriend. There I was, dressed as a woman.

Fuck my actual life.

"Matt, hiiii." I was so caught up with nerves that I'd forgotten I should have been mad at him for not knowing about my dad and the agony I'd felt, all because he'd disappeared off the face of the Earth with no explanation or even a text back.

"Hey, erm—" He looked at Tamsin, whose head popped up and down behind her computer monitor like a *Pop-Up Pirate*. "I think I'm gonna go," Matt said, his speech elongated awkwardly.

"No, don't go. Why did you come here after all this time?" I asked, brushing the ginger strands of the wig off my shoulders.

"I came to apologise, but seeing you dressed like that... I've realised I'm not ready. I really like you, but I'm just not ready." Yet another occasion Matt had so effortlessly hurt me. All of my emotions swirled as I struggled with the feeling of disapproval. If I was ever going to live my life free from judgement, with the person I knew was the one, I had to put it all on the table no matter the consequences. It was a gamble—I could lose him or I could win the jackpot and spend the rest of my life with him, if he'd have me.

"Ready for what, Matt? I don't understand."

"To deal with this."

This.

I was *this*. I was the situation he couldn't deal with. Me being one-hundred percent me.

"You're starting to sound like your parents." My voice cracked as it battled the hurt, and Tamsin squeaked behind her screen, listening to my every word. Matt frowned and stood under the door frame in silence, not responding to my accusation, which was my first counterstrike. "You knew from the very minute we nearly fucked in that bathroom stall—you knew I was camp. You saw me dressed in a fucking black sequin suit. What the hell did you expect?" Tears were drawn to the front of my eyes but with every fibre of my being I tried not to let them escape. I was not about to cry in drag again. Instead, anger escaped, my prickly tone attacking him as I fought so desperately to defend myself. "There is nothing to get. I am me. I'm just in bloody drag. Yes, it's camp, but it's also fun and empowering, and... GOD, do I feel good. If you can't handle me having the confidence of a thousand men or being as queer as the day is long, then you clearly can't handle me feeling the best I've felt in a long time. This is your last chance. I want a relationship, not a flaky fuck buddy who isn't going to be around when I need him. Leave, and if I haven't heard from you by the time I go to Paris in two weeks' time, I'll know we just aren't meant to be. I'll know that a stranger's perception is more important to you than true love."

I caught my breath after giving him all I had. Every little piece of me.

"Okay..." Matt finally spoke.

He was taking the time. He was going to think instead of walking away from us. I'd convinced him not to. Our relationship meant so much to me, I couldn't deny that.

"I don't need time, Liam." He finally walked closer, retreating from the safety of the doorway. "You're right and I'm wrong, just like my parents were wrong. I promise I'll try not to let other people's opinions bother me so much."

"Really?" I shuffled closer to him, waiting for him to ascertain whether he meant every word. This time, his silence was welcomed, and my lips were met with a soft kiss. An electric kiss, sending shivers through my body. A kiss so great I knew he was the one. I was left feeling momentarily reassured, until doubt crept into my mind.

How do I really know if he's okay with this? Are we going to end up in a similar situation again?

I hoped not. Instead of letting my mind run away with my thoughts, I regained control, which was somehow easier to do while dressed in drag. I stayed in that moment and basked in his love.

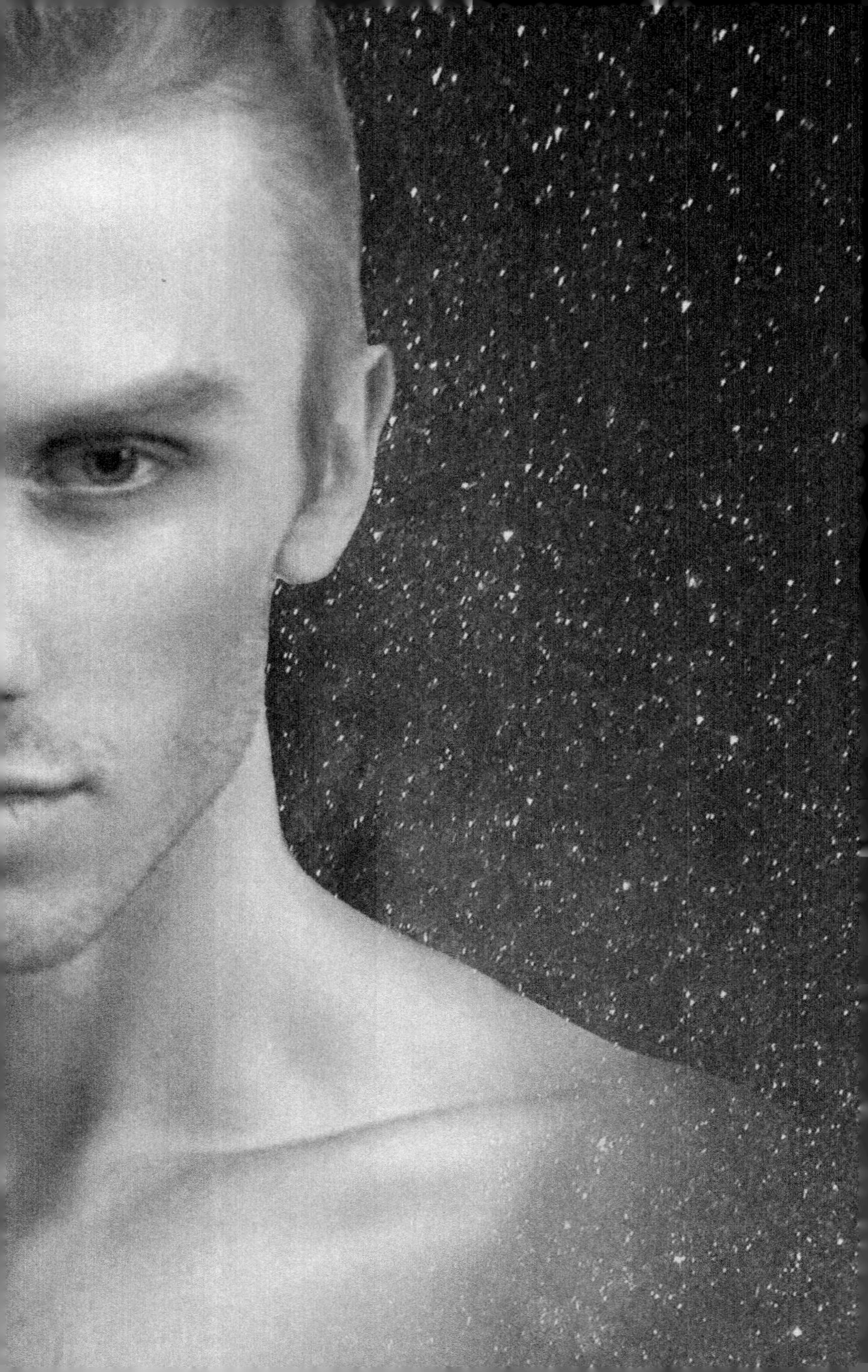

CHAPTER SIXTEEN

When something isn't working, you turn it off and then back on. Sometimes things need to be reset before they start to work properly. I'd seen evidence of this at least twice. The first was in my business, which had broken records for the amount of orders it'd received in the past week. The calendar was a mess of pen, filled with drag names, both famous and unknown. The second was my relationship with Matt. Our small break and then talking about how we felt instead of bottling it up had done us the world of good. Having a serious adult relationship was all new. I was learning and so was Matt. We had to cut each other some slack.

Adults fight. Even those in love argue. Maybe even more.

The cold wind rushed across my face as I filled Matt's car with our packed bags. Matt had planned the whole weekend, giving us enough time to travel back on Sunday to collect my pre-packed luggage and board my flight to Paris that Sunday evening. I couldn't wait to lie in a glass igloo, looking up at the stars that shone brighter above the rural part of Scotland. We'd spend all day on the Saturday basking in each other's company before travelling home on the Sunday.

I'd taken the weekend off and left my business in the capable hands of Tamsin and Joanna, and then Joanna was to fly solo as I dragged Tamsin to Paris Haute Couture Fashion Week. I'd managed to get tickets long before deciding to stick to drag, but I wasn't about to pass up the opportunity to go and see mesmerising pieces of art walk the runway in the fashion capital of the world.

"Have you got everything?" Matt wondered, putting a bag full of sweets in the footwell of the front passenger seat—including my favourites, Peanut M&M's.

"I have. I just need to say bye to Mum and Jade before we go. Are you coming in?" I asked, despite him wanting to take things slow.

"No, babe, I'll pack the rest up so we can get on the road. Say bye from me, though."

I understood, at least I wanted to, but deep down bubbling doubt was filling me, growing from a puddle to an ocean. As the doubt washed around in my stomach, I pushed the wooden front door open. Jade was stood in the living room being dressed for school by Mum, in a white collared polo shirt and skater skirt that she loved to twirl in.

"We're heading off now," I said openly and then knelt down next to Jade. "I'm gonna miss you so much. You be good in school today. No throwing water bottles, okay?" A cheeky grin grew on her face as a look of confusion fell on to Mum's.

"Okay. I promise I won't throw a water bottle," she said, her words coated in sugar but a look of mischief told me otherwise. She was plotting something, and maybe she'd stay true to her word of not throwing a water bottle and throw something else. How could I have been sure without living in the mind of a seven-year-old?

"Love you." I held Jade as tight as I could before hugging mum and heading to the door. Before I could reach the car, Jade yelled down the hallway.

"Love you like twenty thousand and thirty hundred."

Her favourite number, and also mine.

Stunning views of the hillside passed us as Matt drove. Naturally, Matt and I sang along to Madonna songs, Matt putting me to shame as I stumbled my way over the lyrics of some of the songs. Singing with him by itself would have been enough to cope with the long motorway drive without the scenery you just didn't get across the Cheshire plain. Heat poured from the vents, allowing me to enjoy the frost-bitten views without enduring the cold. We even found ourselves opening the car windows, the cold air billowing in along with the crisp fresh scent of the Scottish Highlands. The ground covered in the fresh white of the snow and being with my favourite person, it felt as though I was in heaven.

"We're here," Matt said with excitement after stopping at a small hut at the bottom of a hill. We drove up a narrow dirt track that led us over a hill, with our glass igloo sat proudly on top.

It took me a minute to dispose of the Peanut M&M's I'd shoved into my mouth, and then I scurried out of the car, my foot crunching the ground below that had been kissed by frost. With my camel jacket zipped up to my neck, I pulled a couple of bags from the boot of the car and hurried to the front door, waiting for Matt to use the keys we'd picked up from reception.

My mouth caught flies as I stood in awe of the EcoPod. I'd never been to a place like this—I'd never have been able to afford it, but this time Matt had somehow come up with the money. It was his treat, his way of apologising for his behaviour. His way of showing he'd miss me when I was in Paris. There were no ceiling lights; the curved panels of glass let in enough light, with the bed sat directly underneath—perfect for stargazing. A faux hide sat on the bed, inviting my hand to bury itself beneath the fur.

If there is a heaven, this is it.

"You like it?" Matt said, wrapping his arms around

me from behind. Goosebumps rose all over, not because of the bitterness of winter, but because of him—his being forcing my body to react in unnatural ways.

"It's like a dream come true," I said, turning my torso in his direction and allowing my lips to press against his. Once. Twice. More times than I could count because he was too damn delicious. Each one made me tremble and was more intense than the last. Our bodies fell to the bed next to us, our lips not parting for more than a second. We hadn't been at the lodge for more than ten minutes and already our bodies were clashing in a war of passion. Matt pulled away, breathless, and gazed into my eyes.

"Your eyes are the most beautiful blue I've ever seen," he whispered softly, still holding me and not ready to let me go. "Is it happening? Are we going to try?"

At first, I wondered what the hell he was talking about, caught up in physical attraction, then I realised. We were having that conversation—the conversation every gay couple has at some point.

"Are you sure... Like, are you ready?"

"As ready as I'll ever be." He dropped another kiss on my lips and we began to undress each other, once again hypnotised. In that moment, nothing else mattered but us. Not the birds tweeting their loud song, nestled within the trees surrounding the igloo, nor the fact that someone could find themselves walking past our EcoPod. Nothing mattered.

"Be gentle?" he begged, his eyes never drawing away from me.

"I promise."

We lay on the bed after an eruption of lust. Time ran away with itself. What felt like minutes had turned to hours, and we found ourselves looking at the sunset in the distance. A palette of yellow, orange and red blended perfectly above the hills as the night sky faded to black above us. One by one, stars started to glisten. Each one had their own story, and sparkled in their own unique way. Matt held my hand up as our bare skin pressed together, pointing my finger to different stars. He'd talk about the differences in stars and tell me some of their names. He was the epitome of sexy geek, and he was all mine.

As our eyes adjusted, and the longer we spent under the night sky within the comfort of our igloo, a long cloud-like object appeared in the sky, with clusters of stars and streaks of light around it.

"What's that?" I asked, moving my hand in the direction of the cloud as it spread out in the sky.

"It's the Milky Way. I was hoping we'd get to see this. It's still quite faint because it's not as dark as it could be, but isn't it beautiful?"

I nodded and couldn't tear myself away from its beauty. It was picture perfect, the type you'd see on an Instagram post or in an astronomy museum.

Now I'm in heaven.

We lounged next to each other, drowning in a soft duvet and pillows, underneath the Milky Way. It was perfect. We were perfect. My thoughts collided as the man of my dreams rested by my side, his bicep curled underneath my neck and our bodies as close as they could be. I couldn't lose him. I couldn't allow for something so stupid to continue to eat me up. I had to talk to him, and be open with him because that's what relationships were about. Openness and honesty. I fought with myself to be honest, and I struggled, the worst case scenario sounding in my head as a warning alarm to not ruin this moment—to not ruin what we had. My brain was ready to find out how committed he was to me, but my heart was nowhere near ready to take a punch.

"Can I ask you something—tell you something?" My voice shook with nerves as I tortured myself.

"Anything," he replied casually without a care in the world. He looked the happiest I'd ever seen him.

"So, I know I shouldn't bottle things up. I know that's given us some trouble in the past, and well... I want us to be good—really good. But for me to stop worrying, I need to ask—are you sure you are okay with me? Are you sure I don't embarrass you?" Questions circled my mind as he looked at me, stroking my bare chest and remaining mute. "Like this morning when I asked if you wanted to come see my mum and Jade. Is it you want to take things slow, or is it you don't want to build bridges you're later going to burn?"

"I promise you, I just want to make sure we do this right. I don't want to be spooked again, but I'm one-hundred percent committed to you, babe…"

"How can I be sure?"

Unreasonable Matt could have called me ungrateful after bringing me here. He could have thrown this whole trip in my face, but he didn't. He could have used the fact that he'd given himself to me, something I'd given away too freely in the past, but he didn't.

"I'll prove it. Just give me time."

For Matt, I had all the time in the world, even though I'd given him so much of it already. Some of that time I'd spent down on my knees wondering why I'd allowed love to inflict so much pain, but most of it I'd been made to feel like a prince—a prince who was about to get his happily ever after in his un-conventional fairy-tale life.

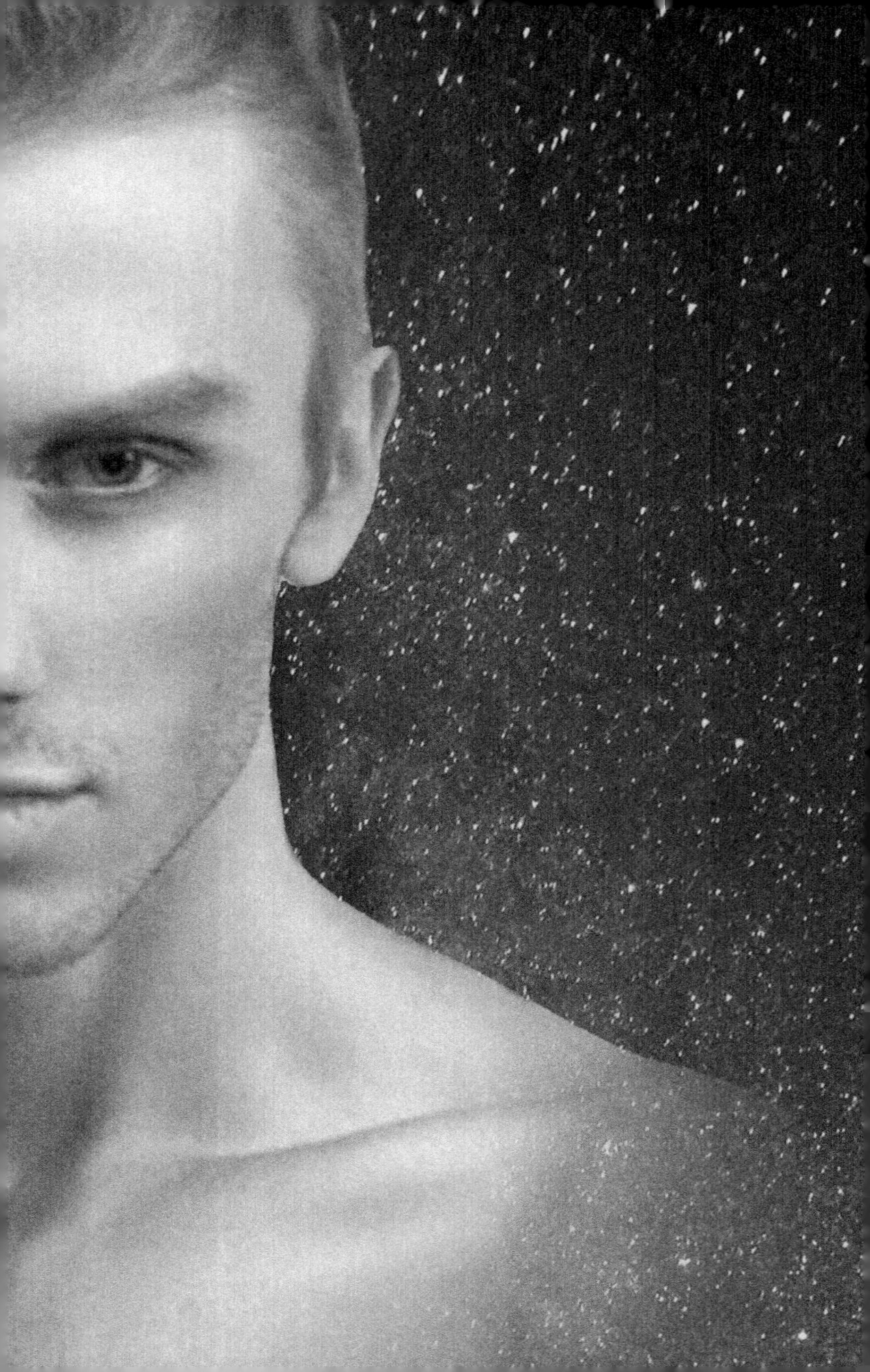

CHAPTER SEVENTEEN

"We didn't have to leave so early, you know?" I watched the world rush past us through his car window, stuffing the remains of whatever chocolate we had left in my mouth because when you're on holiday, you're allowed to eat chocolate in the morning.

"I know. I just don't want you to be late for your flight. You know what traffic can be like on the M6."

"It's a Sunday..."

"Still, all it takes is for there to be an accident and we could be sat in traffic for hours. I'm not taking any risks. Liam Wright, you *shall* go to Paris," he laughed, only briefly taking his eyes off the road to flash a smile in my direction. His grey casual shirt sat so perfectly on him, buttoned to his chest and bulging open, with stray hairs finding their freedom from the concealment of the material.

"You're so pretty." I looked at him, wanting to straddle him right in the middle of the motorway, as if our little break away hadn't been enough. My thoughts weren't helped when his gear changing hand fell to my lap and began to graze my inner thigh.

Take me.

A vibration lingered on my leg, right underneath Matt's palm, the excitement ruined once I'd taken my phone from my pocket to see a picture of Tamsin. I guessed her calling during a heated moment was payback for walking in on Callum and her in the middle of sex last year.

"Hey, Tams. You excited for Paris?" I asked immediately as I heard Tamsin fumbling with her phone.

"Gayboy, I need you. Work has been hella busy and well… I left packing until last minute. Don't shout. Tessa is being horrendous, though. I haven't had a minute's peace and barely any sleep. Callum is doing overtime because he's off while we're in Paris so he can look after Tessa, and of course his parents decided to go on another holiday, so I need a favour. Please can I drop Tessa off when you get home so I can pack?"

"I knew you'd leave it 'til last minute. You're so bad. Look, give Mum a call. I'm sure she'll have Tess so you can get some sleep and then just pack before we have to leave?" She was the most organised person when it came to anyone else, but she was the worst at organising herself.

"Okay, yeah that's a shout. I'll do that. Thank you." She rushed to put the phone down as Tess cried in the background.

"And make sure you set an alarm!" I yelled down the phone before hanging up.

In no time at all, we arrived back at home, with Matt dropping me off right outside my house. It was as if the motorway had swallowed hundreds of cars in front of us, giving Matt a chance to put his foot down.

Matt stepped out of his car, sorted the bags that belonged to me and then stood awkwardly, waiting for me to pick them up from the side of the road.

"Thanks for this weekend," I said, picking up the rubbish bag that had once been filled with treats.

"You're welcome, and thank you, too. Bye, babe. I hope you have a nice time," he said, planting a swift kiss on my lips before hopping back into his car.

"Bye, then..."

Empty.

That's how I felt.

Have a nice time. Bye, babe.

No bloody I love you. No being swept off my feet. No pushing me against the metal of the car to cop a quick feel. Nothing. Was I expecting too much?

. . .

I spent the next few hours with my family, accompanied by little Tess, gargling in the cute baby way she did. Not once did she cry while I was there, which made a change, so I guessed she was having a nice break from her mother's stressy vibes. I told Mum and Jade about our trip, avoiding the subject of sex or the empty goodbye I had just been faced with, before Callum and Tamsin arrived.

Callum took Tess home to feed her—eating was all she seemed to do—and Tamsin and I picked up our bags and strapped ourselves in my car after saying another goodbye to my family.

"Ready," Tamsin said, out of breath as she clambered into my car, as if packing and the travel to my house had wiped her out.

"Got everything you need?"

"Yep! You've got the tickets, haven't you?"

"I do." I pulled them out of my inside jacket pocket as visual confirmation before heading towards Manchester Airport.

We stood at the departures entrance at Terminal One. The airport was nowhere near as busy as I'd seen it in the past when I'd caught morning flights to Magaluf in the heydays of university.

"We just need to find the check-in desk. Can you see Paris on any of the screens?" I asked as Tamsin squinted, patting the pockets of her jacket.

"I think it's over there," she said, moving to unzip her luggage to start rummaging through it, stood in the way of a check-in queue.

"Tamsin, move... What are you doing?"

"I've not got my passport. I mustn't have picked it up from the kitchen counter." Her face looked white in panic, still rooting through her bag.

"Seriously?"

"Yes. Please don't hate me. Do we have time? Can you call Matt to run and get it?"

"I can, but if he's at his Manchester apartment it would be quicker for us to go back. Isn't Callum with Tess? Couldn't he bring it?"

"That would mean getting Tess in the car and she's an absolute pain. Can you just call Matt, please." Her voice changed, anger coating her voice until she begged me to phone Matt.

"Fine."

I pulled out my phone and called Matt, with him answering quicker than he'd ever done in the past. In the midst of worry, wondering if we'd ever catch our flight, I reeled off everything to Matt, not forgetting to rant about Tamsin as if she wasn't there in front of me.

"I'll get it, don't worry." His smooth tone calmed me, and knowing I'd get to see him again before going to Paris was the cherry on top of a bad situation. I hoped this time we'd do goodbye properly. I'd even settle for a quickie in the departure toilets if he was up for it. "Turn around," Matt said, so I quickly turned my torso, catching a glimpse of Tamsin's grin beforehand.

There Matt was, stood with a passport in his hand, dressed in skin tight jeans and a salmon pink shirt. In shock, it took a few moments before I realised he was wearing makeup. Foundation, highlighter, fake eyelashes, eye shadow. The lot.

"You're wearing makeup." I pulled myself closer to him.

"I am. What do you think?"

"That's cute. It looks like Tamsin did it, though."

"I bloody did do it, you cheeky git." Tamsin punched me in the arm and laughter erupted between us, attracting the attention of the commuters around us.

"I wanted to come and say bye to you properly, but I also wanted to prove to you that you don't embarrass me. I'm all in, Liam. I don't care that I look like a man in drag, well more clown like actually, or that Tamsin picked a colour that in no way, shape or form flatters me. I just care that you'll have me in your life forever because... I love you."

"You did all of this for me?"

"Yep. If drag makes you happy, I'm behind you. I don't want to hold you back or change you. You're so imperfectly perfect and that's what I love. Every day is an adventure with you and I don't want that to end. I want to be on that journey with you. Our journey."

"You're the best," I said, grabbing his hand in front of everyone, and not once did he flinch. He may have looked ridiculous, but he was wearing makeup for me. For me.

"Now, I'm not saying I'm gonna do drag. I can't pull it off like you can." His lips wrapped around mine for everyone to see. There wasn't any clapping like in the movies, but it was enough to prove how committed he was to me. I was his one and he was mine.

"Now, I wouldn't rule it out. With some professional makeup skills, I reckon I could turn you into something other than a pantomime dame."

"Dick," Tamsin insulted, peering at the corner of my eye.

"Maybe I'll let you, or maybe you can do drag for the both of us." Matt pulled me inches closer. I could feel all of him and I didn't want to let go. For a second, I thought about not going to Paris. For two seconds, I thought about leaving Tamsin behind and bringing him with me, but we'd have our moment, one day.

"I love you, babe." His eyes were completely dedicated to me and no one else.

"I love you, too." I bit my lip in the middle of a smile as bright as it had ever been. "Quickie in the toilets?" I jested, pulling him jokingly in the direction of the toilets I'd eyed up as I day-dreamed just minutes prior.

"In your dreams. Now, go catch your flight and buy me things in duty free on the way home please."

"You know it." Tamsin and I walked away, towards the desks allocated for the Paris flight check-in. My head turned to Matt's the whole time, only looking back infrequently to ensure I wouldn't trip or fall. That would have been embarrassing. Each time I looked, the more I beamed at his poorly applied makeup. I was sad to be leaving him, but I knew it was only for a few days before I'd be bringing him home a huge bottle of Scottish whiskey from duty free as a token of appreciation for the mini break he'd planned.

"So, had you already packed? Or was it all a ruse to be able to do Matt's makeup?" We approached the check-in desk and stood in the small queue stopping us from handing over our bags straight away.

"Honestly, I hadn't packed either. That's why I was flustered. It was another thing on my list." She laughed and continued. "I realise I'm a bad parent, though. I took Tessa's favourite toy off her so she'd cry just so it was believable on the phone."

"You never! Tamsin Cross, you wicked woman."

My favourite human. Well, one of them.

I sat on the plane, my phone switched off instead of putting it on flight mode. I'd spend far too much time playing on games and automatically clicking on social media out of habit otherwise. As Tamsin played on a game she insisted helped make her smarter, I sat in silence, my eyes closed and my mind free from the dark clouds that had once appeared.

Love doesn't always go according to plan. Not that I'd planned on loving Matt as much as I did, but even so.

I'd already started planning our future in my love-shrouded mind. If I'd learnt anything, it was that most of the time, love is the best feeling in the world, and sometimes, it's a pain you wish would just go away. This time, I had no idea what was waiting around the corner, hidden ever so quietly in the darkness.

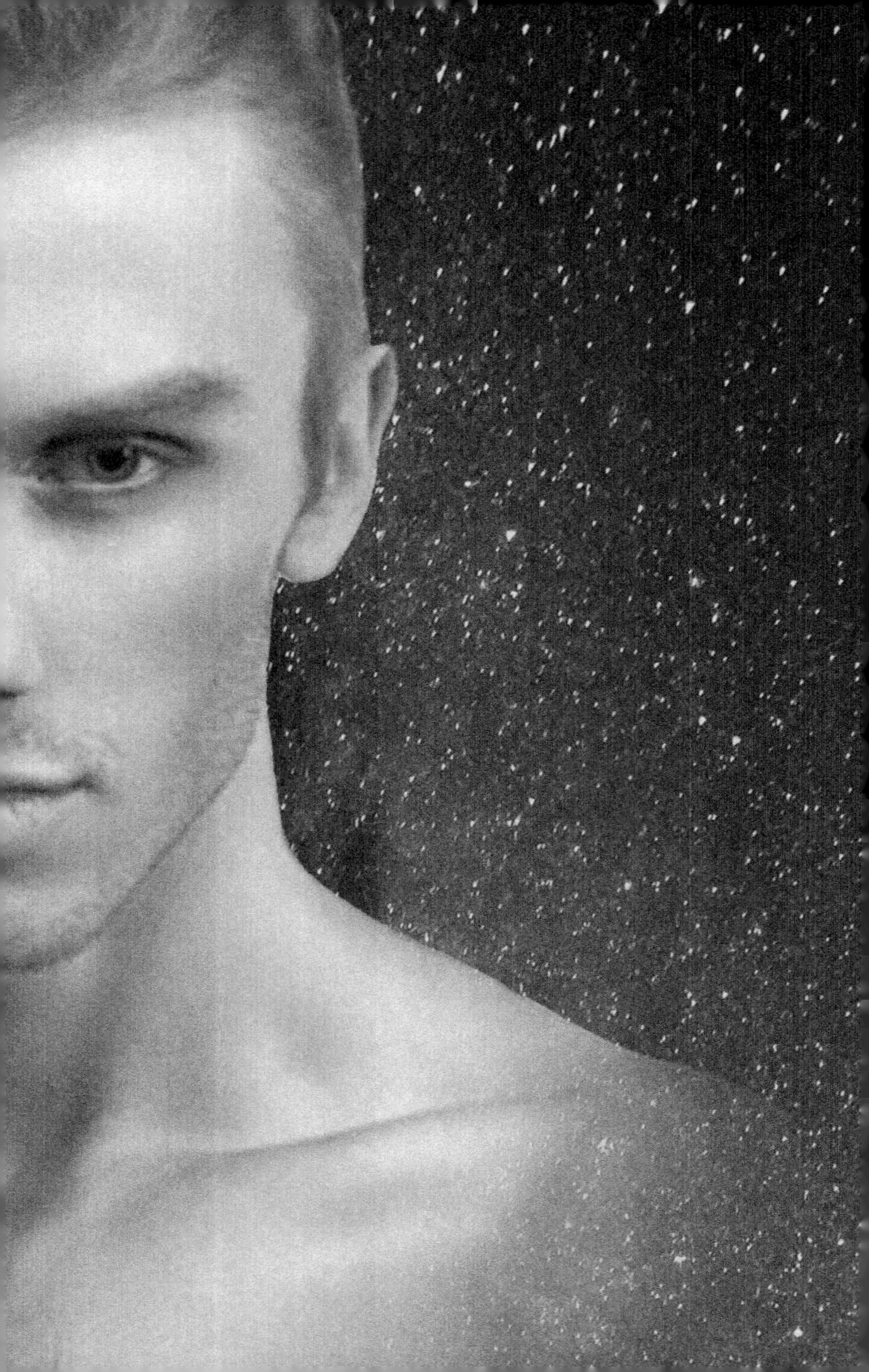

CHAPTER EIGHTEEN

I was at the hotel before I switched my phone back on, waiting for it to switch over to a different network provider. I shook my phone vigorously in an attempt to encourage it to connect quicker. Although the shaking motion had nothing to do with it, I did feel a sense of power as notifications finally started to appear. Some were of importance—like a text from Mum asking if I'd arrived safely. Others of no value at all—like an all too annoying reminder to breathe from a meditation app I'd downloaded but never used. There wasn't a text from Matt, though. I didn't need one, not after the declaration of commitment he'd shown me at the airport, but damn, did I miss him already.

"Oh my god, you can see the Eiffel Tower from the window if you stick your head out at an angle," Tamsin said, leaning over the metal balcony in an attempt to see the Eiffel Tower lit up in a golden orange light.

"Can you? I didn't even pay for a room with a view, so that's good," I muttered, distracted by my phone.

"So, tomorrow I want one of those boards with cheese and ham and stuff on. Reckon there will be somewhere we can get one?" Tamsin walked around the room with her shoulders held high, her spirits even higher. Like being in Paris had given her a well-deserved break, a freedom she'd lived for before having Tessa.

"You mean a charcuterie? Literally every restaurant in France will sell those. Of course we can." I spoke in my best French accent, although it was likely enough to offend.

"Whatever it's called, if it's got cheese on it, I want it." Tamsin and I both hung ourselves over the balcony, our necks extending to see the landmark everyone thinks of when you mention Paris. Her smile seemed brighter than the Eiffel Tower, which sparkled in the distance as the clock struck midnight. Paris was the fashion capital of the world, but it was also considered the city of love. I tortured myself, wondering what would have happened if I'd dragged Matt here instead.

Would he have proposed? If he wasn't ready to meet my family, I had no hope, but I was ready and it would have been the perfect opportunity.

Could I have proposed? I knew he was the one—the person I wanted all my days with, both good and bad, but it would have been too soon.

It was in that moment, with my head hanging out the window and the still bustling streets below, that I decided that I'd be coming back to Paris. We'd be able to hold hands walking down the street without a feeling of sin. I'd be able to get us both underneath the Eiffel Tower's shadow, get down on one knee and declare all my love for him—just like he had in the airport.

The next morning, I woke to Tamsin pottering around the room with the dim sound of music pouring from her phone. I didn't know what time it was, but it was early. The birds were still playing their morning song and the roar from the main road outside our hotel seemed quieter than it had the night before. I pulled the pillow over my head and moaned as the music was interrupted by a call.

"Hey, Cal, you're up early. Is Tess okay?"

There was silence as Tamsin listened to Callum on the phone. I lay in bed enjoying the peace and quiet for a second, when in hindsight I should have been preparing myself. I was lying in the calm of the storm, but it was about to wake me up quicker than I'd ever been woken before.

"What? Is he okay?"

In the safety of my duvet, I didn't absorb what Tamsin had asked, getting only a small portion of the conversation as Tamsin just hummed along with nerves battling her voice.

"Okay. I'll tell him and I'll let you know. I love you."

At this point, I pulled the pillow from my head and

sat up with my fist clenched around the pillow. It tightened as I saw Tamsin's face, darkness shrouding her expression and tears grouped, rolling down her cheeks.

"What's up? Tell me what?" I asked as butterflies fluttered in my stomach.

"That was Callum. He's just spoken to Jackie. They're coming home from their holiday early." Tamsin's voice stuttered with nerves, trying to pull herself back together with each word.

"Oh, right... why?" I sat back, my nerves calming despite Tamsin displaying a look of horror.

"Matt—Matt's..." She struggled with her words, something not allowing her to finish her sentence straight away, as if there would be some consequences. "Matt's at the hospital..."

"What?" I shot up quickly, panic drawing in.

"He's been stabbed."

My breath was caught at the back of my throat, bubbling into something physical I couldn't swallow—couldn't be rid of. Somehow, I managed to find strength and got straight out of bed, ignoring the tired ache in my eyes. I couldn't speak. I couldn't ask if he was okay, nor could I give voice to any of the other questions that had perched themselves in my mind within a millisecond. I pulled on my jeans and grabbed the t-shirt off the floor that I'd worn the day before, entirely fine with the fact I'd be wearing the same outfit twice in Paris. My principles and expectations of myself went out the window when all I could think about was Matt.

Was he alone?
Stabbed? By who?

Instead, I focused on how I was going to get to wherever the hell he was in the shortest amount of time, grabbing my unpacked bag and about to head out of the door. Tamsin didn't hesitate, and followed my lead without speaking. That's how well we knew each other. Once Tamsin had cleared her side of the room, I hailed a taxi, not bothering with the city's metro like the night before.

Why was it that time flew when you were having fun but stopped dead when all you felt was pain? The world still spun at the same pace and the clocks still carried on ticking, yet those minutes and hours felt as though they were in no hurry to end. I could barely speak as I was called through security at the airport, not bothering to use pleasantries as I boarded the plane home. I was too numb, the pain spreading throughout my entire body and allowing the ache to remain until we reached the hospital. Humanity had failed me and I just couldn't forgive it.

"Matt." One of the very few words to have left my mouth since Callum called Tamsin. Had I been saving my voice for him? Storing all of my energy to see him in the state he was in. There were more visitors than doctors and nurses, which didn't seem right, considering all the colour had vanished from his face. There were more machines than people, at least, each one fighting to keep him alive.

"What happened?" I finally asked, each word escaping with caution like I didn't want to know what had happened—if someone were to have told me, it would have made it real.

"He was stabbed. He's got three wounds, and one has punctured his lung. The machine is breathing for him right now, and he's quite weak," Callum said, bouncing Tessa in his arms, Tamsin promptly taking her from him to give him a break. Jackie and Richard still hadn't arrived, but Matt's parents, Angela and Nathan, sat sobbing on the chairs next to his bed.

I wanted this to be a cruel nightmare, a joke my brain had decided to play on me after the wonderful time Matt and I had had together. I had no such luck, and if it was a nightmare, it hadn't finished taunting me.

"So, he's alive? Like, he can hear me?" My voice wobbled.

"He can hear you, Liam," Tamsin said. I could only imagine the pain she must have felt. Hospitals made bile rise to the back of my throat, bringing back the pain of the past. Ever since I'd been bullied at school, and the amount of times I was sent there to be checked for injuries. Tamsin had witnessed her own mum pass away in a hospital bed right in front of her, and I hadn't been there. I couldn't be with my best friend because of those bullies who had installed some sort of trauma in my head that I couldn't shift.

I didn't want to be at the hospital, but I had to. I had no choice. Matt was my boyfriend. He was going to be my fiancé. I had to overcome my own issues for him because he mattered to me more than I could admit. I'd never loved anyone like him.

"We're sorry, Liam," Angela said, holding onto Matt's father.

Had she finally found the love she'd buried deep in her narrow mind? I knew regret must have filled her after not speaking to her child since before Christmas—her own blood. I couldn't acknowledge their apology. They didn't matter—Matt did.

"Why did this happen?" I stood over Matt's bed, watching him frozen in time, still and waiting to get better.

"It happened outside the airport. The police are looking at CCTV, but they said they aren't ruling out a homophobic attack. Apparently there have been other stabbings just like it within the city." Callum spoke softly, his arm placed on my shoulder making me flinch momentarily.

The makeup.

How would they have known he was gay without the makeup?

I was no longer numb, my body allowed to feel everything—every emotion, enough to make me collapse to the floor in tears.

This was me.

This was my doing.

I whimpered on the floor, with Tamsin kneeling down next to me, somehow no longer holding Tess. Her hand ran through my hair as she tried to calm me down. It wasn't the gentle hushed tone of Tamsin or the growing cries of Matt's parents that helped me pull myself together. It was knowing how much Matt would have hated me crying like that, especially as perception meant everything to him.

With Tamsin's help, I pulled myself up off my knees and sat on the edge of Matt's bed. He hadn't moved an inch, his body resting in some sort of coma.

He needed to pull through for everyone in this room, but selfishly, he needed to pull through for me. I wasn't going to lose another person, not someone I'd grown to love in such a short space of time. Someone who had come into my life unexpectedly and turned it upside down and then the right way again. I placed my hand on his, and for a second it was normal. As he moved his hand just an inch towards me, everything was right again.

He moved his hand.

"You need to get better. You need to... Please." I huffed in between violent sobbing I tried so desperately to control. I looked around the room, everyone shedding a small smile before returning to a look of doubt. It was clear to see the room was filled with love, but it seemed as though I was the only one that held onto hope. Hope as I grazed his hand, which lacked the power to do the same back.

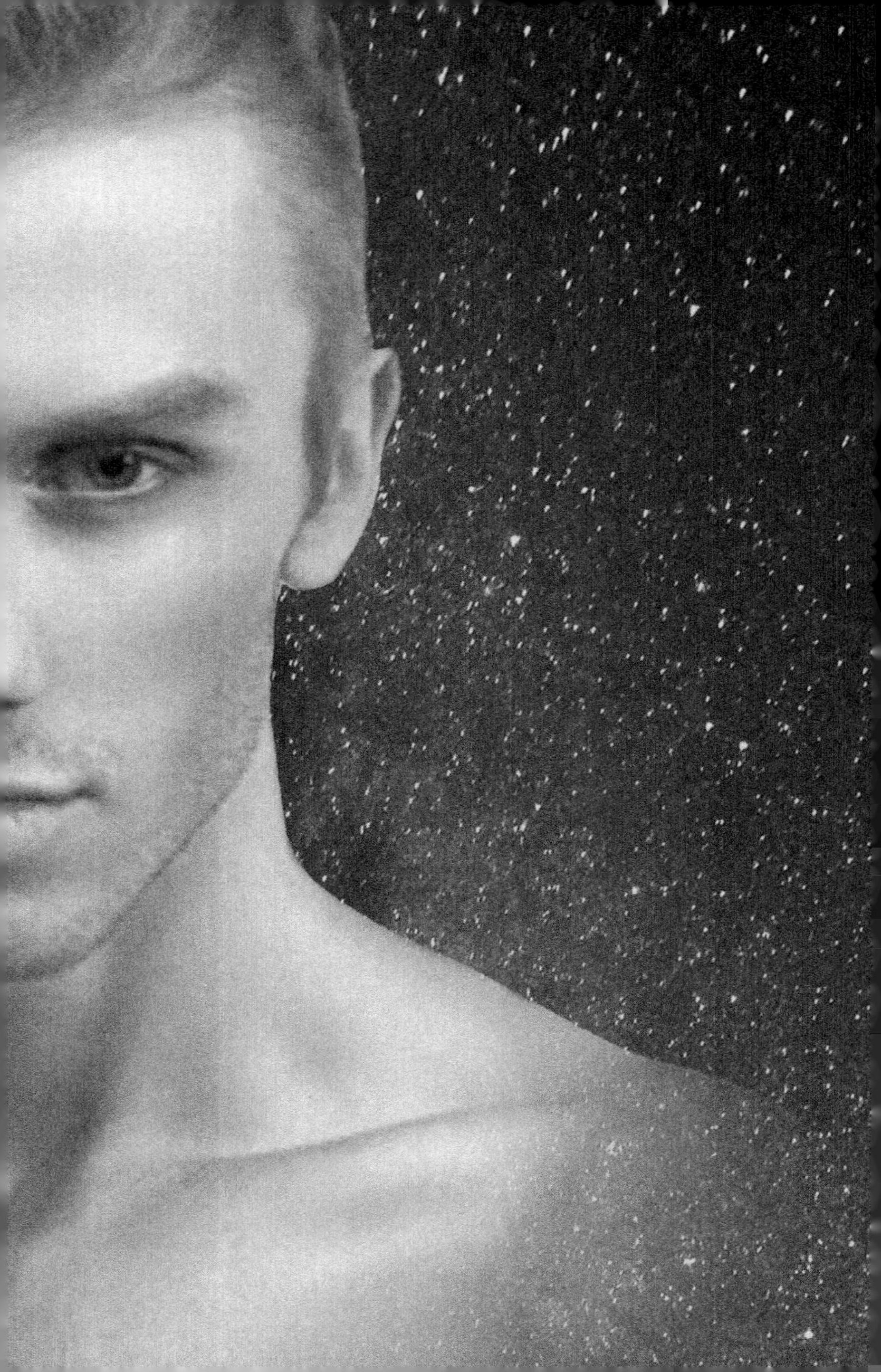

CHAPTER NINETEEN

The world was at odds no more, my faith in humanity restored. That was the case as my mind wandered in an uncontrollable way as I dreamt—dreamt about Matt and I singing Madonna at a karaoke bar in Manchester, holding hands and not caring how people would perceive us. We were gay and not hurting anyone else. We were happy, and that's all that should have mattered. I dreamt of a world where you could be gay without consequence—a world where children could grow up and not have to worry about being penalised for something as uncontrollable as love. A world where if Jade were gay, her friends wouldn't bat an eyelid. I knew it was a dream and it wasn't going to change. Not overnight, anyway.

Awoken by the sound of nurses huddled around Matt in the ICU, I picked up my head from the white cotton sheet draped over Matt and quickly pulled myself out of the tired haze that would normally cloud my mind for most of a morning. I tried to listen to what the nurses were saying, but the words wouldn't decode. It was like a foreign language playing as a hum in my ears. I listened for a while until the hum was no longer a noise from the nurses, but from a machine connected to Matt. An elongated beep. A beep that hurried the nurses into position and forced them to press the emergency button. A beep that encouraged more people to rush into the room.

"He's crashing. We need everyone to leave," one nurse said as another rushed to Matt's side in order to start CPR. I was shuffled out of the room and watched through the blinds without blinking until they were closed.

They were trying to save him.

I stood helplessly in the corridor, with nurses and doctors rushing in to Matt's aid. Callum had taken Tess home, leaving Tamsin by my side along with Matt's parents, and they were just as helpless as Tamsin and me. I couldn't do anything but wait, hopeful that he'd make it through and overcome the evil the world had presented him with.

Hope.

It took a while for the nurses to leave the room. Not one of them smiled. Some walked straight past, not saying a word. Some dripped with sweat.

"I'm sorry. We did everything we could. The injuries to his chest and abdomen were too much for his body to cope with..." One of the nurses spoke to his parents, but I stopped listening. I'd heard enough.

Sobbing filled the corridors.

He was gone.

I'd fucking lost him.

Stabbed because of me.

I'd pressured him into not caring what people would think and if it hadn't been for me, he wouldn't have been at the airport wearing makeup. He'd warned me and I should have listened.

No trip to Paris together and no proposal. No sharing our lives together and creating memories because of one person. Someone evil. I'd have swapped places with Matt if I could, and for a moment I wished with all my might to make that happen. To bring back Matt and take me instead—that was until I saw Matt's parents. They hunched over as a void opened up in their life, ripping out everything Matt meant to them. Leaving them with just memories and the words that had once trailed off his mother's tongue.

'I am no longer your mother. You don't deserve me.'

The words echoed through my mind as I played back what memories I still held of Matt, the only thing life couldn't take from me.

I couldn't wish it was me in Matt's position, not on purpose. I couldn't do that to Mum—to Jade. I couldn't leave them. Not if I had any choice in the matter.

———

In a world with no Matt, things I'd thought mattered for so long didn't seem important anymore. I'd spent more than forty-eight hours back in the safety of my home, accompanied by my family and the occasional visit from Tamsin. I didn't care about my business, or the time I'd booked off to be at Fashion Week. It didn't matter that I should have been there, a lifelong dream of mine, to be sat amongst like-minded people in awe of the creations that walked the stage.

For so long, I had craved love. I'd craved the touch of another man more than I cared to admit to myself. As my head perched on the pillows and I stared at the stars on my ceiling, I couldn't think of anything or anybody else—I didn't want love or the touch of a man. I wanted Matt.

A smile crept on my face as I thought of Matt, the first time I'd looked at the ceiling and not been reminded of Dad. I pictured Matt next to me, my pillow his bicep, as he pointed up to the stars. I could hear his voice and feel his bare skin still next to mine. I could see the Milky Way as vividly as I had once more, and it was everything I needed.

"Roarrrrrrrr." Jade burst through the door in her best attempt at being a lion. I wiped away the few tears that escaped as I saw Matt in the stars above me—the glow-in-the-dark stars I'd wished had been taken down so many times, but were to stay there for eternity.

"Why are you crying?" Her delicate voice wrapped around me like a hug would.

"They are happy tears." I sniffed.

"Oh. Do you want to play with me? You can be the baby lion and I'll be the mummy," she said, stroking my hair as Tamsin had at the hospital. I relived the pain of being in the hospital once more, the ache I'd felt as I blamed myself and allowed my flood gates to open.

"Don't cry, baby lion. I'll make sure you have everything you ever need. You can have all the animals you want to eat. I will give you cuddles and lots of love. Nobody will hurt you because people love lions, especially girl lions. Boy lions are stinky, but you aren't a boy lion." She roared at the end of each sentence. I couldn't help but smile through my tears at how gorgeous she was, in between the blubbering mess I'd become.

"Jade, what are you doing? I told you not to bother him." Diane rushed in after hearing me bawl from her room.

"Sorry, Mum. We were playing lions."

"Are you okay, sweetie?" I sat up in bed and nodded to show I was alright, wiping some of my tears away with my forearm.

Stuart appeared as Diane escorted Jade from my room, holding her hand in order to make sure she didn't come roaring back in.

"You okay, mate?" He placed himself beside me, and then without hesitation he wrapped his arms around me, squeezing as tight as possible.

"Yeah, I'm okay," I lied. I wasn't okay, but I'd been worse. A lot worse.

"It will get easier, you know?"

"Mmm hmm," I hummed unconvincingly.

"When I lost my first wife, I couldn't function right. Jill and I had spent all our time together since we were teenagers, and then one day..." He stumbled, trying to find the right words. "I had to learn to do everything by myself. I had to do things I never thought I'd have to do on my own again, like the weekly shop or just sleeping in bed without someone next to me. It was hard. You're feeling pain, and that's okay—that's normal. But love lasts longer than pain, so once this pain starts to ease, you'll be left with all of the happy instead of all the sad. It does get easier, I promise you."

I needed to hear every single word he had to say. He'd felt pain before just like mine, and he'd pulled through it.

"But... it was my fault. He was wearing makeup because of me." I slumped back in my bed, still choking on my tears, beating myself up to a state of exhaustion so I'd eventually get some sleep.

"You can't torture yourself like that. You don't know that was the reason. He was wearing makeup to show you how much you meant to him. Why are you focusing on all of the pain, when really you should be celebrating how much you touched him?"

"I guess... It's just without me, maybe he would still be here and I wouldn't be moping around." What Stuart said made sense but I'd had too many people taken away from me—first Theresa, my surrogate mum of kinds.

Then my dad, someone I'd fought so desperately to receive validation from but was never given any. Then Matt. Someone who'd fought to stay hidden until he met me, because I was enough. He'd passed away entirely true to himself and managed to stop living a lie before his last day. Stuart was right. I could go on blaming myself, or I could live my life as I would have for Matt, and I knew exactly what I was going to do.

I hugged Stuart once more before leaving my bedroom for the first time in two days, aside from trips to the toilet. I ran past Mum towards my car. She was lucky to have Stuart; we all were. The greatest dad Jade could have ever had, and mine, too.

Once the engine had started, I drove down the road—past Tamsin's house, my old high school and right past the chippy I'd spent far too much time at when I never made it back in time for tea. Just thirty minutes later I arrived, stepping out of my car. I made sure I took a second before knocking at a door.

"Liam, what are you doing here?"

There he stood.

A man I'd not spoken to in months because I was so caught up in things that didn't matter.

A friend who had once meant so much to me.

A drag queen who had filled my university days with so many happy memories.

"I've come to apologise. I'm sorry for ghosting you, and I'm sorry if I led you on. I didn't intend for that to happen. I'm not that slutty guy I once was and I don't intend on giving myself away that freely again, but I need you and I miss you. Will you please forgive me?"

"Yeah, look don't worry. I shouldn't have held a grudge for such a long time. Are you okay? You literally look like shit. Where's your bronzer to cover up that pale skin of yours?"

I stepped inside, his house looking as though nothing had changed—our friendship looked as though nothing had changed, too. I sat on his couch, a place we'd had sex too many times before, and cried. My words were bitter to taste as I brought him up to speed, aching at the sadness yet beaming at times, reliving memories as I told him of the wonder that was Matt Nightingale.

"I'm sorry, Liam," he said sincerely. This time there was no touch of my leg. He knew it wasn't the time or the place. "Is there anything I can do for you?"

"There is actually." I pulled my chest up high, my back straight, and composed myself.

"Anything." He smiled.

"Will you make me a drag queen?"

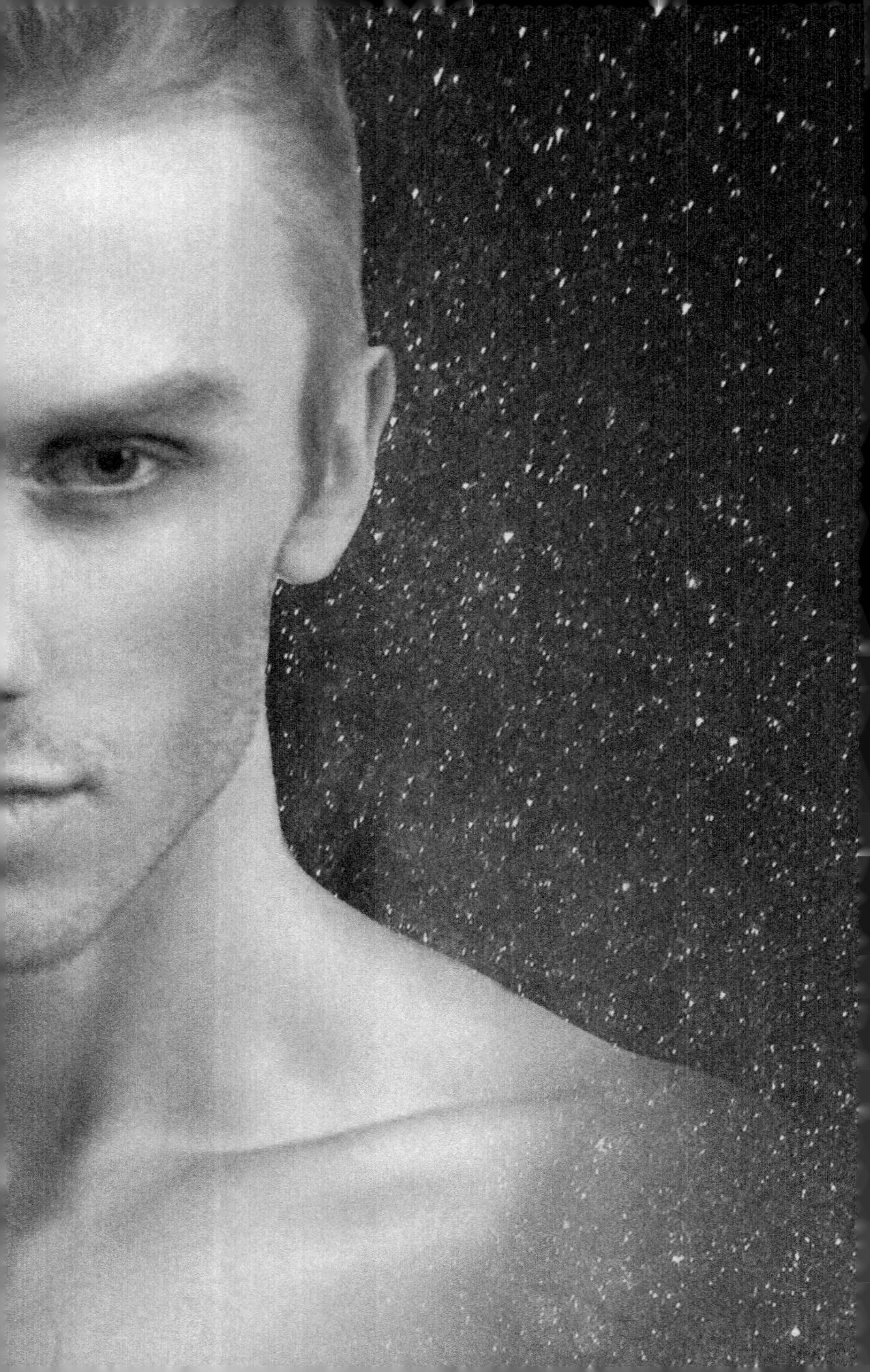

CHAPTER TWENTY

"I've got to admit, I wasn't expecting that." David laughed and pulled me up from the couch, leading me to his spare room.

"Well, I kinda left out the part where I poured my heart out to Matt while I was in drag. Everything just felt right when I was dressed up. I felt like a better version of myself and the world was put right. I need the world right again. I need to feel good," I rambled to him as I stepped into his drag closet, an unused room in his home. Wigs had their own mannequin heads, shoes organised by height on their own racks, and outfits were hung in colour co-ordination. It was an OCD wet dream. My wet dream.

"Help yourself."

"What do you mean?"

"Pick an entire drag outfit, from a wig to the shoes, and they are yours to keep," David said with a grin.

"Are you serious?" I walked around the room in awe. He was built broader than me and could definitely fill the dresses out better than I could, but that didn't stop me from trying on my favourites. His silver sequin dress sat amongst some others I'd designed, placed separate from the rest.

"Why are these not in with the others?" I asked, wondering if our falling out had something to do with it.

"They're my favourites. They are the ones that are just too good to be placed next to the others. I mean... would you put a *Gucci* bag next to a *Primark* one? I don't think so!" His laugh echoed in his make-shift drag wardrobe, as infectious as it was when he was up on stage as Miss Mirage.

I continued trying on different outfits, managing to squeeze my feet into his small size nines while he'd encouragingly say *if the shoe doesn't fit, take painkillers and wear them anyway.* I needed something a little stronger than paracetamol if I was going to wear them for more than a minute. I put on an array of wigs, none of them quite like the ginger wig of his I'd been drawn to and tried on first.

"I think this one is me. Definitely." I stood in front of the mirror, playing with the loose curls that had been styled into the wig.

"You can absolutely have that one. I do not suit a ginger wig, but you very clearly do. It really makes me angry that you are a prettier drag queen than me. Infuriating, really. I think you've found the one," he said after spinning me around and holding me at both tips of my shoulders. "Stunning. So, what's this drag queen of yours gonna be called?"

That question.

Again.

I still couldn't decide, not yet, but I knew exactly what the last name was gonna be.

"I'm not sure about my first name, but I'd like my last name to be Mirage, if you'll have me?" I was sure David would have been offended after all our years of friendship if I hadn't taken his drag name. He jumped for joy, thrilled, and then barrelled into me, holding me, lingering just a little before pulling himself away.

"Oh gosh, I have a drag daughter. Now, hurry and pick your drag name so I can show you off to the world. In just under a month, I've got a drag show in Manchester and I want you to be there, dressed in this outfit, okay?"

I hummed in agreement as I started changing out of the drag outfit, but I was in no way ready to face the world, especially not in drag. *One day at a time,* I reminded myself, because that's all I could do.

That night I stayed at David's house, not in his bed or anywhere next to him, but on the sofa. I wasn't going to risk driving home, not with my eyes aching as they did. I wasn't even sure I'd been in the right mindset to drive to his in the first place.

My eyes closed, allowing everything around me to turn to darkness and my mind to be consumed by the ache I felt for Matt. The pain. I may have been exhausted, but that didn't stop my mind from wandering in a way of its own.

I walked the streets of a city that vaguely resembled Manchester and I was happy. A warmth filled me as I looked around, seeing those around me dressed in rainbow colours. Everyone was so different, unique even, but they all had one thing in common. They all smiled as much as me.

I gripped a rainbow flag in my hand, watching the material flow in the sun-kissed wind. It was summer, my skin a light tan colour instead of the pale white it usually was and my nails were painted to perfection as crowds cheered around us. Small droplets of sweat formed against my forehead above a layer of foundation and ran from pencilled brow down to my shiny lips.

Different music filled the streets as I walked with people just like me, following in their footsteps. I didn't feel alone anymore. I had everyone around me. I felt safe. There were even some drag queens just ahead on a float, which suddenly came to a grinding halt, stopping our celebration.

"Gays to Hell." I could hear shouting in the distance.

I looked to the side of the parade and could see a banner—a banner very clearly aimed at our community. Words painful to read. They'd stopped the parade by lying on the ground, protestors entirely in the way of our march.

"Move out of our way. We aren't doing you any harm," a drag queen yelled from the float to the protestors. "Just leave us be."

"God would not approve of this. You're offending us and our saviour. You call yourselves humans?" a protestor spoke, spitting at the ground. I could just about hear them above the booing of the crowds.

It wasn't long before the parade continued—until the police removed those in our way, although that didn't stop the clouds from darkening above us. No matter how grey the sky appeared, we would still be there waving our flags and brightening the city. We were a family and we stood together.

Once the parade finished, I found myself with a drink in my hand, stumbling down the streets of the city, my vision compromised. The sky was still dark but there were no flags in the air nor anyone wearing rainbows around me. I was alone. I heard footsteps behind me, so I quickly glanced back to see no-one there. That didn't stop my legs from moving forward.

Running.

Faster.

Stumbling underneath themselves.

So fast but still looking behind me, until—

Blood. A knife to my stomach and a burning feeling to match.

Fear. I felt it as I looked at the figure in front of me. I couldn't see them, but they were there. I felt their determination. I could almost see a pair of eyes with a look in them like they'd been meaning to stab me. To kill me.

They pulled out the blood soaked knife and placed it inside me once more, making my whole body heave with pain. And that's when I saw him. Matt.

My body pulled itself out of its nightmare, as a scream leapt from me. I quickly covered my mouth to dull the roar, trying not to wake David as I found myself back on his couch. I panted, drenched in the same sweat that coated my forehead in the dream and placed my hand on my still burning skin. It felt real, but I was still alive.

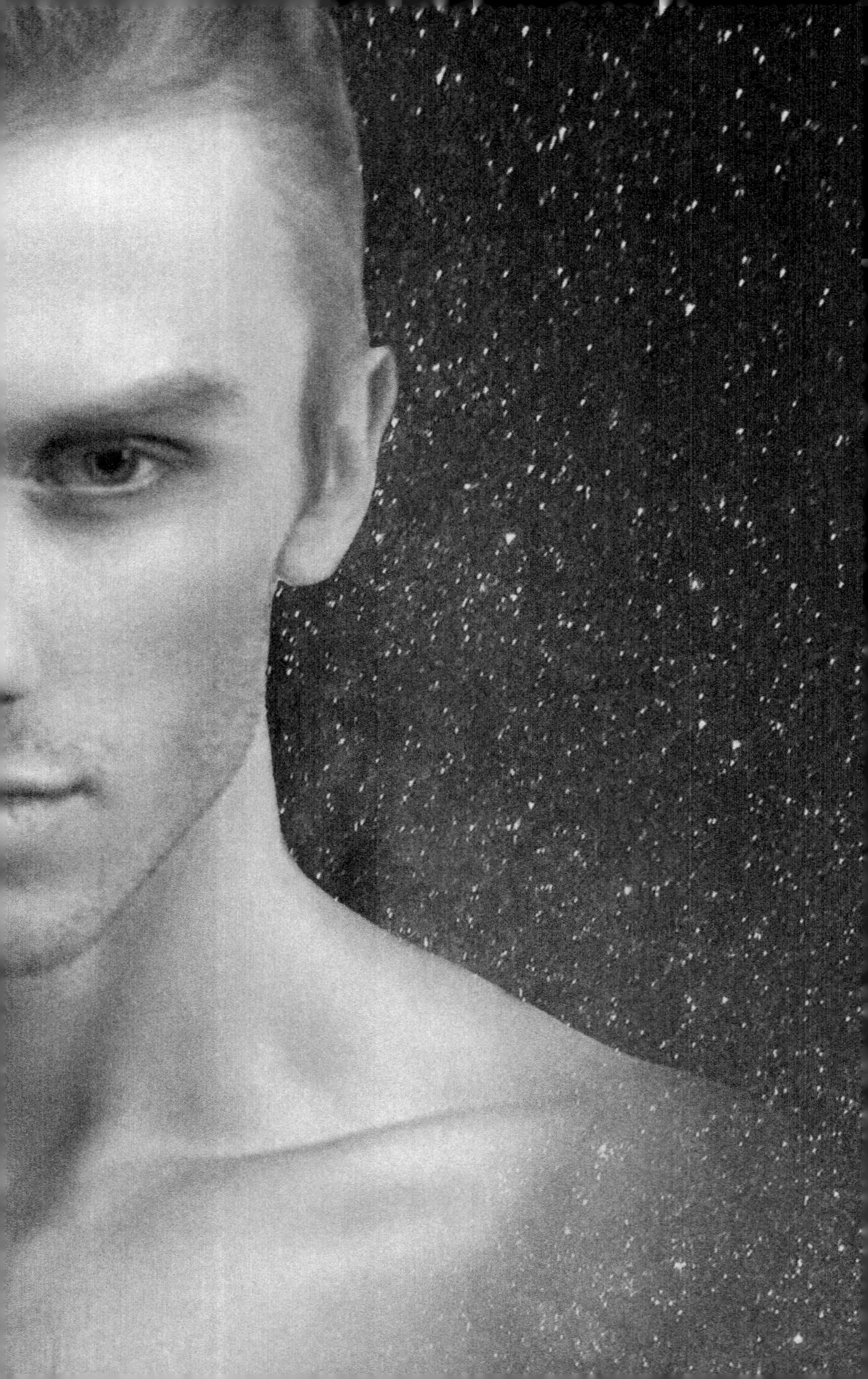

CHAPTER TWENTY-ONE

One funeral.
Two weeks later.
More nightmares than I could count and one nightmare that had become a reality. A nightmare I'd lived before, helping Tamsin clear out her mum's house after she'd passed away—although this nightmare was unexpected. I didn't for a second think that Matt's parents would approach me at the funeral. I doubted I'd even be allowed to go. Their whole bodies shook with nerves as they asked if I'd be able to help them clean out Matt's apartment.

"Why do you need my help?" I shouldn't have asked why. Instead, I should have graciously accepted, but we were all in pain and my walls were up.

"We know we've not been the nicest of people. We didn't understand and we didn't know how to process it, or cope even, but then it turned into losing our son forever," Nathan said softly, people still outside the church on the brightest day of the year so far. Tamsin nervously shuffled beside me as I remained silent. I hadn't forgiven them; I'd not even forgiven myself.

"It's clear that you knew Matt in a way we didn't. In such a short space of time you became a huge part of his life. Jackie told us you even spent Christmas together, and we can't thank you enough for making his last Christmas special while we tore his world apart. We're truly sorry, Liam. Would you please come and help us?" Matt's mum looked me in the eyes the whole time after the limited exchanges at the hospital. She was living with regret, and it was eating away at everything she knew.

"Okay, here's my business card. Let me know when and I'll be there."

It was only a couple of days later I found myself walking from a Manchester train station to Matt's apartment. The city heaved with people, crowds pouring out of buildings to escape the darkness and soak up the Mediterranean heat that was sweeping the country. I flinched each time the noise of someone behind me filled my eardrums, hesitant to look back in case I met the same fate as I did in my dreams.

I tried to focus on the constant hum of the traffic or listen in to conversations from passers-by. My eyes clung to those sunbathing on a small area of green in-between two office blocks, each looking as though they had no care in the world, equally showing off their skin. I was makeup free and my nail varnish had been removed after rubbing vigorously at the layers I'd applied for Matt's funeral.

Nobody could've known I was gay as I walked down the streets. I was wearing slim fit jeans and a simple printed tee I'd dug out of my wardrobe after not wearing it in years. I looked like any regular straight guy.

I squirmed as I saw Matt's parents in the distance, stood just outside of Matt's apartment block. Nerves ran through me at the thought of spending time with them in a open plan room with no escape aside from the bathroom door.

You're meeting your Mum, Stuart and Jade after this. You can do this, I reassured myself. I didn't know what I'd talk to them about and I was sure they felt the same.

"Hiiii," I spurted with a weak smile as I continued to walk towards them. "Shall we go in?"

"Hi, Liam. Thanks for coming," Nathan said, and Angela smiled simultaneously.

I mustered up a smile and caught their gaze. I had no words, only the possibility of vomit if I dared open my mouth again. I couldn't respond, so instead I walked alongside them, remaining mute. We made our way up to his apartment, through the grand lobby I'd been in awe of the first time I was there. The closer we got to his room, the more I felt like I was losing myself––losing my mind once again to the loss of Matt. I stood at his front door, staring, numb from emotion—my eyes stinging like I wanted to cry but there was nothing there.

Numb.

How did we end up here?

Matt's dad tried to take charge of the situation once we'd got into his room, as his mum was clearly in no state to start. She shook uncontrollably by his bed, incapable of doing anything else. I nodded at his dad as he asked me to start with Matt's desk and drawers. His room looked as it had the last time I'd seen it, everything in its place, perfectly aligned. Just the way Matt liked it. I caught a glimpse of someone in his mirror as I sat opposite in his chair. A shell of a human.

Me.

I didn't recognise the person I'd become—paler skin than normal, bags under my eyes and afraid. Afraid of who I was, who I was going to become without Matt by my side. For a split second, I felt like that scared boy lying on the ground once more, with gravel pressed into my face as I endured punch after punch.

I was scared—walking to Matt's apartment with my chest puffed high to seem that little bit more masculine proved that. Matt had made me cautious in a world full of hate. He saw the truth and I tried to forget it.

I spun around on the desk chair and faced one of his walls. The one covered in frames of all different shapes and sizes—the same ones that had been there the last time, but some extra.

Pictures of me.

I stepped up and approached them, finding balance in my legs that had become weak. My finger ran down one of the frames that had felt Matt's touch. I could almost feel him—that's what I wanted to feel, anyway. My finger continued to run across the black of the frame, holding a Polaroid picture within, that had been taken by Tamsin. It was of the day I'd dressed in drag for the second time, with no tears running down my face. It was the day he'd came into the unit and saw me in a cheap wig. It was the day I'd convinced him that I was enough out of drag, but entirely more me in drag. Out of drag I'd been hiding too, just like Matt.

A soft smirk grew on my face, knowing that my picture had been up on his wall all that time and I'd had no idea. Matt wasn't ashamed of me at all. He'd proved that at the airport and he'd somehow managed to prove it again.

I pulled myself out of a daydream and away from the picture, sitting back at the desk to look through Matt's belongings. I felt as though I had no right to be looking, not as much as his parents. Nathan was sorting through his wardrobe and his mum rested against the kitchen counter—looking, staring into space.

"Liam, this has your name on it," Matt's dad said, holding onto something. I didn't know what I was expecting but it wasn't an envelope. He handed it over and I glanced at the sweeping letters that made up my name on the front. There wasn't much weight to the envelope, but it had something inside. Most of me wanted to see what was enclosed, but I still hesitated. I carefully ran my finger underneath the fold and ripped at it slightly.

"What is it?" Angela pulled herself away from the kitchen counter and placed herself on the other side of the bed as I pulled out a piece of lined paper to reveal a hand-written letter.

"It's a letter—from Matt." I gulped.

"Read it then," Nathan said, perching himself next to Angela. Both of them waited in anticipation, nodding their heads to prompt me to start reading. I never thought I'd have something to read from Matt, never mind have to read it aloud. I cleared my throat and began to read, each word sending shivers down my spine.

"Liam, I'm sorry I kicked you out the other day. You didn't deserve that. I was hurting and I took it out on you. I'm sorry. I'm not sure why I'm writing this. We've not spoken for a couple of days and that's already killing me. I guess I'll build up the courage to send this to you one day, and maybe you'll forgive me for treating you so terribly. I needed time. I hope you understand that." I cleared my throat again, struggling to see the words on the paper as tears puddled in my eyes. "I hope my parents will come around to my sexuality. I'm sad I won't be spending Christmas with you, but I'm going home on Christmas Eve to see my mum and dad—if they'll have me. Being bisexual shouldn't be a big deal to them, or to anyone else for that matter, but I understand why they're having a hard time understanding." I looked up to his parents, both displaying a form of agony. "I'm not being greedy finding both men and women attractive, and I didn't choose to be this way. If I could change it, I would. I want you to know that when I chose you over Charl, it wasn't me choosing men over women—it was me choosing you. Every single little, weird and wonderful part of you." I looked up with a smile as I could practically hear his voice over mine, telling me over and over again not to change. It hadn't always been that way, but I know in the end it was other people's views that made him want me to change and not him. "Maybe one day my parents will understand that being bisexual isn't a choice I made. Maybe they'll understand that no matter how many girls they set me up with, none of them would compare to how I feel for you. Anyway, I'm rambling. You left the Madonna autograph on the top of my wardrobe and I didn't realise you left without it. It doesn't feel right for me to keep it, even if we don't work out, so it's yours. Love forever, Matt."

A single tear ran down my left cheek and I ran my hand across it to conceal my emotions in front of Matt's parents. My fingers brushed the paper of the envelope, searching for the Madonna autograph and pulled it out. So many memories flourished as I looked at the mess of pen on the paper—some memories that hadn't happened but I wanted them to be real. I pictured Matt and I in the karaoke bar once more, singing *Like a Prayer*, dressed in an eighties blonde wild child wig and attempting our best Madonna impression. In my head, I was the best, but I knew that wouldn't have been the case.

"We're not bad people," Angela croaked as sadness consumed her throat. I knew I'd have been distraught to have heard that in their shoes—to hear their son's pain, having no hope of fixing what was broken.

"We're so sorry. It all seems silly now that he's gone, but we are truly sorry. We'd do anything to take back what has happened," Nathan said, holding onto Angela. Her eyes were the brightest red, streaming as a way to get rid of the angst she felt inside.

"No, I'm sorry. I shouldn't have read that out loud to you both. You didn't need to hear all that, especially not feeling like this," I said with sincerity I didn't know I felt at the time. The last thing I wanted to do was make things awkward, or upset them.

"No, we did need to hear it. We have a lot to learn. We may be old and wise but we want to understand—we need to." Nathan widened his eyes reassuringly.

"Okay, well he wrote this letter because he was in pain. I know how hard it is to hide who you truly are away from the real world because I've done it in the past. I guess it's the same as me not being as true to myself as I could have been, unlike when I've been dressed in drag. But aside from the pain, he still loved you. He wouldn't have hidden himself away from you if he didn't—he wouldn't have cared what you guys thought if that was the case. My dad didn't react in the best of ways when I came out either, but that didn't stop me from loving him." I fidgeted and looked to my lap in sadness. They didn't say anything. Angela rested her head on Nathan's shoulder as they seemed to contemplate their life. I waded through the remains of Matt's belongings still sat within the drawer, and spoke without thought.

"You two should come and meet my family. They're meeting me for coffee, if you fancy it?" I said to mask the awkward silence, created in agony on their part. It was the least I could do for allowing me to be part of that day, because if I hadn't, I may never have forgiven myself.

Once I'd helped Nathan load some things into their car, I placed myself next to Angela who remained in the room. She looked into the mirror that sat on the dressing table, and used a face wipe to clean her tear-soaked skin.

"Are you sure you want us to come?" She coated her face with a fresh layer of foundation and prepped her eyes for mascara.

"Absolutely. Besides, Jade, my sister, will cheer you up effortlessly. She has this weird infectious power about her."

"A little like you then." She allowed a small smile to grow on her face, grabbed her bag and ordered Nathan to follow us down to meet my family.

"Gayboy!" Jade yelled at the top of her voice, with

gasps from everyone in the vicinity, including Matt's parents.

"Hey. You know only Tamsin is allowed to call me that," I said, picking her up with both arms and launching her into the air. The skirt of her dress ruffled in the wind, the pink tulle sent flying above her head. It was too cold for her to be wearing a dress, and I knew Mum would have put up a fight to get her in pants and lost.

"Mum, Stuart—this is Angela and Nathan. Matt's parents." They all exchanged pleasantries, my mum still upset she never got the chance to meet Matt.

As we walked away, Angela faced Nathan and whispered into the crook of his neck, just loud enough I could hear.

His sister knows he's gay. Surely she's too young...

"She knows." I turned and spoke directly to them. The drag queen in me took control and gave me all the confidence I needed. "It was important for her to know. I told her, and I wouldn't change it. I couldn't have her finding out any other way, like walking in on me with a guy—" I winced at my last comment. I shouldn't have said that. It was too raw but spoken with truth. Angela's face softened at my comment. She really started to listen to me, so I had to make her understand. Now was my chance to convince her, an opportunity I never got with my dad.

"I think the point I'm trying to make is that it's much better for her to learn that being gay is okay, and the earlier she learns that, the less impressionable she'll be when others try to change her mind. There are more than seven billion people in the world, and there won't ever be a time when every single person has the same view, but if one more person than the day before understands—if one more person can live their life with a little less scrutiny, then that's a win in my eyes."

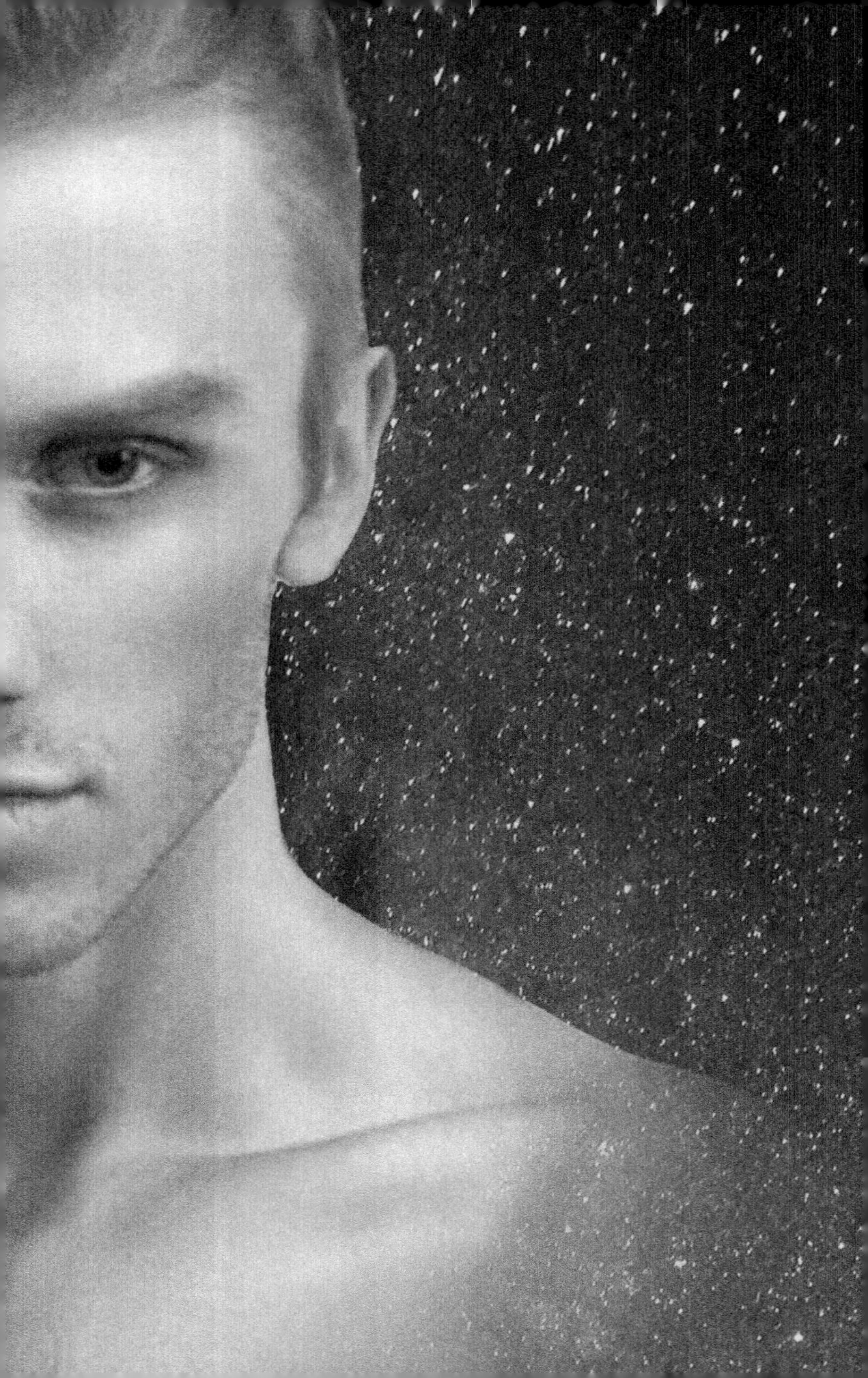

CHAPTER TWENTY-TWO

I procrastinated, consumed by my phone so easily in an attempt to not get ready for Miss Mirage's Comedy Night—to stay in the comfort and safety of our hotel room in Manchester. We were only a few streets away from the venue, yet dread bubbled under my skin at the thought of walking the streets of Manchester in drag. I'd be wearing more makeup than Matt had worn, wearing a wig and clothes that made me stand out. I was even more afraid to admit that I was gayer than him.

"Here, drink this and then get ready. It'll be okay," Tamsin said, handing me a large glass of Prosecco. She could see the angst I was feeling. She probably felt it, too.

It was a safe place. I'm not going to be alone, I had to remind myself.

This feeling I felt was a worry I'd had the luxury of

not feeling before, something I guessed I was naive to. I knew there were people who didn't understand about our community, who didn't want to understand for that matter, but I'd never feared for my own life before.

Was this the same fear women felt?

All those times I'd told Tamsin to text me when she was home, when I should have walked with her. I was going to in future—I wasn't having her feel the same way I did.

About an hour and a quarter later, I was ready, wearing the gorgeous outfit David had gifted me and dolled up in all things makeup. I didn't know why he wanted me dressed in drag that night, and at first, I was dead set against the idea until I remembered that I was entirely more me in drag. I needed a release, some laughs instead of loss, but most of all, Matt had asked me to do drag for the both of us, so that's what I was going to do.

I stepped out onto the street from the safety of our hotel room and made my way towards the venue with Tamsin. I walked in the shadows of the buildings that towered above. I even tried to conceal my long painted nails behind my back. It wouldn't have made much difference wearing a vibrant ginger wig. I could be seen a mile off.

I flinched at every noise, just like I'd done in my dreams, although this time I had Tamsin to protect me. Pathetic that I relied on her really, but that's what friendship was for. She had been my saviour ten years prior, and to that day she still was, and she had no idea how much I needed her there.

I saw another guy dressed in drag on the other side of the street, clearly walking to the same venue we were. They were smiling, laughing with their friends, oblivious to the dangers of the world like I'd once been.

I wanted to go over, to warn them, but I was being erratic. I knew what had happened to Matt didn't happen often, but that didn't make it okay. I knew that the odds of something happening was a million to one or more, but that didn't make it easier to walk the streets and feel safe.

I hesitated, but eventually pulled my arms from the arch of my back and stood tall. If the other drag queen could do it, so could I. I walked into the venue with Tamsin. There was a large open space at the back for people to stand, with a few rows of seats at the front that lined the stage. A few heads turned as I walked in, dressed the best I'd ever looked in drag, so I shuffled to the back of the venue as close as we could get to the bar. Thankfully, I wasn't the only one in drag—a few other men had as much makeup on as me, which calmed my nerves nearly as much as the double vodkas that seemed to go down too easily.

A few more drinks and smiles down, the lights dimmed and the crowded theatre screamed for Miss Mirage. She appeared on stage, a single spotlight highlighting the mass of makeup and enormous eyelashes she wore. Tamsin made a joke underneath the bustle of the crowd saying, "Her eyelashes look like tarantulas on her face," loudly enough to make me choke on my drink, inhaling the liquid while laughing.

She started with a lip sync, a performance including topless men dancing. It looked as though Miss Mirage had applied baby oil to their torsos before hopping onto stage.

"She's so bloody good, isn't she?" I said rhetorically to Tamsin, my voice raised just above the noise level of the audience so she could hear me.

"I know, and those men." She practically drooled at the sight of them, even more abs than Callum.

"Dirty bitch," I said, laughing. For a couple of minutes, life was good—normal, in fact. The song came to a close, leaving Miss Mirage on stage by herself, the lights dimmed to just a twinkle.

"Now, I don't normally do this, but I want to talk to you all about one of our very own. His name is Matt." My heart sank, listening to her speak directly to the audience—to me. "He lived here in Manchester, and a few weeks ago his life was taken. He was just twenty years old and someone thought it was fine to attack him because of his sexuality—something he had no choice in." I could just about see Miss Mirage on stage through my tears, her face as serious as the day we'd had our fall out. "These acts of homophobia have got to stop. Matt had a bright future ahead of him. He was someone's son, nephew, cousin, friend and even boyfriend, and some depraved waste of space human thought it was fine to do this! We are a family and we stand together. One day I hope they learn that these acts of terrorism will not persevere. That's why all the proceeds from tonight's event will be donated to Stonewall, a charity that campaigns for the equality of the LGBTQ+ community." David stood still and remained strong for everyone in the room. He remained strong for me, a blubbering mess. There was silence for a short while, and then clapping echoed throughout the hall that seemed to come from near the front of the stage.

"So, I want you all to know that there's another Miss Mirage in the audience tonight—a mini Mirage if you will. Let's welcome her onto the stage." David smiled underneath his makeup and waved me up onto the stage.

"What's happening," I asked, but nobody bothered to reply, and instead were clapping, chanting even.

I stood in front of the audience. The small stage light seemed brighter than the sun, and sweat dripped off me. I didn't know if the sweat was due to nerves or the heat from the spotlight.

"This is my drag daughter, and I've been telling her for a few weeks now that she needs to hurry up and pick a first name otherwise I'm disowning her." David spoke to the audience at first and then turned to me. "Now you're under pressure, tell them what your drag name is."

I stood in what was my new found identity, a persona I could put on and take off whenever I wanted or needed to. Adrenaline rushed through me from my very core, so I did what I was good at, something that the bullies had allowed me to do so well. I was the class clown. I was good at making people laugh.

"See how quickly I got up on stage? Bet you aren't used to that waiting for this old hag to climb those stairs," I jested to the crowd in front of me, and it came so naturally.

The crowd roared, sounding almost like Jade when she'd play and pretend we were lions. I traced back to her, stroking my head, reassuring me that she'd give me everything I needed, and she had. I was a lion and I could do this, no matter how many people tried to kick me down in the past.

"Now, I'm gonna to tell you all my name shortly, but first—the venue had a stair lift fitted especially for our old lady Miss Mirage, but she broke it on the way up. I just need to call the emergency response team otherwise this bitch ain't got no chance of getting down."

The audience continued to laugh, and in that moment, I paused. I'd not seen them from the back of the venue, but stood on the stage I could see them perfectly clearly. Sat on the front row were Matt's parents, both of them smiling even through the tears they must have shed for Matt during Miss Mirage's speech.

Maybe they'd changed and were sorry for all they'd said. Maybe this was their shot at redemption in order to forgive themselves. Either way, it must have taken some guts coming here, even if they'd been invited.

Nerves started to fill me and sweat continued to pour off me under the spotlight, my inch thick foundation starting to melt. I looked to the ceiling, needing a minute to compose myself—something I couldn't do looking to the audience, some of my favourite people in the world along with Matt's parents staring at me. I half expected to see stars on the ceiling, just like in my bedroom, but instead it was dark and dingy and hadn't been painted in decades. I couldn't help but think the place could have been brightened up with some glow-in-the-dark star stickers.

"You guys are too kind. I'll definitely come and join you all again if Miss Mirage is able to fire up her dial up internet and get in touch." My final joke before I went to leave the stage after an unexpected invite. "One very special person once told me that every star is unique, each one sparkles and shines in their own way. Well, you guys are all stars being here tonight." I paused for a second, cleared my throat and straightened my back, standing tall and proud. "You've been watching Mattonna Mirage, a nod to the queen of all queens, Madonna of course, but most importantly a tribute to my boyfriend, Matt. If it wasn't for him, I wouldn't be stood on this very stage. I may not have even found myself. Because of him, I'm going to be a star, too."

The crowd roared, cheering me on—some shedding tears and others laughing with huge smiles on their faces. I'd done that. I tried to glance at everyone in the audience, trying to take a mental image of each one and how I'd made them feel that night. Just by chance, I looked back up to the ceiling of the poorly decorated theatre to see it lit with stars, all glistening in their unique way and then glanced at Mum and Stuart sat on the balcony, holding onto Jade—stood on the chair in the middle of them, flailing uncontrollably.

My lioness.

Jade.

She gave the loudest roar of them all.

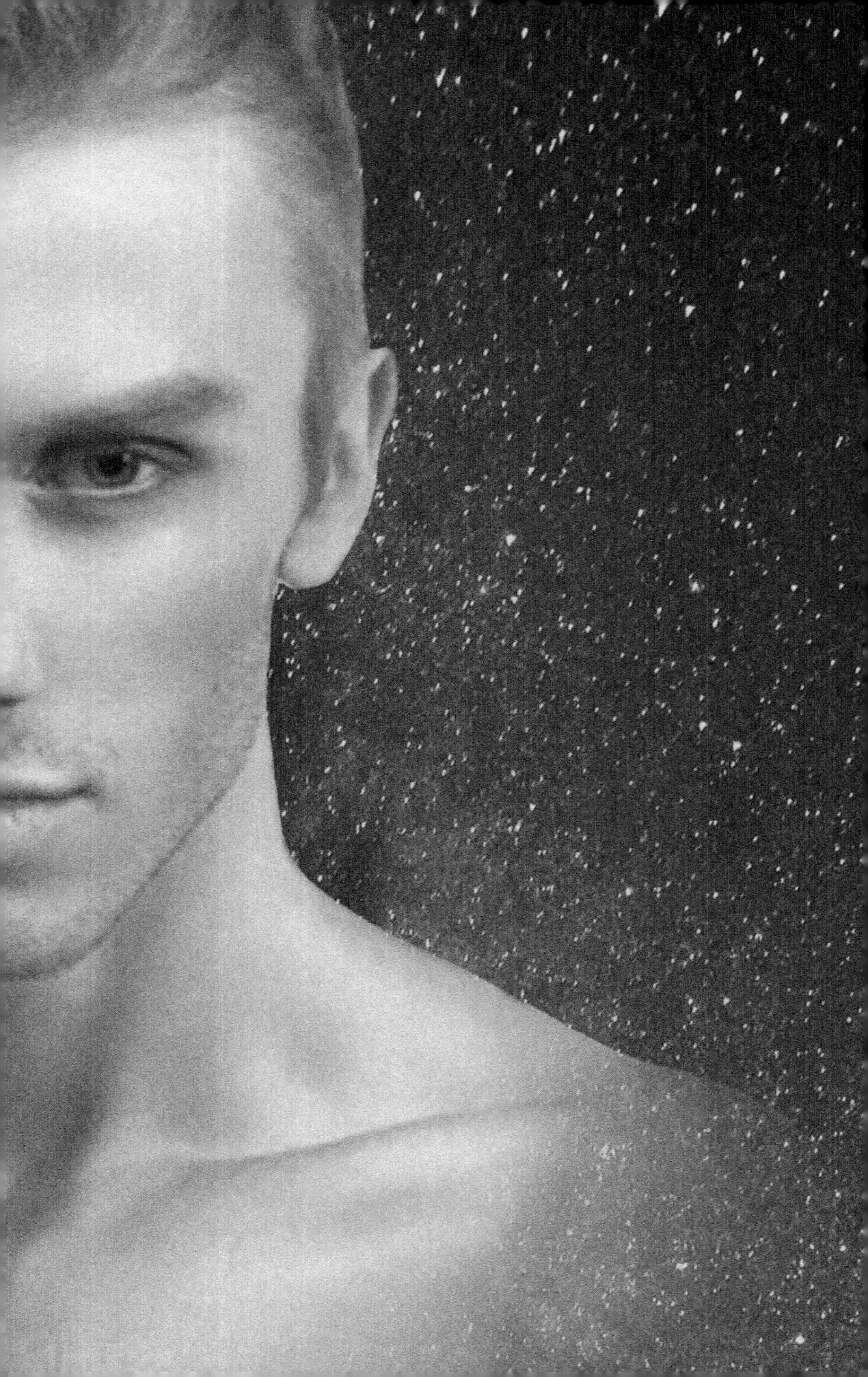

EPILOGUE

I'd made it. All those times I'd sat back and watched, not for one second had I ever believed I'd be on television myself. I wasn't on television for Wrighteous, even though it was growing quicker than I could have imagined and I'd hired another person—it was safe to say our jobs were safe. I wasn't even on television because of all the campaigning I'd done for the LGBTQ+ community—for Matt, Instead, I was going to be on television, dressed in drag.

My drag.

I walked onto the set for the first time, stage lights blinding and the most noise I'd ever heard when they weren't filming, and when they were filming—silence. Mattonna Mirage had become a star. I had become a star. I even had a double act of sorts with the original Miss Mirage, but none of that mattered when I got the call. A calling to my future as a drag queen, an opportunity to represent myself and all of those in our community. Wrighteous was going to reap the rewards, whether I was to win or be the first out, I was going to make sure of it, but I wasn't there for that. I was there because I'd found my voice—a voice I'd lost, stolen from me little by little as I'd grown up.

I sat down opposite the most beautiful drag queen I'd seen in all my life—flawless makeup, towering bronzed legs crossed at the knees and accessories paired beautifully with her dress. I was envious of it all, just as I knew she was envious of me, dressed in my custom-made, grey-glittered, lace dress with a flare. I shook her hand in the midst of shaking nervously while the crew around us was set to cue us in. Nervous to be in front of the cameras, absolutely, but to be in the presence of the one and only Mona De Lisha, that was something else. I was about to be interviewed prior to my entry into the biggest drag competition of them all, before meeting all of the other queens. My competition.

"Thank you for being here," Mona said, her hands rested on her crossed legs in front of her.

"No, thank you for having me. It's an honour." I looked at her, away from the camera at all costs as according to the crew, that was rule number one.

"So first off, tell me about your name. How did you come up with it?"

They knew the answer already. It was included as part of my audition reel—this was all for the cameras. For the show. Entertainment.

"Well, I once had the privilege of dating the most gorgeous man, Matt. We only managed to get a few long months together, before he was stabbed because of his sexuality." No matter how many times I'd said that, it still hurt my throat as the words came from my mouth. "I'm here today because of him. He adored Madonna, so I thought it would be a perfect tribute to both of them. Mirage is my drag mother's name. I'm sure she'll be rooting for me to fail so I can go back and still do our double act show."

"I'm sorry to hear that." The sound of Mona's voice softened and there was a pause, a miniature moment of silence for my one true love. I didn't know if it was going to be aired in that way, but it was nice while it lasted. I fiddled with my thumbs out of shot, so viewers wouldn't be able to see my nerves. "Do you think you'll ever find love again?"

The room was eerily silent. Nothing from the crew behind me, not even a cough. No words came from my mouth as the question swirled my mind.

Did I even want love again?

I'd be lying if I said I didn't want to feel the way I had done for Matt. Even so, the thought of meeting someone else hadn't crossed my mind until the question left Mona's lips. Before speaking, I cleared my throat and composed myself after a long pause I hoped they'd edit out.

"Who knows? Maybe? I've definitely gained perspective. I have all my family, my crazy best friend, and so many other people that fill me with love. Would I like to meet someone who makes me feel the way Matt did? Absolutely, but I'm in no rush to search for it. I'm here today because I'm happy, and I'm happy because I found me—the real me in drag." I didn't have to lie for the cameras. I was finally happy and I knew who I was. Meeting someone would be a bonus, but if it hadn't been for Matt, I might never have found myself.

"It's truly wonderful to see how much drag means to you, and the impact it's had on your life after only a very short space of time." Mona smiled, her teeth as white as moonlight. "I have one final question," she said with another pause for suspense. I almost felt as though I was in *The Hunger Games* being interviewed by Caesar Flickerman before heading into the games to fight for my life. "Tell me about this most beautiful dress. Look at that detailing. Stun-ning!"

I looked down to my dress, ran my fingers across it seductively, the lace delicately clinging to my slightly padded hips.

"Oh, this old thing?" I flapped my hands and gave a twinkle to the camera. "I made it."

"I want to rip it off you it's so gorgeous. You made that?" Mona almost seemed shocked, her eyes caressing the detailing of the gown.

I turned the bottom of my dress upward, revealing a hand sewn label with my logo, beautifully scribed onto the fabric.

"Yep. Wrighteous Couture Drag." Life was good. I'd

made it—successful drag queen, as gay as the day was long, but my priorities were straight. I even had the business of my dreams. Who said drag queens couldn't wear high fashion? Who said they couldn't look as good as me?

I looked to the camera, breaking rule number one because when had I ever been good at following the rules? "Guess what world? I'm wearing me."

ABOUT THE AUTHOR

D J Cook, or Danny, lives in Cheshire with his annoying yet lovable partner, and even more annoying siblings. He has a Special Guardianship Order for his sister since his Mum lost her fight with cancer in 2013. Danny uses books as an escape from reality, because who wouldn't want to be in House Tyrell, sipping wine and watching The Hunger Games unfold before their very eyes? When he isn't consumed by a world full of books, he binge watches TV series and plays Xbox. If he disappears, you'll either find him at IKEA or in the bath.